BECAUSE OF YOU

Tick-tock, tick-tock, tick-tock . . . midnight.

The old millennium turns into the new. In the same hospital, two very different women give birth to two very similar daughters. Hope leaves with a beautiful baby girl . . . Anna leaves with empty arms.

Seventeen years later, the gods who keep watch over broken-hearted mothers wreak mighty revenge, and the truth starts rolling, terrible and deep, towards them all. The power of mother-love will be tested to its limits. Perhaps beyond . . .

DAWN FRENCH

◆

BECAUSE OF YOU

Complete and Unabridged

CHARNWOOD
Leicester

First published in Great Britain in 2020 by
Michael Joseph
London

First Charnwood Edition
published 2021
by arrangement with
Michael Joseph
Penguin Random House UK
London

*A catalogue record for this book is available
from the British Library.*

'Catching of happiness' taken from 'Born Yesterday',
in *The Complete Poems* by Philip Larkin, is reprinted by
permission of Faber and Faber Ltd

ISBN 978–1–4448–4754–3

Published by
Ulverscroft Limited
Anstey, Leicestershire

Printed and bound in Great Britain by
TJ Books Ltd., Padstow, Cornwall

This book is printed on acid-free paper

For my kids,
Billie, Lils & Olly,
because it's all about being a mum

For my kids,
Billie, Lila & Olly.
Because it's all about being a mum

In laudem matrum

Start

Try to imagine two more different couples than these. You can't. They are as opposite as it gets. Oil and water. Salt and sugar. Always and never. Lost and found.

As midnight came and went, so too did Julius's hope of Anna giving birth exactly then, with the bongs and fire-cracks of the new millennium heralding the baby's arrival.

'Any chance you could push a bit harder, babe?'

'I hope you're joking, you weapons-grade twat,' Anna panted.

'Course!' Julius chuckled.

(He wasn't joking.)

It would've made a perfectly neat nice story. There might even have been some coverage, which could have boosted Julius's stalling profile. Yes, there might. But the baby didn't come then. So there wasn't. And his disappointment was palpable.

Anna felt the culpability stronger than the waves of intense pain that flooded her body with each contraction. She found herself perversely welcoming the rhythmic spasms as something that was at least tangible and immediate. It was real, and happening right now, and it needed managing, something Anna was supremely skilled at. It gave her an undeniable focus, a job to do, with a result at the end of it. Something to show for her efforts, something to infill the fissures in the marriage, someone she could guide and administer. A little

1

person who would surely listen to her, look up to her and make her feel as though she mattered. Someone to dress nicely. Someone to live because of. A purpose, finally, that wasn't primarily about him. No one could deny her part in this. In this, she shared equal responsibility, if not more. She didn't have to be only Julius's wife. She could be a little child's mother. Finally, she would have made something. With any luck, the next step might be that she could feel something . . .

Something.

Anything.

'Seriously, Jules, please give it a rest.'

'Bloody cheap crap, should've researched it better. Piers has got a brilliant one, got it in the airport in Dubai. Should've done that.'

All the time Anna was attempting to feel something other than groaning birthing pain, Julius was attempting to film his perfect family finally becoming a reality. His irritability about the missed opportunity of a stellar midnight birth was eclipsed by his irritability with his new camcorder, which seemed to be refusing to zoom. The zooming is the most important and impressive element of any successful birth video, surely? Despite Anna's protestations imploring him to 'put that effing thing down, please', and help her instead, he continued to fiddle with it.

Sarah, the older and more experienced Irish midwife, rolled her eyes at her younger colleague as they both witnessed Julius resoundingly deflate their perception of him.

'Could you just move a bit, thanks?' he said, rudely shoving Sarah with his elbow. 'I need to get

2

a good shot of this . . . '

'This,' emphasized Sarah, 'is your good wife, and quite frankly, sir, I don't think she's wanting any close-ups of her noonny right now, am I right, lamb?'

'Yep. No,' Anna confirmed between puffs.

Julius took no notice. So Sarah rudely shoved him back with her elbow as she explained to the young trainee midwife, 'Some of our daddies forget themselves in the excitement and, sure, they become utter feckin' pillocks.'

Julius was oblivious.

Sarah was disappointed that he was so singularly NOT the solid, supportive, wife-loving emergent politician he purported to be. Yes, tall, verbose and shiny black, but no Martin Luther King this, she thought. Sarah saw that Julius was a behemoth of self-interest. It was evident that no one could love Julius more than Julius loved himself. An interesting and somewhat terrifying prospect as a potential father . . .

'Oh dear,' Sarah muttered to herself. 'Oh very dear.'

★ ★ ★

In another room down the corridor, a very different baby is also being hatched.

This room felt almost sacred. Even Hope's occasional muttered blasphemies were holy in their quietly focused devotion. She was praying and cursing in equal measure, to a God that she was eternally grateful to. This baby was a happy surprise.

3

Ever since Hope moved to London, away from her family in Bristol, she had felt singularly singular. Her loneliness was compounded by the thrust and bustle of so many busy people all around her, all the time. Everyone was going somewhere with a clear sense of purpose, rushing and forever unfriendly. She pretty quickly gave up trying to catch anyone's eye or even smiling. It was a thankless and vaguely humiliating effort, and left her with the sting of rejection to bolt on to her already aching isolation.

Hope was and always would be a natural stickler for high standards. After various placements heading up different cleaning teams, she had been promoted to manager of a fifty-strong team in this very hospital. Hope liked to think that the reason this establishment had a good record regarding MRSA was because of her diligence. The last inspection had been the best they'd had for ten years. Hope was commended.

Hope was delighted.

Hope knew the big move to London was the right thing to have done for her work. The pay was far better, almost three times what she could earn in Bristol. More importantly though, she had been promised the chance of promotion, which was virtually impossible in the smaller city in the relatively monopolized world of commercial cleaning. She would only ever have been a zero-hours contract cleaner there. Offices, universities, schools: wherever the contract sent her, she went. She didn't aspire to a desk job, no, she wanted to work hands on, but she desperately wanted to run her own team and that's what she could

4

do in London. The main reason Hope wanted to head up her own team was because that was the only way she could ensure the job was done right. It bothered her to be shoddy. Especially when it came to cleanliness. This job was the most natural and satisfying one she'd ever done, however lowly others might regard it to be. She cared not a jot. She wanted to be captain of her small and clean ship. She wanted to steer it, and London was the best port for that opportunity.

And now Hope was grateful to know that she was giving birth in a clean hospital. In a room where her own team made extra visits to make her laugh and prove to her that they were continuing to do their job well in her absence. They put googly eyes on their mops and drew funny faces on their industrial rubber gloves. In two years, these folk were the closest she had come to friends. A disparate group of people, from almost every nation on earth, come to London, like her, to make a decent living. Some spoke very little English, but Hope always found a way to communicate. Sometimes she drew diagrams to help everyone understand her instructions. It was the silly faces from these diagrams that resurfaced on the rubber gloves of her playful work-mates when they popped in on her.

Time for visitors was past, however.

The young, newly qualified midwife Fatu was keen to engage Hope's partner Quiet Isaac in conversation about his home in Sierra Leone. Fatu's own mother was from Freetown and she had visited there for the first time the previous year and wanted to share all her holiday 'Yes! I've been there too!' whoops of recognition with him.

Hope was pleased that Quiet Isaac could relate so easily and happily to this stranger. He rarely had the opportunity to regale anyone with stories or news of his home. Of 'Sa Lone'. Most people only showed a passing interest in this young student's heritage, nothing more than that. He relished the chance to drop into his native Krio to share greetings: 'Cushah'; and when he asked her how she was — 'How de body?' — he squealed and snapped his fingers with delight when she answered, 'De body fine.' He hadn't heard that familiar reply for too long. It was a warm blanket around his homesick heart, and it was Fatu's way of representing her mother.

Hope was grateful she could be momentarily distracted from the pains that increasingly racked her body. But another wave built; Fatu held her hands. 'Slowly. Steady. Breathe.'

★ ★ ★

Down the corridor, things are more urgent. Baby Florence is demanding she be born. Pronto.

Julius was impatient. The sooner she arrived, the sooner his 'picture-perfect family' would be complete. Julius sees everything through his own lens, including how his life should look. His heart wasn't really in this, and he was unaware of that particular tragedy.

Florence as a name had been hotly contested between Julius and Anna. It was one of many arguments during the past nine months. Julius didn't entirely approve of the fustiness of it, but

6

was prepared to concede that it was nicely traditional — enough, probably, to help secure a place for her in a decent school in their over-subscribed West London catchment area. He was a lapsed Catholic who found his faith again very quickly when he discovered that the best free schools in his area were denominational. He also had the priest on speed dial to baptize her as soon as possible since he learnt that the selection process favours those who are baptized first, and of course, all the Catholic EU incomers were quick out of the traps on that. The authentic continental Catholics don't hang about. They don't give the devil a single slice of opportunity to claim the souls of their innocent babies; they know how sneaky and sly he is, and they act quick. If Julius had his way, the baptism would occur on arrival, along with the first blessed breath. In yet another rare moment of assertiveness, Anna had put her foot down. NO. The baby would be baptized in the usual way, in the same flouncy dress worn by her parents and grandparents and great-grandparents going way back. There would be hats and tears and keepsake thin candles to keep Satan at bay. And there would be presents, thank you. A cushion with 'Florence landed here on 1 Jan 2000' embroidered on it, possibly. And some silver napkin rings with any luck, that can tarnish, neglected, in a drawer for years. Or a posh teething ring not meant for actual teething. Meant for a box under a bed which won't be looked in again, until her room is being turned into a spare guest room when she hopefully departs for a decent university. Those kinds of presents. After all, Anna had given up smoking and alcohol for nine months; surely it wasn't THAT selfish to expect a party for all her efforts. Florence would be baptized in due course, Julius reassured himself, when the celebration could be properly curated for maximum effect and optimum impact. Could there even be a *Hello!* magazine deal . . . ?

Anna's breaths were short and shallow now. She glanced at Julius, who was busy applying mint lip balm. Anna spluttered a laugh but it really hurt, so she stopped. She often laughed at him. AT him. Not with an 'Isn't he charming with all his quaint eccentric ways' kind of laugh. More like an 'I'd better laugh to dilute how awful he is for everyone else' kind of laugh. Giving everyone permission to see him as a loveable buffoon, thereby defusing and allowing his frequent faux pas and insensitivities. He had recently been with her at her best friend's father's funeral. So disinterested and unmoved by the whole sad circumstance was he that afterwards, at the wake, spitting a mouthful of flakey pastry prawn vol-au-vent, he'd enquired of said best friend how her father was keeping . . . ?

Even then, Anna had over-laughed to bridge the awful moment and to somewhat mollify her beloved grieving chum. It was fairly exhausting to be a constant smokescreen for his blatant idiocy, but she persisted. It was an exercise in damage limitation in which she failed to realize that she herself was the most damaged. The relationship was broken, but they were both clinging to the wreckage.

Well, she was clinging to the wreckage.

He WAS the wreckage.

8

Back in Hope and Quiet Isaac's room, the air is starting to thicken.

The anticipation of an imminent arrival was quickening, as Hope's breathing became deeper and she started a low, rhythmic moan. Quiet Isaac was stroking her hair and whispering encouraging words close to her ear: 'You are amazing, Bubs, that's it, nearly there, my beautiful girl.'

Hope and Isaac had always worked well together as a couple.

Quiet Isaac was an unashamedly emotional young man. He spoke of his inner thoughts easily and often to her. Hope was very attracted to this. It was not something that she'd experienced often in the Jamaican-based community she was raised in back in Bristol. Although her dad was white, she was always surrounded by her mother's family, some of whom were born and bred in Jamaica, and swagger-proud of their roots. She loved those older uncles, with their hats and sass and sucky teeth. They were the ones who taught her to joust verbally in patois. They reminded her who she came from and why she should never apologize for it. Her nanna, Beverley, was their mother. She was long gone now, but she was so evident in Hope's momma, Doris. In fact, she was emerging more and more clearly on Doris's face every day. Hope only had the faintest memory of her, but it was as if she was slowly returning to remind them who started it all. Yes, Hope loved her loud, confident family. She adored their jokes and their teasing, but it was the very clatter of all that crazy volume which caused her to notice the quite different, dignified, calm nature of Quiet Isaac when she first saw him.

There had always been something other about him. He held his own in a slow, considered way. Nothing was ever going to rush Quiet Isaac and very little would cause him to be noisy. He was a stander-back, a 'watch, learn and step up when necessary' sort of man. Self-effacing. Reliable.

And handsome. Unmistakeably Liberian, after his father. Tall and striking with a high forehead, a wide-open honest face, and a curious pigment flaw on part of the iris of his right eye, which in certain lights looked like a tiny flash of green lightning, cutting across his dark brown, deep brown, brown brown eyes. Quiet Isaac was very noisy with his eyes. He could be on the opposite side of the room from Hope and speak to her very easily with only the looks he chose to give her. He didn't even need to use his whole face, his eyes were so expressive. He joked with Hope about *ifa mo*, something his father taught him, meaning 'do not speak it'. He told her that Liberians are predisposed towards secrecy, unlike his Krio mother born and bred in Sierra Leone, and that his dad was part of a male secret society called Poro, and it suited him to keep everything on the down-low, so signs and subtle eye movements were the stock-in-trade of his family on his dad's side. He liked it. It was conspiratorial, mischievous and skilful. Hope got it. Hope got him. More than anyone he'd met before, which was strange considering how very different their backgrounds were.

It had been a huge shock to find that she was

10

pregnant. They were still in the first year of their relationship and Quiet Isaac was a student and pretty much penniless. So much had been sacrificed at home for him to be here in London at Imperial College. There were scholarships available to international students like him, but it seemed that the Nigerians were the wisest to the process and all the scholarships for his master's degree course in General Structural Engineering had been filled. So his family had had to provide as much as they could for his tuition fees and his living costs. An evening job in a coffee shop near King's Cross Station helped a bit, but it ate into his study time and left him wrung-out-rag tired. Sometimes Hope met him after work at 2 a.m., and they went together, unallowed, back to the halls of residence where he lived. They sat side by side on his single bed and slurped noodles from paper tubs followed by slightly stale muffins he was allowed to take from work if they hadn't sold. Usually honey muffins. They were the least popular, for some reason. Quiet Isaac had eaten so many that they were definitely his least favourite. Sometimes he moved a couple of the blue-berry ones to the back of the glass dome where they were displayed, to try and hide them from customers in the hope they might survive 'til the end of the day and become his booty, but they were too obviously delicious and nearly always sold. Cheap noodles and honey muffins became the taste of their newly formed relationship.

He'd thought they'd been very careful with contraception. He wasn't a huge fan of condoms, but she insisted so he obliged. He was aware she was

11

also on the pill, so he reckoned that wearing the condom was the least he could do, considering she was putting chemicals into her body. They were covered, he thought, so it wasn't discussed much. In fact, she didn't stay the night with him for several months after they met. She wanted to know him, to trust him. After all, he would be her very first lover. She wasn't prim, but it mattered very much to her that it mattered to him, that it was to do with love, not lust. They waited. He didn't mind. He wanted her very much but it was daunting, because it was also the first time for him. He didn't tell her that until it was over. He reckoned she wouldn't know because she had nothing to compare it with . . . which, for him, was a giant relief. He needn't have worried. Hope and Quiet Isaac fumbled their way through that first time with extreme tenderness, and both were glad it was the other, and no one else.

Once that first time had happened, they had fallen into an easy intimacy and made love often. Sometimes they were both so very tired that sleep nabbed them before they could, and when they woke up they couldn't believe they'd missed out. Hope could only imagine that it must have been in this kind of fuggy stupor of fatigue that the sex happened carelessly, without any protection, and this must have coincided with her also forgetting her pill. Shocked as they were to discover her pregnancy, and worried as they were about telling their two families, nothing could dampen their excitement. It wasn't planned, far from it, but it was still undeniably wonderful. They had no idea how they were going to manage a baby,

12

let alone afford one, but they knew for sure, right from the positive pregnancy test, that they would do it somehow, together. They talked endlessly about how their lives would change.

'I won't go home when I get my degree,' he'd said. 'I'll find work here in London.'

'Are you sure?'

'Yes, so sure. Maybe we will get married? That way I will be able to stay. And we will be together, so we should get married anyway, if you want to . . . ?'

'Are you sure?'

'Yes. I'm sure. Maybe before the baby comes.'

'Really? So soon? Are you sure?'

'Yes. Maybe you should meet my parents first? And I should meet yours?'

'Before the baby? Or after? Are you sure?'

'Maybe we should move to Bristol? Then you could be near your mum?'

'Yes! Are you sure?'

'Yes, or we could stay in London. The pay is better here . . .'

'Yes . . . Oh, I want this so much, Isaac, I didn't know how much 'til now.'

'You're sure?'

'I'm sure.'

* * *

But that was then, and this is now.

In Anna and Julius's room, the tension was palpable. A change was happening. Anna's face was altering. She locked her gaze on to Julius and followed him wherever he moved to in the small room. He was shuffling about quite a bit; he took and made phone calls from anxious family and friends; he looked out of the window at the dark city; he looked out of the door into the corridor; he opened every drawer and cupboard; he scrutinized all the machinery in the room. Anna knew he was restless and bored. Patiently waiting wasn't Julius's strong suit. Neither was tenderness or compassion, or any of the virtues Anna could've sorely done with at that moment. Julius's strong suit was Julius, and this birth stuff didn't concern him directly, so his being here was chiefly duty. And show.

Even the phone calls at this late hour annoyed him. Why couldn't people wait to hear from him when he had something definite to say? It wouldn't be long, by the look of things.

The look of Anna, the way she looked right now, and the way she was looking at him, were unusual to say the least. She was clearly zoning out into some world of her own pain whilst her gaze was firmly clamped on him. It made him uncomfortable. He could ordinarily escape her if she became too focused or dwelt on difficult subjects or pinned him down in any way, but even selfish Julius knew it would be wrong to escape at this particular moment. He was expected to be here, so that was that. Did he want to be trapped in this fuggy room with his irrefutable duty? No, he didn't. Given a free rein, he would go and do something else, almost anything else, and come back for the big finish. Anna's eyes told him everything about how much of a mistake that would be, especially now as she started to enter

14

the serious stage of labour. He could see that she was trying to cope with the huge unlocking that was happening inside her. She was trying to stay in control.

Anna had had no idea it would be like this. She was on the edge of panic. Some of the contractions felt like a jackhammer was trying to break out of her. Some felt like waves of searing hurt ebbing and flowing through her. As the baby started to move down, she felt sure she would tear apart and the sound she could hear in her ears was herself screaming although she knew she wasn't. She was grunting and moaning. The screaming was inside her head, very loudly inside her head. She wasn't screaming simply to herald this new baby's arrival, she was screaming about everything . . .

About Julius's avoidance of her.

About his endless crass infidelities.

About his smug entitlement.

About how this baby now meant they were joined forever.

God.

About all the faking.

About the toxic marriage.

About her own weakness in not leaving.

About all her lost opportunities.

About all the 'I told you so's' from her family and friends that she hadn't cared to hear.

Somehow the pushing and the pain and the clamour gave her a massive sense of relief. This, at least, was real. She couldn't at that moment distinguish anything else that was. Certainly not Julius. He was a big fat fake, but this wasn't. This was truly happening, gulping her up and spitting her out to deal with it. A raw, real thing was happening. Right now.

She pushed. She tore. She sobbed.

She pushed again. She gasped for air because she'd forgotten to breathe.

One last gut-wrenching, eye-bulging effort, and the baby was out. The midwife immediately placed the sticky brown bundle of arms and legs on to her mother's pale skin, high up above her breasts, near Anna's neck. Her eyes were tightly closed and her hands tightly clasped below her chin; there was a furrowed expression on her little face. Florence was here at last. Furious, but here.

Anna looked up to see where Julius was. She couldn't see him anywhere. Seriously? Had he really left the room at this critical moment . . . ? Sarah indicated to Anna to look in the corner of the room. There he was. Big proud Julius the father, the seed-giver, the root, the origin, the man, was crumpled in a heap on the floor. He had fainted.

Sarah looked Anna squarely in the eyes and, with her assured Irish breeziness, she said, 'Well, you've got yourself a proper soppy bollock of an eejit there, haven't cha?'

Anna had to agree, but here, with her wriggly little new daughter on her chest, skin to skin, brown to white, she had someone else to concentrate on. Florence was immediately an astonishing bright light and she utterly eclipsed Julius from the very first moment.

He mattered oh so much less all of a sudden.

Florence was all.

Instantly.

All.

16

The circumstances of her birth were not Florence's fault. All she did was come to be. She couldn't know that she'd been born into such a volatile situation. All she knew was that there was a big close-up moony-pink sweaty face looking at her, making satisfying cooing noises and laughing. She knew that she was warm, and she knew that EVERYTHING was different. The light, the noise, the air on her, around her. It unnerved her a bit and she made a screechy noise which hurt her tiny throat, which made her make more of the screechy noise, which hurt her throat . . . Something tugged her belly . . .

Sarah tried to physically haul the dopey Julius up, so that he could welcome his little daughter. 'C'mon, mister man, let's have you upright, eh?'

'Umm, yeah.' Julius stretched and yawned. 'Could do with a cuppa.'

'Could ya? Perhaps after you've acknowledged the miracle that's happened over here . . . ?' She nudged him towards the mother and infant on the bed.

Anna and Florence.

Julius peered at the baby, finally realizing what had happened. For him, what had happened was that he had missed the photo/film opportunity of his first child's birth, dammit.

What had actually happened was a wonder: a beautiful and unique girl was born . . .

For her, for Florence, what happened was that a large brown face came too close to her . . . and then disappeared out of view to the side . . . as Julius fainted again. This time, it wasn't the gore that overwhelmed him, it was the thudding realization

17

of the huge responsibility.
(Soppy bollock.)

* * *

Hope is too lost in the business of birth to notice a miniscule, hardly perceptible change in Fatu's otherwise calm demeanour.

Her body was shaking now, and she was doing all she could to control her breathing and bring this baby into the world with the least possible stress. To do that, Hope had to take herself inside for now, into her own huge interior where she could centre her thoughts and be elsewhere from the pain. She wanted to be in charge at this critical moment, she wanted to drive it. She was whispering little comforting mantras to herself.

'Let her have my strong back.
'Let her have his crazy beautiful eyes.
'Let her have my sister's curls . . .'
And on . . .

She was imbuing the little life with all the good stuff. She was making wishes. She was cherishing a future . . .

But the ever-alert Quiet Isaac was hyper-present. He watched every move Fatu made with the vigilance of a hawk. He searched every flicker of expression on her face for a clue. He felt it in the deepest place he had, he knew something had changed: it was no longer going along the same path, this labour . . .

He saw the worry in Fatu's eyes when they met his briefly . . . a stinging, still pause . . . and then, from that alarming moment on, everything that

18

happened was a blur, a chaotic jumble.

Hope snapped out of her deep focus very quickly when the tempo of the room changed. The volume, the light, the whole atmosphere altered. It was suddenly urgent. Hope felt her teeth tighten. What was wrong?

The calm was gone.

The panic was palpable. However controlled they were all pretending to be, she felt it rising in her; she knew she'd caught it.

What? What? What was it?

Please let them all return to the moment before when it was right. Not this. This is wrong.

'What's happening?' Hope gasped. A question she really didn't want the answer to. Her eyes darted between Fatu and Isaac, and she knew there was fear. Slices of it.

'I'm just going to call in the consultant and one of the senior midwives. Nothing to fret about. I just think Baby is a bit . . . worried . . .'

With that, Fatu pressed a button by the bed. Very quickly the room was fuller of people. Sarah had left Anna and Julius's room and raced down the corridor. The words were a jumble to Hope; she heard snatches of hurried sentences, as everyone was talking to each other, but no one was really addressing her . . .

Bleeding heavily
No movement
Heartbeat faint
Placental abruption
Acute hypoxia
Stress on baby

19

No oxygen
Forceps
Ventouse

Quiet Isaac was right at her side and gently slipped his hand around hers as the tension increased.

'Isaac . . . what's going on? Please . . . '

'Don't you worry, darlin'. I'm here. I'm here. I'm goin' nowhere . . . ' He was aware that he was reassuring himself as much as he was comforting her.

Hope couldn't see the ever-expanding pool of blood on the bed between her legs. He could, and he started to breathe very deeply to steady his shock. The consultant swept in and was quickly gowned-up by the other nurses as they apprised him of the situation.

The situation . . .

Which was clearly getting worse by the minute. The words were being repeated again, but now louder and faster, so that he could take instant decisive action.

Abruption
Hypoxia
Zero heartbeat

The consultant took hold of the forceps and skilfully manoeuvred them inside Hope, explaining what he was doing all the time, but not once looking her in the eye. He couldn't. No time. He had to concentrate. Hope's heart was beating fast. She was in hell. For the first time, she felt like an animal. The tugging below, the stroking and patting above by Isaac, with everyone focused on the unseen baby and how to get it out quickly: it all felt overwhelmingly savage, bestial. She was still pushing and breathing hard when she looked to Isaac for any sign of comfort, and she saw that he had tears rolling down his face. Fear tears.

Quiet Isaac saw that she had noticed, and he quickly wiped his face dry and attempted a pathetic smile. He found himself suddenly noticing all the small things in the room. He was mentally pinching himself to stay strong. He focused on the top window blind, then the tap in the sink, then Hope's cross around her neck, which was now dipping into a tiny pool of sweat gathering there in the bowl of her throbbing throat.

And in that appalling, gut-wrenching instant when he couldn't meet her gaze, Hope knew.

Like a switch flicking, she shifted immediately from physical pain to mental pain, which was a jump from a puddle into Niagara Falls. The doctor was still tugging away at her, but Hope knew it was too late. That baby had climbed out of Hope's heart and was gone.

By the time the dead infant was delivered and the consultant turned off the monitor and quietly confirmed, 'I'm afraid this little one hasn't made it. I'm so very sorry, folks,' Hope had pulled up a drawbridge. No one from across the moat was coming into her grief. Even the lifeless child placed in her arms didn't stir her. She was numb.

The room went completely quiet to honour the awful moment. No one spoke. There were no words big enough. This should have been the cue for whoops and cooing and crying for joy and happy kisses. Instead, it was a breathless room for a breathless baby.

Time stopped for a few brief, respectful, hushed minutes. Hope handed the little bundle of lifeless limbs wrapped in a white hospital blanket over to Quiet Isaac, who took it so tenderly.

'It's a girl,' said Fatu. 'What will you call her?'

Hope looked at her, astonished and bewildered. 'Call her . . . ?'

'Yes. It's good to give her a name. You'll be glad you did. She's still your daughter, even though . . . she wasn't here long.'

'I was going to call her Minnie. If she was a girl . . . ' said Hope, in a daze. Her brain couldn't make sense of anything that was happening.

'She is a girl,' said Fatu, 'she is.'

'OK,' said Hope, agreeing just to get this strange moment over and done with. 'OK, then she is Minnie . . . '

'Yes. Minnie. Good. That's good,' chimed in Sarah, who had rushed in to help. She smiled at Hope, and Hope's face smiled back, although nothing in her body had directed her to do so. It was habit. Manners.

She mirrored Sarah's smile and felt a tiny infinitesimal drop of comfort. Throughout all of this muffled interaction where women were helping a woman, Quiet Isaac stared down at his tiny dead daughter. Her little face was relaxed, her eyes tight shut; she seemed to be sleeping a deep deep sleep. Born sleeping. He couldn't believe how beautiful and perfect she was. Still warm. Nutty brown with lots of black black hair. He was jolted

22

into the horrendous realization of it all, the terrible truth, by the piercing cry of a newborn — by Florence — somewhere up the corridor.

Quiet Isaac couldn't be quiet any more. He pulled his lifeless daughter tight to his chest, threw his head back and howled. His pain was as big and loud as a whole wide world of sorrow. He was helpless to save his daughter, helpless to remove Hope's anguish, and helpless to stop the torrent of sadness that flooded out of him. Here she was. A real baby. His own flesh and blood. In his arms. A miracle. Everything about her was right, except . . . except . . . she wasn't there.

Eighteen Years Later

Eyes shut, nose pinched tightly, Minnie was counting in her head underwater. She'd done this in the bath ever since she was small. She was eighteen now, but she was still no better at it.

Twenty-one elephant.

Twenty-two elephant.

Seconds are elephants. Or Mississippis. Or Minnie Moos.

Could she get past thirty for the first time ever?

Feel like a pearl diver?

Feel like she's flying?

Yes, nearly, twenty-eight elephant . . .

Gah! No, she had to sit up and surrender.

Why was she so rubbish at it?

She'd always felt as if she had less lung power than her friends. She ran out of breath before them if she did any exercise, especially dancing, which she loved. She managed one song, then she had to make excuses, sit down and watch instead. No fun whatsoever.

Minnie gulped the lovely air as she lumbered herself awkwardly into a semi-upright sitting position in the small bath. Her body was so unfamiliar now that she was six and a half months pregnant. She was amazed at how quickly her belly had grown. The first few months had been relatively uneventful physically, besides some nausea and a constant feeling of tiredness. She was tempted to believe she wasn't even pregnant at times. Then it started, a gradual swelling until this huge and remarkably defined lump settled on the front of her.

Everything, everything, everything seemed to be happening fast. It was all so different now.

She let her head rest back on the hard rim of the bath, and she could feel the coolness of it on the back of her skull, even through all the thick, wet curls.

Gradually, the water stopped sloshing about and, along with her slow and steady recovering breath, it became calm.

All of her senses were staggeringly alert.

Touch: the warm water slightly tickled her skin at the edges where it met her. The mix of the heat beneath the surface and the immediate nip of the colder air above was curious. She could feel her pores reacting. Those that had been lulled into opening below the water versus those that were closing quicksharp in the shivery crisp air above, causing goose bumps. She moved ever so slightly to tease the skin on the very edges.

Smell: the bubble bath was Matey, for children. The familiar gentle soapy aroma was heaven, and no other bathtime fragrance triggered all the happy memories like this. She'd not been without the jaunty sailor bottle on the side of the bath for her whole eighteen years. It promised that not only was it hypoallergenic, but that each bath was going to be an actual adventure. She loved it.

Hear: in the distance, she could hear Lee on his beloved PlayStation committing mass genocide in his efforts to rid the virtual world of mutant baddies. In the near, she could hear the tap dripping in the basin, and her own steady breath in

25

the damp air.

Taste: ever since she'd realized she was pregnant, she'd craved toffees. Cadbury chocolate éclair toffees. Lee supplied her regularly with many crinkly new purple packets and it was rare that she didn't have one in her mouth. She'd swallowed the latest one minutes before her breath-holding challenge, but she could still taste the remnants stuck in her teeth. Little sweetie jewels to mine with her tongue.

See: as she looked around the bathroom, her eyes were drawn to the bright green fluffy towelling dressing gown on the back of the door. Her mother's. In her mind's eye, she sees her mother wearing it. She loves the image. Then Minnie looks down along her clammy body, at her silky brown skin, flawless apart from a few stretch marks on her swollen breasts and her tight extended stomach. Past the hills of her bosoms is the mountain of her belly, and she can see nothing between or beyond. This is her baby landscape.

This is my body, Minnie thought. It belongs to me and to no one else. This is my baby, Bean. She lives in me, and I'm the container for her. Everything she is, all of her, is contained in me right here. We are part of each other. I'm her mother, and all of my future happiness will be in her happiness. Oh God, please let her be happy. Let me be a good mum. Like my mum.

She looked back at the green dressing gown. Her beautiful mum. How had she felt when SHE was six and a half months pregnant with Minnie? Had she lain in a bath like this, wondering these same things?

26

She wished she could ask her now.

But she couldn't. Not right now.

She COULD feel close to her though. A bit . . .

Minnie broke the stillness of the water, and pulled herself up and out of the bath, tugging the plug out with her toes on the way. She carefully stepped out on to the bathmat and reached out for the green dressing gown. It hardly fitted around her big belly, but it was big enough to gather her in and comfort her. As her mother had always done.

Minnie stood still as she allowed herself to drip on to the mat and realize that this home she lived in was not really a home without her mother.

Home is people, not a place.

Home is somewhere distance isn't. And she felt homesick. In her own home.

Back to the Start

Hope was not keen to hold the baby again, however much the midwives encouraged her to 'take as much time as she wanted'.

Fatu took her little body from Quiet Isaac, who was now gently sobbing.

Hope watched him. She felt so very sorry for him; it was a terrible sight to see, the lovely man so utterly bereft. He had no resources to deal with this sudden trauma. He had never known shock like it.

She felt very separate from him. They were ordinarily so close, their thoughts and feelings in tandem, sharing absolutely everything. He was sitting right next to her, but that wasn't where he was at all. He was worlds away in his own vortex of loss; he was unreachable.

Hope was hyper-aware of what was happening in the room. She knew someone was sewing her up. She knew the baby was over on a table, being put into a tiny yellow Babygro. She knew the senior midwife, Sarah, was writing out some kind of form. She knew the doctor was signing it. She knew all this because among the low buzz of activity in the room, kind people were telling her what they were doing. She watched it all. She heard it all, but Hope, like Isaac, was elsewhere.

Because detachment was familiar territory for Hope.

She had learnt very young that there is a way

to be somewhere else if you don't like what's happening around you in that moment. She became a skilled traveller to that somewhere else inside her head, where she was always much happier. She knew how to split away very successfully. She hadn't needed to do it for some time though, not really since her early teenage years and when life in her family home became too difficult to sit in the same room with. No one beat her. No one molested her. It was nothing like that — almost the opposite really. Instead of being the focus for any abuse, the abuse itself stole the focus from her, because in Hope's childhood home, the priority was heroin.

Her father Zak was a gentle man, a drummer, the only white member of a ska band who had never quite made it, but who took drugs as though they had. Weed at first, *irie* and easy, no problem, but as the fortunes of the band dwindled and then plummeted, so Zak's need to find his highs had increased. He was dangerously available for any diversion. Some were good. He wrote poetry, he helped people fix their cars, he kept an eye on Hope and her sister Glory when Doris went out to work, cleaning at the University of Bristol. He tried to quieten his frustrated inner voices with keeping busy, but inadequacy is a ferocious loud nag. The only time he had any peace from his demons was when he was sucking on a sweet sweet joint, when time stopped for a sweet sweet while. Then that wasn't enough.

Zak had easily been persuaded to try heavier drugs. He liked the stories of how 'golden' his old band-mates felt, and how nothing bad inhabited

29

them when they had these kinds of remarkable high. He was so desperate to forget his troubles that he only listened to their stories of ecstasy; he totally overlooked their sunken eyes, their loss of energy, and teeth, and reality . . . and loved ones. He craved the release from all responsibilities. At first. Then he craved it for itself. For its greedy jealous hold over him. He forgot to love his family more than the drug and, before long, the ravenous drug was almost his only love, to the painful exclusion of everyone else including his beloved girls. Heroin stole all his love.

Hope's mum Doris had smoked a bit of weed occasionally back then, but she had been too afraid to get involved with smack. She watched Zak disappear into the fug of it, though, and rather than face up to the devastating impact it was having on them all, witnessing him gouched out so much of the time, she turned to her friends down the pub for support and comfort, those who had already turned to alcohol for support and comfort. She was too ashamed to confront her daughters with the awfulness of the situation, so she escaped to the pub and to vodka with orange. Her new best friend. Over a period of a year, Hope and Glory experienced the creeping neglect of both parents.

It might have been easier if Zak and Doris had been unkind parents you'd be glad to have less of, but that was palpably not the case. Zak was still the gentle funny dad they'd always loved; it was just that now he was the comatose version, either off his face or desperate to be, or very shaky and ill because he had been the night before. Their mum was still their mum, but either the embarrassing loud and drunk one or the grumpy hungover one.

When she was fourteen, Hope had had to go to Glory's parents' evening because neither parent showed up and Glory rang her in tears. 'They bloody promised they'd be here, Hope, PROMISED, to my face! How could they do this to me?'

'Hang on, don't move. I'll be right there.' Hope had raced back to the school, hugged her furious, hurt sister, and then hurriedly explained to the various waiting teachers, 'Sorry Mum and Dad can't come, they've both . . . got . . . a terrible bug, so if it's OK, I'll be Glory's stand-in mum for now. I'll tell them everything you say, yeah?'

No one on the staff had been fooled. They had taught both girls since primary school and knew the family well. Of course they'd noticed the girls weren't quite so fresh any more, they'd both become tattier and definitely a bit thinner. There were rumours in the staffroom about the well-being of them both, and about their home life, but they remained rumours; no one came calling to check on the sisters back then. There were so many more critical cases than theirs for the social workers to consider. So they slipped under the radar, these two valiant sisters, and Hope grew up very quickly.

Sometimes, on the days her mother was particularly frail and groggy, Hope would skip school to accompany her to work. No one seemed to mind that Doris's daughter was with her. Furthermore, no one seemed to notice that it was mainly Hope doing the actual cleaning on those days while Doris slept it off in a chair. When she was sober, Doris was massively grateful to Hope, and she would apologize by buying her delicious pizza on the way home. They would laugh and walk arm in arm as they always had, and for a tiny while, it would all be like it used to be, and Hope would have a small 'catching of happiness' . . . until they walked in at home and Dad was out for the count . . .

The family kept doors firmly shut to outsiders. The secret of these darker notes in their life was to remain exactly that: secret. Even Doris's family were kept at arms' length, meaning that the sisters were starved of contact with their cousins and their uncles whom they loved so much. Occasionally there would be a ruckus when one of Doris's brothers would turn up to confront them. They shouted from outside when their entrance was barred, imploring Zak or Doris to open up or at least let the girls out to spend time with the family. But no. Sometimes they would hide so as not to be thought at home. Hope longed for the doors to open, to let the light and fresh air in, have a barbeque, put music on and be with people she loved, laughing and dancing. That's why Hope was determined, in adult life, that hers would be a doors-open house where all were welcome. There would be nothing to hide in there . . . would there?

Still, it was back in those old days of her childhood fears that Hope had learnt to detach from the 'now' life, to travel to the 'could-be' life in her head. Hope wanted her mum and dad back, and she had no idea what to do to make that happen. She chose, with her juvenile best thinking, to find the good in everything. She ignored the dark fug of their home, the lack of food in the cupboards and fridge, the detritus of her dad's drug use on

32

the table and floor all around him, the smell of unwashed underwear beneath unwashed clothes, the lack of telly due to electricity cut-offs, the stumbling about of her parents. Instead, she invented a world for Glory and her to play in, usually in the peace of their bedroom where they made up fantastical stories and built towns from cushions and boxes, where dolls could live the bright and happy life the sisters couldn't. They had a theatre of delights at their fingertips.

It was the night-time when Hope had felt most sad and frightened. She knew her parents loved her in their misguided way, but she always had a nagging fear in her belly. This way of living wasn't right: there was no light, no safety, no joy. She would stay awake feeling anxious, so to try and combat the fretting she learnt to float away in her mind to a deep place where only she needed to look after her, where she felt wrapped up and cherished. By herself. She learnt to detach and self-soothe.

So, in the painful now of this hospital room of the dead, with Isaac crying and no baby to take home, she splintered off into her own world of coping, where she was inwardly stroking stroking stroking her broken heart. She wouldn't be able to carry on otherwise.

Fatu placed the baby back in Hope's arms. She was now dressed in the yellow Babygro Hope had brought with her, and she was wearing the tiny woollen hat Hope had knitted. It was her first attempt to knit anything, and it was a bit wonky, but it was made with love, in stripes of pink and yellow. Hope stared at Minnie for a few seconds.

'No,' said Hope, 'she won't need this,' and she gently removed the hat, and handed the baby back. She didn't want to hold her or look at her any more. What was the point? Hope wasn't in the now place, and she wanted to be done with now. Now was indescribably dire.

The midwives took the baby and started talking about funeral plans in hushed tones, about how someone would be in touch, and how there were organizations they could turn to for some support.

The doctor came over to close by her side. 'I'm so very sorry about this,' he said as he handed her an envelope, 'but it's best to get it over and done with, let you get home, so . . . in this envelope there's a form, a certificate which I've signed. You will need it when you go to register the . . . incident. All the details of where to go and everything are in there. It's best to register it within five days. Now, there may be a post-mortem, but only with your permission, and only for medical purposes. We'd all be grateful if you consented, but there's no obligation. There's no mystery surrounding this; the certificate simply says 'intrapartum', which means during labour. The reasons are unknown, as is so often the case, I'm afraid. It's tragic, inexplicable, but as I always say, there are more things in heaven and earth. I do hope we will see you back here again with a happier outcome. You're healthy and young and there's no reason to think that won't be possible one day. So. All the best. Such a lovely couple. Chin up and all the best.' With that, he was gone.

Quiet Isaac was open-mouthed with astonishment at the sheer machine-gun-fire speed of the doctor's well-meaning information. At least the surprise of it had brought him back into the room with a jolt. He reached out to Hope and took her hand.

Hope allowed the gentleness of it, although she filtered out any sympathy with which it was offered. If she allowed that she would be toppled.

No pity. No, thanks.

A tiny dollop of comfort? OK.

Hope took the pain-relief tablets she was offered and laid her head back on the pillow. It felt damp to her neck; it was the sweat from all the effort earlier when her baby had still been alive. She chose to ignore it, close her eyes and rest. She could hear them all faffing around in the room. She prayed that when she opened her eyes again, there would be no baby anywhere to be seen.

She prayed that when she opened her eyes again, Quiet Isaac would be composed and strong once more . . .

She prayed that she would sleep a little and maybe when she opened her eyes, all of this might have been a nightmare and she would start giving birth all over again, this time to a live baby . . .

As she prayed for all this, she wondered whether her prayers were ever heard?. She had doubted like this before, when she was younger, but she had rejected those thoughts because she so needed God to be on her team back then; she couldn't face the thought that he might not exist. She took massive comfort from the idea that God, the big real God, was *in loco parentis*, that He was look- ing out for her at a distance, the way her real dad wasn't.

35

There, there, she was stroking her heart.

Now here she was years later, doing the same again, but this time, however much she yearned for the comfort, the doubt chipped away at her. What kind of father-God let this woeful cruelty happen to her? To anyone? Surely only a vicious and vengeful God? Did He hate her or something? Did she do something so wrong? Had she offended Him? It was unfair on her, on Isaac, and especially on little Minnie. Little dead Minnie. Who deserved a life, who was innocent and perfect and who had tried so hard to live. Why didn't He help her have that? Why did He forsake her at that very last moment?

Hope felt the anger boiling up inside her; she heard the distant roar of it. She didn't want it any closer, so she shut it down quickly. She just wanted her baby.

She wanted it so much.

She kept her eyes tightly shut and forced her mind to sink deeper, below the agony, to some rest. The heavy painkillers helped her, they were sedative and eventually sleep claimed her as she fell deeper and deeper, pulled further into the arms of Morpheus by a thousand chubby babies' arms, tugging tugging her drowsy drowsy down.

★ ★ ★

In Anna and Julius's room, further up the corridor, there was a low-grade hushed argument kicking off, threatening to gear up into a full-blown row. Julius was beginning to raise his voice: 'All I am saying is that if I call Kirsty now, she can

36

action the release of the press statement about the birth. I did bother to prepare it, so why wouldn't we push the button?'

'Because, Jules, and please keep your voice down, it is three o'clock in the ruddy morning — what is the point of waking Kirsty up now? She's exhausted enough as it is. Surely it can wait? Come on now. And shush, please.'

'The whole point is to catch the early editions. We need to get amongst it. Pronto. Or sooner.'

'Jules, surely it is more of a priority to tell the family? My parents will be waiting by the phone. Call them first? You did promise. And leave the papers 'til tomorrow. Please?'

Julius harrumphed like a spoilt six-year-old. This meant he would be forced to talk to Anna's parents, who would no doubt want all the minute details about the birth. He genuinely had zero interest in talking about all that guff; besides which, he hadn't really witnessed it, since he was spark out for most of the time.

'Jules, seriously, it's not just my ma and pa — oh and my bro please, and Jo: I promised her — it's your bloody mum too, and your sisters, for God's sake. Surely they're your first bloody call?' Anna whispered loudly.

'OK, OK. Yes, OK,' he replied, annoyed, and immediately called his best friend Piers instead. 'Piers, wake up, mate. Yeah. A girl. Filly and foal doing fine, yeah . . .'

Julius was no stranger to arguments. In fact, he enjoyed them. As Julius wandered out into the corridor to continue his conversation, it annoyed Anna that he was so loud despite the fact it was

37

very early and the hospital was cocooned in the unmistakeable early-morning shush that happens just before a building properly wakes up. Other people must surely be giving birth, this was the maternity ward after all, she thought, but nevertheless it was quiet. And Julius wasn't. He was laughing as he strutted up and down, boasting loudly for all the world, sleeping or awake, to hear. These phone calls weren't just to inform or celebrate as far as Julius was concerned. No, they were his calling card to anyone he told, a calling card which, were it to be printed out, would read:

Julius Albert Lindon-Clarke MP
Tory. Husband. FATHER.
Seed-giver. Success.
Very. Important. Indeed.

At last, he had achieved fatherhood, which was very important . . . for his job. It authenticated him. It helped him to be regarded as stable and faithful. The British public needed to trust him, and the new little wriggly bundle was a key part of that package.

He had been extremely worried when no baby came along earlier in the marriage and he was nervous when Anna suggested getting help in the form of IVF. He'd turned his feelings of failure and frustration into an offended childish stomp-off. It was some time before Anna tentatively suggested it again. Five years and a pressurized but sparse love life later, Julius had agreed to go and see an IVF specialist with her. By the time Anna had booked the appointment, she was pregnant. It was

38

truly miraculous — they so rarely shared any intimacy — but he had come home one night in early April after a 'late session' in the House, smelling of cannabis and very interested in her. She knew deep in her honest heart that he'd been unfaithful many times, but she couldn't accept it in her day-to-day trying-to-stick-to-the-marriage-vows-and-just-get-on-with-life state of mind. She didn't want to confront him with it — he had a quick, ferocious temper and the poisonous tongue of a thousand snakes. He hadn't displayed this side of his nature for some years when she first met him.

But.

Then again.

There were many hidden parts of Julius Albert Lindon-Clarke. Anna couldn't have known when she first met him, but he wasn't a whole real person. He was a construct, a convincing, attractive façade. Julius had scars. He had been the butt of many jokes when he was young. It wasn't obviously to do with his race, there were plenty of other black kids at his school and they were respected and powerful. It was to do with his snobbish attitude.

Snobbery, whatever colour it's wrapped up in, is pretty galling. As he saw it, he was truly entitled to any level of importance he desired. He saw no limit to any of his many aspirations and he genuinely believed that those who did were fools, and he pitied the paucity of their ambition.

Julius also had actual scars, from heart surgery he'd experienced as a very young child. The marks across his chest were testament to a very serious operation he'd undergone to correct a rare heart defect. The staff at the hospital in London where he was born noticed how blue he was and how little he fed. His breathing was shallow and he gained virtually no weight in the first few weeks. The doctor eventually told his mother the frightening news that he had something they named 'coarctation of the aorta', which they explained to her meant that part of his aorta was too narrow, thereby causing the left ventricle of his heart to have to work much harder. It could mean a problem with lack of blood flow to the lower half of his body if it remained unresolved, so she agreed to the proposed surgery. Julius was plumbed in wrong; basically there were serious errors in his piping. During the substantial surgery, the surgeon had to excise the section that was too narrow, and stretch the remaining tissue around the small Gore-Tex tube which replaced it. The operation was entirely successful and little Julius was soon able to go home with his mother and grew up without any further health issues other than the odd check-up. By the time his two younger sisters came along, Julius was fighting fit, and at age five he was pretty much assuming the role of the man of the house. The father figure he longed for, he became.

Except he wasn't very fatherly. It was the position and status he desired, not the emotional responsibility, but being the only boy and the eldest, and the most prized by his mother (in no small part because she felt she almost lost him very early on), he had the figurehead role bestowed upon him, and he liked how important that made him feel.

Julius was going to MATTER, whatever it took, however many other people might have to be swept aside to achieve it. Ironically, Julius didn't notice that those he was repeatedly sweeping aside, namely his mother, his two younger sisters and his wife, were in fact the very people he mattered the most to. They were ultimately the ones who endeavoured to love him best, despite how challenging that was, especially as he began to gain some purchase on his meticulously planned career path. The first whiff Julius had of any kind of status he might gain was when he took part in a school debate about the death penalty and why it was abolished in 1965. He was the only candidate to propose the return of such a penalty in cases of murder. He was extremely dramatic and persuasive when he recounted the grisly details of various murders he had researched, mostly brutal ones. The sixteen-year-old Julius re-enacted the events with great showmanship and plenty of vigour, eventually pleading with the audience of fellow fifth-formers at his grammar school, as if he were the prosecution attorney in an edgy crime series:

'And so I urge you, upright citizens that you clearly are, to consider the moral justice of capital punishment. Look inside your own hearts, your own consciences, and surely what you will find is the incontrovertible truth that if, God forbid, someone killed your mother brutally, like this, it would be the only right thing to do, the biblical and justified RIGHT thing. That, my friends, however unpalatable, would be the neat and correct ending to any murderer's life. I rest my case.'

When, inexplicably, he received a round of applause for his impassioned argument, Julius's world changed. The possibility of power was no longer a whiff, it was a graveolence. Julius reframed himself in that instant as a potentially significant person and he relished all the attention it brought him. Little did he realize then that this kind of limelight is the worst poison for a psychopath such as he.

It would feed
  feed
   feed
    feed his monstrous ego, and it would lead him to seek out his approval and his love in all the wrong places.

And it would also allow him to repeatedly and selfishly forget all the sacrifices his family had made to help their golden boy on his way.

Julius finished his loud phone calls and came back into the room where his wife and baby were. The midwives had gone for now; the baby was wrapped up tight and dozing in the see-through plastic crib next to Anna's bed. He flumped down into the chair at the end of the bed and, without a single glance at his daughter, yawned a huge, cavernously loud yawn, uttered, 'God, I'm knackered . . .' and promptly fell fast asleep, mission accomplished.

Anna, barely resisting the urge to sleep, was trying to remain upright so that she could share this precious time with Florence.

She didn't even want to blink really, so as not to forgo a moment where she could be looking at Florence's beautiful little face. She couldn't stop staring. 'Look at you, tiny one,' she whispered. 'Who are you actually? I know you, you lived inside me, but now you're here, I don't think I do know you after all. You are yourself, aren't you? A whole new person of your own, bless you. Welcome, darling Florence. There were two of us. Now there's three. And you're the best one of us all . . .'

'Bah.'

A strange involuntary grumble coming from her conked-out husband made Anna look over to him. She watched Julius as his head slowly lolled forward on to his chest, and he started his familiar caveman rumble of a snore, leaving her to watch over Florence. Anna imagined that this would be the first of many nights just like this, where she would be alone with the responsibility.

She didn't know that there would never be another.

1 January 2000

The tinkling of a hospital teacup woke Hope up. It was still early, around 6.30 a.m., but Quiet Isaac was clearly in the new day in such an affirmative way. He smiled at her as he slurped his milkless tea.

'Hey. Sun is shining,' he said, risking a tentative smile. Hope looked at the window and indeed it was — shining brightly. She could see dust particles dancing in a beam hitting the far wall. To anyone else, this would be entrancing. Beautiful even. But for Hope, no. She didn't like to see dust anywhere, and definitely not here in the hospital where she was in charge of ridding it of exactly that.

She and Isaac were the only people there. The baby cot was empty. So empty. Except the atoms of dust. The dust that might have also once been on her baby.

She sat up and took the fresh cup of tea Isaac poured for her from a sludgy green teapot. There was no sugar in it. She liked sugar, did Hope. She liked it far too much. But there was none on the tray, so she settled for tea with just the milk. It was hot and vaguely tea-ish, and that was enough to rehydrate her, which was all she wanted, because her head was pounding.

All Hope knew was that she needed to get out of that room, that ward, that hospital. She felt a strange mixture of sadness, shame and embarrassment. What had happened to them was supremely

44

personal, and she wanted to hide away so that she could nurse herself.

As she moved her legs out from underneath the warm sheets, she felt the sharp sting of pain where her stitches were. Ow.

Quiet Isaac saw her wince and moved to help her.

'It's OK. I'm fine. My clothes . . . ?'

'Let's wait for the nurse. She said she'd be back soon.'

'I just want to . . . get home . . . '

'I know. I know, but be careful, Bubs,' and he reached out to her.

She looked him in the eye and they both understood just how much it all hurt, and Hope let him hold her. As her face nestled into his chest where he stood at the side of the bed, she could hear his heartbeat, strong and steady, like the Isaac she knew before all this, the Isaac she came into the hospital with. He was back, strong and supportive, and she was gratefully glad of it. Perhaps they might just get through everything as long as they were together . . . ?

Fatu came back in and explained that Hope was free to go whenever she felt ready to. She gave Hope a packet of pain-relief tablets and an antibacterial wash to keep her stitches clean. She sat next to Hope on the bed and, very very sensitively, she said, 'I have a pack here for you, Hope. It has some information about a support group for people who have been through this similar situation. They're good at their job, so lean on them if you want to, yes? I know you want to leave, but if you would like to see the hospital chaplain, I can call him ... ?'

'No, no, it's far too early.'

'He would never mind, honestly.'

'No. Thank you. It's OK. Thank you.' Hope knew she wouldn't be able to stomach another sympathy-tilted head. At least Fatu had been there in the room with them through it all. Others couldn't possibly understand.

'And lastly, Hope, this envelope is for you to pass on to the funeral director, when you are ready. It has all the details of where little Minnie will be kept for now ... '

'What do you mean, 'kept'?'

'Where she will wait to be collected ... '

'Where is she then?' Hope asked.

Fatu paused. The word was hard to say, but she knew she must. 'In the hospital mortuary. Safe.'

Fatu had kept it together valiantly until this moment of raw reality. She was a young midwife, and stillbirth was relatively rare, so witnessing Hope and Isaac's shock and pain was dreadful for her. She wished it had turned out differently for them, but there was nothing she could do other than offer her sisterly giant heart in a professional manner.

Fatu put her hand on Hope's hand, which was in turn on Isaac's hand, and for a small frozen moment, the three of them shared the heaviness of the grief. When Hope lifted her head to look Fatu in the eye and thank her, she saw that Fatu wasn't coping with the sadness.

'I'm so sorry, sista.' A fat tear rolled down Fatu's cheek and sploshed on to her hand.

Hope reached up to Fatu's face and wiped away

46

any wet that was threatening to congregate and make more tears. ''S OK. It's . . . yeah . . . OK. It is this, it's what it is and nothing can change it now, so save your tears. But thank you. From me and him and . . . her. Thank you. You did nothing wrong. We know that.'

'Oh, thank you for sayin' so . . . I wish — '

'I know,' Hope interrupted her. 'My grand-mother would say this is God's wish. I dunno what I think right now, but we need to go away and work out how to live without her . . .'

'I don't know how you're goin' to do that, but I get the strong feelin' it's goin' to be all right, I really do.' Fatu tried to reassure her with what she undoubtedly felt was the truth. 'You want some breakfast?'

'No, no, we will go if we're allowed to . . . ?'

'Yes, you are free to leave, but, Hope, please take it steady. Can I help you to shower . . . ?'

'No, no, thanks, I can manage . . . ' And with that Hope released their hands and stood up. She wasn't an invalid; she could get herself ready. She was a bit sore but she could manage. Hope was a tower of strength, and even if, like now, there were times she wasn't, boy could she fake it. She had reached that moment when if she didn't move for-ward somehow, she knew she would tip back into the awfulness of what had happened a few hours ago. Nope. That was NOT going to happen. She needed to motor on. She needed to get out.

Quiet Isaac went to pick up the two large bags they had packed to bring in. One was full of baby clothes, blankets, newborn nappies and everything they could possibly need to bring their new little

47

one home. Isaac wanted to get this bag especially out of Hope's eyeline and out of the building into the boot of his tatty old Honda Civic parked in the hospital's basement garage. The zip was tightly closed on that one; it hadn't even been opened once. It would return home packed. The saddest bag in history.

Quiet Isaac picked up the other overnight bag, but Hope stopped him.

'Best leave that one. I'll put my nightie in it, and there's my washbag stuff . . . ' she said, touching his arm.

'OK, I'll take this,' he said as he went to the corner of the room and picked up the baby car seat they'd bought to make sure the tiddly infant was safe homeward bound. He was a pitiful sight. A man so loaded down with the defunct detritus of his tragedy.

The seat was a pastel purple colour with a pattern of ducklings on the padding. The bag was pale yellow with cheerful pink hearts all over it. The man was brown, with a black and blue interior. He attempted a valiant last smile; then he was gone.

Hope was grateful the delivery suite had its own bathroom. She closed the door behind her. This was the first minute she'd had entirely alone since . . . well, since.

Everything inside Hope was trembling. She felt that only her skin was keeping the shaky jelly in, and her skin was extra thin right now. She wondered if people might actually be able to SEE the wobbling mass she was just beneath the surface, if they were up close? She turned the shower on, and she stepped in.

48

Something very strange happened to Hope as the water hit her upturned face. It gave licence to Hope's tears, the first she had cried. Hope had cried before in her life, many times; she'd had some pretty lonely moments trying to be both parents to her sister, and worrying herself sick about her mum and dad, but she'd not experienced anything like this. These tears came from a bottomless well she didn't know was there. How could something so recent, so new, feel like such ancient sorrow? It was as if she'd lost her oldest, dearest darling, the closest soul to hers. Some of her, of herself, had died. Unexpectedly.

She opened her mouth and as the shower water gushed in, she let out a choking yelp. She held on to the wet, cold tiled walls for balance as she looked down at the water disappearing into the plughole, taking with it all the hopeful skin she had yesterday, when life was so differently better and so full of happy anticipation. Hope's tears joined in and swirled around the drain along with all of her joy and she watched it vanish. She was emptying out. She felt weak. And raw. And strangely heavy. Surely all these tears escaping should leave her lighter, in every way? And yet she could barely stand, owing to the weight of the concrete sadness in the pit of her stomach. She placed her back to the wall, felt the cool of it with a wince and slid down until she was crumpled up in the shower tray, curled in on herself with the hot water pounding down on her. She started to slap the wall with the flat of her hand, and soon she was on her knees thwacking the wall repeatedly and howling out her pain.

49

When, finally, Hope's breathing was back to calm and regular, she stepped out of the shower and vigorously rubbed herself dry with the merciless over-bleached hospital towel. She rubbed very hard. She wanted that top layer of baby-hopeful skin gone. She wanted her hair clean of the baby-pushing sweat. She wanted no single remnant of any of it. Her skin felt raw but it helped somehow. Even the way it stung felt right. The inner anguish boiling away, filling her up and pushing out through every pore.

Fatu popped back into the room and heard the noises coming from the bathroom. 'You OK in there, Hope?' she enquired as she knocked on the door.

'Yep. Yep. Fine. No problem,' Hope shouted from within her own private wet hell. 'I'm nearly done . . . '

'Take your time, no rush,' Fatu answered. She hesitated briefly in order to listen closely at the door, just to be sure Hope was all right. She heard nothing alarming, so she carried on with her work.

Home was definitely where Hope wanted to be now. She wanted everything familiar around her; it might help to anchor her to the earth again because, sure as hell, nothing in the hospital seemed normal. Even though it was her place of work, it felt like a completely strange and hostile other planet. She was glad it was early and she might avoid seeing any of her cleaning team as she left. She'd promised that she would present her new little one to them on the way home, but she couldn't face telling them. She couldn't face the pity; it would tip her over the edge. She wanted to dodge them all and get straight down to the car and waiting Quiet Isaac.

Home. Home. Home.

Hope looked in the mirror, and saw a strange, drawn face she barely recognized. She was only twenty years old. How could a twenty-year-old woman look like the haggard, haunted person staring back at her?

Working in the hospital, Hope saw every day how illness affected people. She regularly saw the brutal ravages of cancer and the toll that pain took on so many patients. It was a difficult truth to face so often, but she was aware that she had come to normalize it a bit. She had to. She had to learn to work alongside difficult circumstances and she had to avoid showing any scintilla of shock. She had to be able to walk into any room, and see any sight, without flinching. Illness and how it took shape: she could cope with that; it was the awful trauma on the faces of the visitors that stopped her heart more often than not, and their brave, unsuccessful efforts to hide it. The fear was visible in the eyes of wives and husbands, sons and daughters, all having to realize that their worlds might be about to change beyond all recognition, that yesterday was going to be vastly different to tomorrow. And that it was probably going to be worse.

Hope had often wondered how those people fared after they left the hospital, both through the front and back doors. They went home changed, but what happened then? Did they learn to live differently? Did they cope? She only knew the part of their stories that happened in this building, but she'd always wondered about that next crucial part.

And . . . here she was, glimpsing in the mirror a ghost of a person, shaken with shock, forced face down into a heap of horror and now looking back at her with unmistakeable injury. Her eyes had seen the worst sight she could ever imagine and she couldn't understand how she would ever unsee it. The baby. The sleeping baby. The dead baby. The image was there forever. She could hardly keep herself together thinking about it for an instant, never mind having it seared into her heart forever. She wasn't going to cope or be OK or be fine. She was going to be swallowed up by it. She was going to see it every waking moment and most sleeping moments. It was going to be torture, an unbearable torture.

Hope dressed quickly, trying to put aside any hurtful thoughts. As she leant down to pull up her skirt, she whimpered quietly. She heard the noise and knew she had made it, but was surprised to hear it. She stopped for a moment to calm herself, and it happened again.

'Stop it. Stop it. Come on . . . ' she whispered to herself, and as she did, more of the little sobs surfaced, almost as though a hiccup and a cry had conspired together. Hope was emptying. She'd known it would happen soon, but she'd hoped she might have made it home first. She felt dizzy and helpless to contain it. All of the anguish inside her was bubbling up, wanting to explode, be acknowledged.

She sat down so as not to fall down, and she tried to piece herself together again. 'Come on, Hope, get it together,' she was repeating over and over, but she was full to the brim and her brain was not listening. Hope tried to think carefully, in an orderly way. It wasn't working. Her mind wasn't receiving the transmissions her heart was making. A trauma bomb had exploded inside Hope's head. All normal thoughts or processes were utterly shattered. Her head was a skullful of splinters and her world was collapsing.

Hope clasped her chest. She knew that her heart was beating very fast. She had the distinct feeling it might actually burst. Was that what the breaking of a heart felt like?

The rending of a heart?

The ending of a heart?

Was it going to simply stop? And then, would she also . . .

stop? For a tempting moment, she even embraced the idea. It would be better to be dead than to feel like this. This was terrifying. She wouldn't be able to stand it much longer. Was she going mad? Was this what full-on crazy was like?

She wanted Isaac. She had to get to him as soon as possible.

If she could stand up. And walk. And talk. And seem ordinary.

'Come on, come on, it's gonna be OK . . . OK and fine, that's what we are . . . ' She tried the mantra. 'OK. Yes. And fine. OK and fine . . . ' And somehow she managed to finish dressing. She flung her last few items into the remaining bag. She held on to the walls, the bed and the cupboard to steady herself, and somehow, soothing herself all the while, she was ready to leave.

'Shall I come with you down to the car?' Fatu

53

was standing in the doorway.

'No, no. Seriously. I'm OK. Thank you, Fatu. Again.' The two women hugged.

'Don't forget your coat, sista, it's cold out there.' Fatu took Hope's red coat from the hook behind the door.

'Yes. Good. Good. Goodbye . . .' Hope said as she manoeuvred out of the door, awkwardly holding the overnight bag straps in one hand, her red coat in the other and her handbag over her shoulder. Off she went, out into the corridor, heading for the lifts and her escape from the graveyard of her beautiful daughter. She could feel the yelps rising inside her again, but she was determined to make it to the car.

No one who met her that morning would see that, in that moment, Hope was broken.

Hope was hopeless.

The Chance

Hope was hurrying down the corridor, anxious to make a swift exit, to leave here and somehow, eventually, convince herself that none of this had happened.

Her legs were carrying her along quite fast, although the quicker she moved, the more she felt the sharp pain between them; the sting was vicious.

But nothing compared to the earthquake happening inside her. Hope was split away from her real, true self. This wasn't Hope rushing down the corridor; it was a mess in Hope's flesh, parading as a normal human. She felt dizzy and disorientated, so she let her hand brush against the cool wall to steady her as she raced along. Her head was thumping; she could feel her pulse, beating too fast and irregularly, and her own confused blood swirling in her veins, hammering around in the chambers of her hurt heart. She was in many pieces. None of her was joined together properly; she didn't feel real. She was a numb, walking-dead zombie. Except zombies shuffled. Hope wasn't shuffling; she was zooming along. Too fast, too fast. She almost tripped and had to stop for a second to steady herself. She leant heavily against the wall and hung her head down momentarily while she caught her breath. She kept looking up to check both directions of the corridor, like a nervous cat. She didn't want anyone to see her like this. She wanted to GET OUT.

She was relieved to see that no one whatsoever was in the corridor. She could see as far as
the nurses' station at the end by the door, and it
seemed that nobody was there, even. She could
hear some faint sounds coming from behind various doors along the hall, the sounds of birth, in
different stages. These were noises she herself had
been making only a few hours before. Hope really
didn't wish to listen to another second of anyone
else's miraculous moment, but she was shattered,
mentally and physically finished, and could hardly
move.

Hope looked at the door next to where she
had stopped. There was a long window in it, and
through that, she could see a large slumped man
sleeping in a chair in the corner. His mouth was
wide open and she could hear his loud snoring
through the thick door. She could see the end of
a hospital bed and, just beyond that, she glimpsed
the edge of a see-through baby cot, just like the
one she'd had in her own room. The empty one.

But this cot wasn't empty; she could see two
tiny little feet paddling against the Perspex. The
baby was awake.

The door Hope was leaning on wasn't a sliding
door . . .

Yet it was.

A giant, inexplicable universal magnet drew
Hope into the room. She was utterly helpless to
resist. A cosmic grappling iron had been thrown
out, latched itself to her heart, and was now reel-
ing her in.

She leant against the door and it opened silently,

56

causing her to almost fall into the room. As she stepped forward, slowly and quietly, she put her bags down, and Hope took in every detail of the room as it revealed itself to her, inch by inch.

The big dark man was definitely sound asleep.

The baby was sleepy-eyed, but gurgly happy, wriggly and blinking at her first daylight.

The mother was turned towards the wall and breathing very deeply in her exhausted slumber, with her blonde hair splayed across her sweaty face.

The whole room was bathed in winter morning light.

There were bags and phones and jackets and bottles of water and a banana skin and a brush and a car seat.

All the same sort of normal stuff Hope and Quiet Isaac had had in THEIR room. In readiness for THEIR baby.

The car seat. Yes.

Isaac was sitting downstairs in the underground car park waiting for her. She needed to go, but something kept her in this room, watching the family just being, being together, as if she were entirely invisible. She could hear them all breathing in their very different ways. She saw the same dancing dust in the light. She noticed that was the only movement besides the rise and fall of the man's chest and the woman's ribs, and of course the happy writhing of the infant, which she was so drawn to.

Hope risked a step closer. She had to see the baby up close. She wanted to look. A step wasn't enough, so she took another. And another, until she was standing right next to the bassinet. The newborn saw her and immediately stopped gurgling as their eyes locked on to each other. Lovely open eyes. ALIVE.

The baby was exquisite. Unmistakeably female, she had flawless bronze skin, a mass of curiously straight black hair, large deep brown eyes and the most deliciously dribbly kissy lips. She was perfect. She was life. And she was looking right at broken Hope, who could physically feel her heart mending as they gazed at each other. The longing was mammoth. Here, staring at Hope, was her missing piece, everything she surely needed right at that moment to be happy. It was precisely then, in this crazy stopped slice of time, that Hope suddenly became aware that she was lactating. She felt the wetness from her nipples making stains on her blouse. She looked down, and confirmed that it really was happening: her body wanted to feed that baby.

And it was precisely then that little Florence reached her hand up. Her perfect hand with her beautiful tiny pinkish nails, trying to connect with Hope. The wrist was so small, and circled with the hospital wristband identifying her name. Florence was looking for her mother. Hope wanted to be that more than anything, ever. In an instant worthy of a fresco by Michelangelo, Hope tentatively reached out her hand, into the bassinet, and into the tiny perfect fingers of Florence Lindon-Clarke, who immediately grasped her. This was Hope's could-be life. Hope knew instinctively that the baby wanted to be picked up and held close, and that in a matter of seconds she

58

was probably going to yell for that to happen. She mustn't cry. The man and the woman would wake and find her there.

Boom. It happened. Without so much as a second thought, Hope snapped. She crossed the line. In the fuzzy haze of Hope's dreadful sadness, she couldn't possibly discern the boundaries of right or wrong. How can a person know their own mind when their own mind is absent? Hope's whole body was doing what it NEEDED. For her, right then, it was indisputably right.

In less than ten seconds the baby was lifted out of the cot and into Hope's big overnight bag, nestled on top of Hope's nightie, zipped up and heading out of the door.

Out.

Quick.

Out.

Hope made sure the door closed gently behind her with a soft flump, nothing to disturb either parent. As she raced up the corridor, her feet hardly touched the ground; she was fleeing over dangerous hot coals.

The nurses' station seemed deserted, but as she crept by she heard the low mumblings of someone on the phone. The desk around the station was at chest height, and all Hope could see was the top of someone's head, who was clearly deep in conversation. Never had Hope been so pleased with the purchase of a pair of trainers. The particular ones she was wearing had been on sale in a Nike shop in Carnaby Street a month prior. She was passing by with no intention and pretty much no budget to go shopping, but they were in the window, these Air Max 270 Flyknits, brazenly daring her to buy them, and tempting her with a third-of-the-original-price tag combined with their irresistible air-soles and ultra-breathable orange uppers. She was a goner. Instantly in love with them. She adored them for so many reasons, but she didn't know the true depth of the love until now, when they were the perfect getaway vehicle because they were . . . s . . . i . . . l . . . e . . . n . . . t. Only her breath and the airstream she was creating in her wake would give her away. With that in her mind, alchemy in her soul and prayers in her heart, Hope wondrously became

> as small as a mouse
> as thin as paper
> as fast as light
> as invisible as vapour
> as breathless as a dead baby

and somehow . . . somehow . . . all the gods and wizards of kindness and fortune conspired to help her reach the ward door unnoticed. She burst through, and as it flapped shut behind her, the phone-busy nurse looked up, too late to see her, and too distracted to try.

At that precise moment, an early-shift midwife emerged from a room near the station, and started to make her way back down the corridor towards Anna and Julius's room. She yawned and peered through the same window in the door that Hope had looked through just moments before. She saw a sleeping exhausted father, a sleeping exhausted mother, and she saw the very end of the bassinet where the blanket was bunched up in such a way that it looked just like a perfectly safe sleeping baby's covered feet. Reassured, she made the most giant career-threatening error of her life. She moved away, to get on with her day.

Hope decided to avoid the lift just in case the baby made a noise, so she headed for the stairs and cursed the fact that the maternity ward was on the eighth floor. She knew she had to get into the basement garage and she wasn't sure this stair-well would go all the way down. Would she have to divert back into the main body of the hospital to find the exit to the underground parking?

As she descended, it was clear that the hospital was kicking into the top gear of a fresh day, as one, then four, then eleven and more members of hospital staff arrived on to the stairs at various floors, rushing up and down to their jobs. Some greeted her with a quick 'Morning!', most took the stairs three at a time, and absolutely none genuinely looked at her. Although she worked in this hospital, the sheer size of it meant that the staff count was in the thousands. Nobody really knew her, and she realized that she didn't even know the building very well, because she typically stuck to the floors where she had always been assigned, and to the service lifts accessing those couple of floors. She was a stranger on these stairs.

Hope had to be careful not to slip because she was going so fast. She could hear the faintest sound of the baby responding to the jiggling of the bag, but no one else would hear it against the thunder of footfall on concrete steps.

When she reached ground level, Hope noticed

a side door off the main stairwell, indicating 'Parking'. She slipped through the door. It wasn't easy to manoeuvre with the awkwardness of all she was carrying, but she managed it.

The stairs down to the garage were different to the ones above. They were narrower, darker and had that unmistakeable putrid uriney stench. This deeply offended her. Nothing in her hospital should smell like this. The stairs weren't the most common route to the parking area, the big lifts in the main concourse were; but, nevertheless, some folk would be using them. Hope muttered to herself as she moved along, 'For God's sake. This isn't a nightclub. It's a hospital. Who gets out of a car to visit someone and thinks, Oh I know, I'll just have a quick wee on these stairs . . . ? There are tons of loos a minute away inside the building! I mean, honestly, who does that?'

Hope was glad her baby was cocooned away inside the bag, protected from the rancid pee particles she might inhale. Hope didn't want this awful stink to be in her baby's memory as a sensory souvenir of her first day on this earth. If she could, Hope would ensure that the little one breathed only good clean air. Maybe one day, at the seaside even . . . ?

For now, the only mission was to safely get her home. Hope was a parent now; she was focused in a way hitherto unknown to her. This was what she was on earth for, to love and protect, she absolutely knew she was going to be supremely good at it, but . . . first things first. She had to get her baby back to the flat, safe and sound. She had to remain calm and clever and quick-witted.

Down, down two flights of revolting stairs, through a big blue door, and into the gloom of the car park. More fumes. Exhaust fumes. Even more perilous than pee. There was no doubt that the absolute best way to transport a baby was in a bag; it was brilliant for so many reasons.

Hope looked left and right, but there was no sign of the familiar rusty silver Honda Civic with Quiet Isaac in.

Damn, where was he? Hope could feel a panic rising but she needed to remain cool and in control if this was going to work, so she took a deep breath, including the awful fumes, and she started to walk among the cars looking for him. Suddenly, she stopped, when the thought occurred to her that, of course, he would probably be waiting near the entrance to the lifts. That would've been the more likely place for her to emerge. She could see the big red doors on the other side of the car park.

She started to walk directly towards them.

She changed her mind; she needed to be cleverer.

She wended her way between cars and pillars.

She made sure no one saw her.

She kept low.

She moved stealthily.

She checked the bag didn't bump anything.

She avoided a chatty family.

She watched them from behind a pillar and only proceeded when it was safe to do so.

It came easily to her to be furtive: she had the best of reasons.

Hope could see Quiet Isaac fifty yards away, near the lifts. He was sitting in the driver's seat of the old car, with his head leaning back against the headrest and his eyes closed. Was he asleep? He looked wrecked. She checked that the coast was clear and when she was sure, she moved fast towards him. In behind, out in front, and around cars, she was on her victory slalom run with her eyes on the prize. At last, she arrived at his car and opened the front passenger door, shocking Isaac awake. He said, 'Ah, hey. Wanna put that bag in the boot?'

For a brief surreal moment, she considered it.

'No,' she replied, climbing in and securing the bag full of baby on her lap with the safety belt, 'just . . . drive.'

Gone

Over twenty minutes went by before baby Florence was reported missing. All the mothers on the maternity ward, except one, took their new little ones home with them. That mother was going home to rest, on the paediatrician's advice, before returning later to visit her poorly baby in the premature baby unit.

And, of course, Hope. But Fatu had discharged her and reported that she'd left very early, way before anyone believed the baby had gone missing.

Prior to any alarm being raised, a fresh and keen midwife, who'd just come on duty and already been briefed by the departing two nurses about the sleeping Clarke family, took it upon herself to slide the 'Do not disturb' latch across outside the door. She wouldn't ordinarily do this unless there was a doctor inside or an emergency going on, but she completely agreed with her colleague that this family could do with the rest, and that they should be allowed to grab it as long as their baby was sleeping.

The baby was seemingly 'sleeping' for a while, which suited everyone on the ward just fine. They were short-staffed and all the other rooms were filling up quickly with new couples buzzing with fear and excitement. All of the maternity staff were busily distracted.

As two of the nurses passed each other in the

corridor, one handed the other a Kit Kat. 'Here, darling, keep yer sugar levels up, yeah? 'S gonna be another hectic one.'

'Thanks, Karen. I'm putting the kettle on. I'll leave yours on the side for when you can grab five minutes, OK?'

'Yeah, like when hell freezes over.'

'Yeah. Ha ha.'

It was hell when Anna finally woke up from her deep deep sleep to find her baby gone and her entire life tipped into a hell-pit of confusion.

She took a while to wake up. The painkillers contributed to her drowsiness, and for a few minutes her groggy brain had no idea where she was. As she slowly allowed her memory to float back and fit together piece by piece, she happily remembered the seismic hugeness of what had happened. She had become a mother at last. She had given birth to a perfect, beautiful little girl. Yes, Anna had finally come to matter. No longer simply an add-on to Julius or a faintly disappointing daughter to her parents. She was significant. Finally. It felt wonderful.

She looked over to see her husband. She noticed a small line of drool making its way down his chin. He was still slumped uncomfortably on the chair in the corner, his head lolled down. Ooh, that's going to ache when he wakes up, she thought, and then her next thought was, Meh, serves him right. She didn't feel kindly towards him any more, and hadn't for some time. BUT. He WAS Florence's father, and they would be forever linked, so she was going to endeavour to give family life her very best shot.

The baby was still sleeping; she could see the blanket all bunched up in the bassinet. She was longing to have another look at her this morning, but it was probably best to let her be for a few minutes more, while she was so peaceful. Anna was still horizontal, and couldn't easily see into the plastic cot. She started to hoik herself up the bed, trying awkwardly to rearrange the thin pillows behind her to prop herself up. As she moved, her clammy body alerted her to the fact that it had recently been a boxing ring for a baby to punch her way out of. Everything inside was jangled and bruised. She squirmed at the discomfort but she had no complaints; this was what happened when you were the arena where a miracle had happened: a temporary hurt which connected them profoundly forever. Only the two of them had shared it. Birth. A phenomenal, powerful agony. Florence had ripped Anna on her way out in her violent struggle to be born. She was clearly determined to have life; she'd fought for it with laudable vigour. Nothing was going to come between Florence and breath, not even the safety of Anna's body. Florence wanted to get out of there and be in the world. And she was. And Anna didn't mind in the least that her body was the collateral damage. She was honoured to be injured; she was delighted; and she was proud to have created such a resolutely purposeful little warrior. Long may she live.

Anna was desperate for a pee, so she swung her legs over the side of the bed and gradually stood up. She hadn't been in an upright position for some time, she realized as soon as her feet hit the ground and the cruelty of gravity took charge.

'Ow.' All of her organs jolted into their rightful, painful places. For a brief instant, she felt slightly dizzy, so she steadied herself at the side of the bed, the opposite side to the cot with all the bad news in it, as yet unseen, unknown.

Anna shuffled into the bathroom, had a painful pee, yawned and went to the sink to wash her hands. She washed them using the liquid soap from the wall dispenser, dried them using the wall-mounted blower, and squirted some antibacterial gel on to her hands, as directed by the strict notice on the wall. It amused her that the bathroom was so uniquely hospitalish. She could be nowhere else. The long red alarm cord, the heightened loo seat equipment on the floor next to the toilet, the pile of sludge-brown papier-mâché bed pans, the very thin extra toilet paper roll, the carefully placed rails screwed to the cleany-clean tiled walls. Yes, it was very clean, she noted gratefully: they did a good job, the domestic-services staff in this place; it was exemplary. She was delighted that her daughter had been born in such a hygienic environment — it was one of the issues she and Julius had discussed when they were debating whether they should go private for the birth.

Julius had been the one with the conflict: he'd desperately wanted the status, the comfort and the cleanliness he imagined they would only have if they were in a private hospital, but he was hugely aware that he OUGHT to use the NHS like everyone else, since he was a public figure (albeit solidly backbench). Therefore, he would be accused of all kinds of hypocrisy and harassed in a way he didn't want. He intended to bring plenty of attention to the arrival of this child, so, much to his annoyance, he'd had to think better of his preference to go private. He announced, 'OK, Anna, you win. There is, as of now, an annulment of the decision.'

'Don't be so pompous, Jules. Seriously. You should be delighted to have the baby inside the NHS. All of my family have been born in NHS hospitals. Bloody hell, I'd be crucified if I went private. No, ta.' She'd known that Julius had capitulated for the wrong reasons, but she was relieved nevertheless that she didn't have to fight him on it, or her family. In that second, the spotless bathroom confirmed her correct choice, and pleased her.

As Anna washed, dried and antisepticked her hands, she caught a glimpse of herself in the mirror, dishevelled and puffy from sleep, and she thought she looked closer to forty than the thirty-five years old she actually was. She didn't care. This is what an older mum looks like the day after she's given birth. Not everyone can be as miraculously beautiful as Princess Diana by the next day, much as they'd love to. Anna smiled at herself. She hadn't seen her own reflection since Florence was born, so she really looked closely.

Yes, she appeared tired, but there was something . . . different . . . new . . . changed. What was it? She leant in until she could see the huff of her breath on the glass. Was her skin better? Did she dare to imagine she could see the 'glow' people speak of? Well, she was quite flushed, but she thought that was mainly due to how warm it was in the room. They were high up in the building and therefore not permitted to open a window. It was ludicrous. No, it wasn't the glow. Was it her eyes? Did she now appear to be wiser or more knowing or something like that? Would that literally happen overnight? No, it wasn't that, although she did notice that the inner part of her left eyeball was quite bloodshot, giving her a rather zombie-ish appearance. She must have burst a small blood vessel with all the pushing. It wasn't a great look, but that wasn't the change . . . what was it?

As she stared at her face, she knew. Her face, exactly as it looked right that minute with all its flaws and unsymmetrical quirkiness, was the exact face Florence saw. The first ever face she saw. This was now not just Anna's face, it was Florence's mother's face. The face she would know and trust and love for her entire life. Or at least, until Anna died . . . oh God, no, she mustn't ever die. She had a daughter now to live for, to protect and to nurture. Anna decided exactly then that, as long as Florence needed her, she simply would NOT die.

More immediately, and with a familiar feeling of dread, she thought about how she was going to have to slap on some make-up. Julius would surely want a photo shoot of them all for *Hello!* magazine.

Anna was overcome with a desire to see her baby again now. She wanted to hold her close and look into her gorgeous eyes and know that they would forever be looking at each other. This face. And that face.

As she left the bathroom she had a passing worry that her newly gelled hands might be a bit too astringent to touch the baby with. Perhaps she ought to call the nurse for advice? She giggled at the fact that this was probably going to be the first of many ridiculous over-worrying moments she would have in the lifelong pursuit of trying to be the best mother ever. That's what darling new bud Florence deserved, and that's what she was going to have: the best mother Anna could possibly be, flaws and all. Florence didn't know that Anna often felt as if she was unloveable and ugly on the inside. The enduring toxicity of her dysfunctional relationship with her mother had confirmed those assumptions years before.

An inordinately jealous woman, Anna's mother had never quite recovered from the trauma of giving birth to someone more beautiful than her, so she constantly pecked at Anna's confidence until there was very little remaining. But Florence wasn't going to know that. Florence would think Anna was strong and beautiful. So that's what she would be, for her beloved daughter.

But as Anna approached the cot, she could see that the blanket was just blanket. There was no baby.

Life stopped.

Anna's heart suddenly had a noose around it and she felt a brutal tug.

'Jules,' she said. Or rather, she didn't say, because although her lips made the shape, no word came out. She made breath, but no sound.

'Julesss!' she managed to sputter on the second attempt. Still, he didn't wake. He was so sluggily asleep.

'JULES!' she squealed in a pitch she didn't

recognize, since she'd never made the sound before. She leant over and thumped his arm. Julius lurched forward in his chair and into wakefulness, shocked and angry.

'For Christ's sake . . . what're you doing . . . ?'

'Shush!' she scolded him, instantly realizing that she was pointlessly trying to prevent him from waking the baby that wasn't even there. 'Where's the baby?'

'What? What? In there.' He pointed at the cot.

'No. She's not. She's not there . . . ' Anna was barely able to control her rising panic. Tug. Tug.

'Yes, look.' Julius rose from the chair and lumbered the couple of steps towards the cot, reached in, and picked up the blanket.

He had to admit that she was right, there was no baby, but he wasn't a gun-jumper, he was a considered, logic-wrangling man. There had to be a simple explanation.

'They will have taken her for something . . . ' he offered as his first attempt at a guess.

'Taken her for what? Who?' Anna was having trouble remaining upright now, the heart-noose was constricting her and something odd was happening to her legs, both of which were suddenly boneless. She held on to the frame at the bottom of her bed.

'I'll call the nurse. They should've told us. Can't take a baby without permission, however important . . . ' He was ranting on as he fumbled around the bed looking for the alarm button they were shown when they first arrived.

Anna wanted to stride over to the door and shout out into the corridor for help, but her legs

72

simply wouldn't let her. She knew instinctively that she would fall if she let go. When Julius finally found the alarm button, he pushed it and then immediately strode to the door anyway, yanked it open and yelled out, 'Nurse! Hello? Nurse!'

'Shush,' repeated Anna, this time utterly conflicted between the embarrassment of his loud bellowing and the certain need of it.

'No. Someone needs to explain . . . ' He shot a furious glare back at her as he stomped off to find answers.

'Shush,' Anna whispered to herself. It was a tiny hopeless soothing for her, for the baby, for her pounding, tightening heart, a barely-there lullaby, a trace of comfort, a desperate hope. Let him be right. Let the big annoying know-it-all be right. She would be overjoyed to concede to his smugness if he was right this time.

Let there be a simple reason.

Let her have cried out and let a midwife have scooped her up and out, to let them sleep.

Let her need a blood test.

Let her need to be weighed.

Let her need to be measured for a hospital trial.

Let an inexperienced trainee have come in and taken her to the wrong place and then realized her stupidity, and be heading right back this minute.

Let anyone have been helpless to resist a sneaky cuddle, and naughtily have thought it OK to walk up and down the corridor rocking her and smelling her wonderful sweaty baby head.

Let someone have entered the wrong room, picked her up thinking she's the baby boy next door called Arran or something, and be mistakenly taking her for her first sickle cell assessment.

Let someone be dyslexic and not know how to read the wristband on her lovely chubby wrist.

Let someone be foreign and not know how to read the wristband on her lovely chubby wrist.

Let someone be stupid and not know how to read the wristband on her lovely chubby wrist.

Let someone be blind and not see . . .

As the creeping certitude of dread started to engulf her, Anna heard the pounding of footsteps thundering towards their room and the sound of raised voices. She didn't want to hear any urgency whatsoever. She wanted to see and hear that lovely calm exterior that all aircrew have on planes. Utter utter confidence in the fact that ABSOLUTELY NOTHING IS WRONG. The faces of the people who burst into the room in a tornado of alarm told her otherwise for sure.

One after another, the midwives, the receptionist and the doctor stampeded in and past her to stare at the empty cot, as if only seeing it with their own eyes made it the truth. What were they seeing? A full, horrifying nothing. They looked at no baby. The first midwife in shook the blanket, maybe hoping the infant had shrivelled up and hidden in the smallest fold. She passed the blanket to the doctor, who also examined it closely. Perhaps when the unthinkable happens, our brains tell our eyes to keep searching while the awful truth is sinking in. The receptionist was even checking the floor, the bathroom, opening the door of the bedside cupboard as if Florence might be a missing handbag.

'Where's our daughter?' roared Julius. 'What

are you going to do . . . ?'

'Shush,' muttered Anna. She leant against the wall and closed her eyes. She wanted the world to stop.

'Get security immediately,' ordered the doctor as he moved to push the room alarm on the wall panel behind the bed.

'Shush,' Anna tried again, but her legs buckled under her and she slid to the floor at the bottom of the bed. She was trying to quieten her screaming heart, but it was too late: the noose had strangled it. She allowed her head to fall back and she let out the loudest howl she'd ever heard.

The Journey Home

Quiet Isaac's car pulled out of the gloomy, fumey car park and into the bright light of a nippy yet sunny 1 January day. Not just the start of a new year, but the start of a new millennium and the start of a bold new life for Hope, unbeknownst to him.

London was untidy. The detritus of the celebrations from the night before littered the streets and blew about in the chilly gusts, messy souvenirs of a party city.

Quiet Isaac loved his car; he had bought it from a departing Nigerian student who'd graduated the year before. Quiet Isaac paid two hundred pounds for it. The previous owner had paid three hundred pounds for it, and so on back through many students. Somewhere twenty years before, the car must've been worth it, but now it was an ugly but reliably functioning rust bucket. Luckily Isaac's father taught him well about cars, and in particular Japanese ones, which he admired so much for the ease of replacement parts and for the longevity. This vaguely silver Civic was an example of how hard it is to kill a Honda. It just would not die, however ancient, and Isaac already had a clutch of first years nipping at his heels to buy it for a measly hundred quid, when the time came that he was through with it.

Quiet Isaac looked across at Hope. He had spent his waiting time in the car thinking about how he might possibly be able to comfort and support her, wondering if he would find the right words to use. As he glanced at her, he imagined her beautiful wide-open face might be a bit crumpled, but that wasn't what he saw. Hope's eyes were sparkling; she was bolt upright and fresh as air. Isaac hoped she wasn't in some kind of shocked trance. She was looking straight ahead, clasping her bag close to her, balancing it on her knee.

'You OK, Bubs?' He squeezed her hand. She didn't take his, which was unusual, but she did let him touch hers, which she kept firmly clamped to the bag. She was holding on to it as a teenager hugs a cushion when they watch a horror film.

'Yeah yeah,' she replied, a bit too distracted.

'D'you wanna go find some breakfast . . . ?' he offered, in the hope that it could be a treat for her. He wasn't sure if she would be up for it, was almost certain that she wouldn't, but he still wanted to offer, in the belief that there could still be some joy in their lives after this shattering tragedy.

'No, no. Home. Please.' Hope sounded urgent. He could see that she was breathing deeply. Had she been running? That couldn't have been wise after all she'd been through. He wished he was a rich man who could whisk her away somewhere on holiday to recover, instead of a poor third-year engineering student without two farthings to rub together.

No matter, he would do whatever was in his power to make sure Hope was all right. 'Twas ever thus. That's who Isaac truly always was, and now, as he was driving, he felt reflective. It might have been the case that the pregnancy was a surprise to both of them, totally unplanned, but in all the months leading up to the birth, he had been in no doubt that they were a strong couple. Their endless chats about how they would somehow manage to be good parents had really focused his mind on their relationship. However much Quiet Isaac was falling for Hope, the pregnancy clinched it; he fell right in, the moment she told him.

He remembered what had happened: he had been due to go over to her flat in Kensal Rise to see her on that day. He let himself in with the keys she had given him months before. He was chuffed that she'd had a set cut for him, that she trusted him enough to let him come and go as he pleased in 'her yard'. On that day, he struggled to get the wretched rusty Yale lock to move with the key. It was old and stubborn. He made a mental note to fix that for her with some WD40. Once inside, he awkwardly manoeuvred past the bike belonging to the hermit bloke in the downstairs flat, which was forever illegally parked against the wall. Hope rarely saw him, he rarely used his bike, but always left it there, exactly where it was the most inconvenient. Hope had guessed that it was a prized possession, so she didn't want to confront him about it. Plus, the small communal hallway which serviced both flats often smelled of weed. It seeped from under his door. Hope knew that smell well, and she consciously stayed away from him, leaving him to what she imagined was his mellow stoned state. He was no bother to her, or she to him, but she decided not to seek him out, or provoke him.

Quiet Isaac had carefully shuffled past the

prized bike, and up the narrow, cheaply built and therefore very hollow-sounding stairs to her flat door at the top. The carpet on the steps was threadbare, and non-existent in some parts, so the sound must've been major in the flat below, and definitely heralded any arrival in Hope's flat. There was no chance of surprising her. He didn't really need to; she was expecting him that day.

The lock to her actual flat was easier to operate. One turn and he was in. The flat was very small. A living room with a bay window at the front looking out on to the busy road below, a bedroom just behind that, a small bathroom behind that, and a half-sized kitchen at the back with double doors that opened out on to a fire escape with metal stairs going down into the shared garden space. He called out immediately.

'Hope! 'S me. Where are you?'

No reply. The flat was quiet. He listened. Perhaps she was in the bath? Or on the loo? No sound. He walked to the kitchen first, and immediately put water in the kettle and turned it on. There were two chairs at a small table at the far end but otherwise the kitchen was uninviting, which was all wrong, they thought. Hope told him that any home where she lived should have a kitchen you can hang out in, but this one was too small and shoddily put together. The saving grace was the door out to the stairs. Hope was specifically told by her landlord that, by law, she WASN'T to block the access on these stairs, they WERE NOT for her recreational use, they were a fire escape ONLY. They weren't even the proper access to the garden. To get into the garden officially, legally, she was supposed to go out of the flat, down the clompy entrance stairs, out of the front door, turn right on the street, turn immediately right again up an alley to the narrow lane at the very back, which ran along all the yards, and which contained everyone's bins. There was a door into the garden yard from there, and THAT was the one she was supposed to use . . .

Yeah. Sure.

Just like Mr Bike Hermit wasn't supposed to keep a bike in the hallway . . .

Of course, she used the fire escape. She often left the door wide open, and she had commandeered the slightly bigger top step to put plenty of planted tubs out. She grew herbs for cooking there. She had mint and basil and chives and rosemary. She had a honeysuckle which was growing vigorously up and twirling around the railings, and which had a heavenly perfume that blew back into her flat on summer evenings and helped to combat the sickly sweet cannabis aroma that wafted up from Mr Below, the Bike Hermit.

Quiet Isaac opened the door. It was April then, and warm enough to let the fresh air in. He walked back up the narrow corridor to Hope's bedroom. He glanced ahead into the tiny front room to check she wasn't asleep or something in there, but no. So, he opened the door to the bedroom. It was a small room, but Isaac loved it. It was where they were intimate, so even the lovely musky smell of the room as he opened the door excited him; there was always love in this room.

The curtains were open on the small window and the top half of the window was ajar a few inches. It was impossible to open the door fully since Hope had insisted on having a double bed in a room so small that a single bed was pushing it, space-wise. The double bed took up all the space and pretty much touched the walls on three sides. Since there was no room to walk around the bed, Hope had put shelves up everywhere so that whatever might be in bedside cab-inets was now on shelves all over the walls. It made for a cluttered, cheerful room. Pride of place, above the head of the bed, was a painting Isaac had brought with him. His mother gave it to him just before he left Africa. It was the side-on silhouette of an African American in a high collar, circa eighteenth century, with a majestic clipper ship beneath, and the words 'Captain Paul Cuffee 1812' written around it. This was his mother's hero, a black Quaker ship's captain who assisted free blacks in America to emigrate to Sierra Leone, and played a huge part in abolishing slavery and establishing a new colony in Freetown. Quiet Isaac's mother often told him that this was a man to aspire to be like, a courageous traveller who NEVER FORGOT HIS ROOTS. Isaac had heard the stories of Cuffee's bravery all his life, but the overriding message was about returning. His mother wanted him to arm himself with all the engineering skills he could, then bring them home.

HOME.
HOME.

Her message was powerful and Quiet Isaac fully intended to honour her wishes . . . It was testament to his high regard for Hope that he had brought the painting from his campus room to here. He knew it would be safer here, and this was where his heart was. Hope had placed it there, and next to it on the shelf, she put two small flags she'd made and coloured with felt-tips. A Union Jack and the tricolour green, white and blue flag of Sierra Leone. Isaac whooped when he first saw them and it had made Hope very happy.

So here he was, entering the room he loved so much. As he flung his tote bag on to the bed, he noticed a blue shoebox there, with 'OPEN ME' written on it in Hope's unmistakeable bold clear handwriting. He looked closer.

As Quiet Isaac bent over to examine the curious box, Hope held her breath. She was hiding in the small wardrobe in the corner of the room, just behind the bedroom door. The cheap built-in cupboard had slats on the doors, so she could just about see him. She didn't want him to have a single clue she was there, so she had been sitting as still as a statue in the cramped space ever since she heard his key in the door downstairs. She was hot and uncomfortable, but she was determined to witness his true reaction at this crucial moment. She really needed to know how he would take the news.

Quiet Isaac picked up the box. It was the one she had brought her new trainers home in. Was she saying something cryptic about them . . . ? The box was too light to contain trainers; it didn't seem to weigh anything at all. Was it empty? He opened the lid to find lots of white toilet roll bunched up to be wrapping paper. He delved a bit deeper. There was something inside. He pulled out the central package, wrapped in the same paper. He guessed it might be a pen; it was that kind of shape and size.

It wasn't a pen. As he unwrapped it, Isaac took a couple of moments to understand just what he was looking at. He had never seen a pregnancy test indicator before. Inside the wardrobe, Hope almost passed out with the tension and her breath held too deeply and for too long.

He had his back to her, so she couldn't quite tell what he was thinking. He seemed to hold it in his hands and peer at it for an age, but gradually, she saw his shoulders sink and his head lolled forward on to his chest. Her heart sank; he seemed sad. She couldn't hide away any longer, so she flung the door open, and rushed to him. 'Isaac, I'm sorry . . .'

Quiet Isaac almost jumped out of his skin with fright at the sudden shock. He yelped, and his arms flailed up in the air like a berserk windmill. Hope dodged an inadvertent clout by millimetres. She flew at him and flung her arms around him, knocking the test out of his hands and pushing him to the bed, all in the propulsion of one bear hug.

'Whaaa!' he shouted.

'It's just me!' she yelled as they fell on to the bed.

'Be careful, Bubs, watch out.' He was worried. He quickly sat her up next to him on the bed and she could see that he still had a tear on his cheek.

'Are you OK? I'm sorry. I thought we were careful . . . I'm so sorry . . . ' She tried to reassure him. She felt panicked. She didn't want to lose

83

him — Quiet Isaac was the best person she'd ever known. Maybe this was a disaster for him?

He spoke breathlessly, 'Yes, yes, it's OK. I just . . . You scared me then. I didn't know what the hell . . . but this . . . '

He leant over and picked up the pregnancy test. 'This doesn't scare me. No. This is us. You and me. It's not your fault. It's not anyone's fault, because it's not a fault. A life can't be a fault. God makes life, so it can't be wrong. Can it? We made this life together . . . right here in this bed. It's gotta be good, it's gotta be OK. It's beautiful, Bubs. You are beautiful. Don't worry. We'll do this together; we'll manage it somehow. We're blessed. Now I need you to be careful. No falling down . . . ' With that, Isaac started to well up again and Hope saw that his tears were a kind of gratitude, not the anger or sadness she had supposed. She pulled him in close to her.

'We can do anything, Isaac. If we're together,' she reassured him quietly, close to his ear, but as she said it she realized that so many reassurances in her life, both told to her and by her, were no more than words of comfort, often without any real truth to them. Her mother's hollow drunken reassurances, however constant, weren't that real. Doris forgot them by the next day. Hope's own reassurances to her sister in difficult times were her dearest wish that the two of them would be OK, not her certain knowledge. However, this, now, with Isaac, was the incontrovertible truth and, as such, was a beautiful relief. Yes, together they would be mighty, and inside that strength would be a great place to be a baby.

Hope had felt her fear flood away back then.

She wasn't frightened with him alongside her, and he made it clear he wasn't going anywhere. She had a rock to stand on. Solid and reliable . . . and quiet. Isaac.

And Isaac had known, at that precise moment, that for the first time ever he was surely in love, with both Hope and their baby she was carrying. Abundantly in love.

* * *

Now, here, in the car as they drove home from the hospital with an empty baby seat, and an empty Hope, Isaac seriously prayed that she would still believe in his love . . . and that he would also. He had come to know and adore Hope for all the good stuff she clearly was. He hoped that it wouldn't matter that there was no baby. He hadn't known the baby before she died, of course he hadn't, not in actuality, but the two of them had spent many hours imagining so much, thinking about her, and who she might turn out to be. Wondering what name might suit her, and how they might raise her. They'd thought about her all the time. They'd called his parents and told them. It was a shock, but his mother especially was supportive, so long as he promised to bring the child home at some point. Hope told her sister, and left it for her sister to tell their mum and dad. She was better placed than Hope to choose the right moment, when Doris was sober and receptive and when Zak was cheerful and present, rather than in the depressed paranoid slump he so often lived in. So, everyone knew this baby was arriving.

Sitting together side by side in the car, they both tacitly understood that they would have to explain what had happened that night to everyone. It would be difficult but it had to happen.

Hope had been very quiet for most of the journey. She was trying to process what she'd just done and she was frantically working out how she would tell Isaac. She clung on to the bag and its precious cargo, her heart in her throat fearing that the baby would cry out, but miraculously she didn't. A couple of times, she heard some contented gurgling noises. So Hope reached over and turned the radio on. The old radio in the old car was stuck on Radio 1 — it hadn't moved from there for two years, according to Isaac — so they listened to Zoe Ball excitedly sharing her favourite tunes in her new job, on the new day.

The journey was only twenty minutes or so, but Hope was fidgety throughout, Isaac noticed. He supposed she might still be sore from the birth; perhaps that was why she was so restless in her seat? In actuality, Hope was attempting to cradle-rock the baby to keep her nicely soothed. It seemed that the baby had no problem being cossetted in such a small dark space. Hope imagined that perhaps it was because she had so recently been born. She had, after all, spent nine months in a tiny dark safe place and only a few hours in the light. The bag was likely very comforting. Maybe every new mother should put her baby straight into a bag to zip up and transport about for a while at the beginning.

Hope purposely kept her thoughts occupied with ridiculous ideas like that. After all, if she halted her frantic mind even for a few moments, and let herself consider the other woman's pain at that exact time, she would surely have had to return the baby? She knew this deep down, but her need was greater than her conscience so she shushed it with distractions, until at last they were home.

They pulled up outside Hope's flat. Isaac said, 'You go on up, I'll bring the bags and everything.'

She climbed out of the front seat, carefully guarding the all-important bag. Isaac had quickly nipped out and, in true gentlemanly style, he tried to help her by offering to take the heavy bag.

'No, no. I'll take this, you bring the rest,' she said, keeping the bag handles firmly clasped in her hands. She was a tad sharper than she might ordinarily be.

Hope took her key out of her bag expertly with one hand, and once she'd given the lock the familiar extra flick she knew it needed, it opened immediately. It helped, of course, that Quiet Isaac had in fact squirted WD40 in there months before, as he'd promised he would. She pushed through the door and carefully past the annoying bike propped up in the hallway. It had never irritated her as much as it did today. It was DANGEROUS, for goodness' sake; it would have to change.

She mounted the stairs tentatively, being sure not to bash the bag in any way; she opened the flat door, and she was in. HOME.

Quiet Isaac loaded himself up with the remaining bags, but decided against bringing the car seat up; it was just too sad. He put it in the boot, locked the car and started to head into the flat. Hope had left the door open, so he went in and battled past the bloody bike, and on up the stairs. Halfway up, he stopped. He took a breath and wondered why these stairs suddenly felt like a mountain he would never reach the summit of. He was so so sad. He let the sorrow flood through him for a moment, leaning against the wall. Then he heard it. He heard the sound of a baby. He shook his head. He must be imagining it. On he went. Up the mountain. Into the flat.

Anna's Pleas

Detective Inspector Mike Thripshaw and his sidekick Constable Debbie Cheese (as if her life wasn't difficult enough) had arrived at the hospital with a flurry of activity.

Julius was shouting, 'We've told you the entire situation four times now. Seriously. You need to cease with the questions and get on with finding my daughter. Immediately.'

'My' daughter? Even through her fug, Anna wondered why he had chosen to be so possessive. Florence wasn't only his daughter. If she had felt any urge to be generous, she might have considered this to be a slip of the tongue indicating his extreme personal despair. She didn't.

They were still sitting in the same small hot delivery suite. Anna and Julius had been asked to remain there until the police arrived and now the officers had been questioning them for nearly an hour, all crammed into the room, sapping the oxygen and creating even more heat than the bright morning sun was, as it blasted rudely in through the dirty windows.

Anna was sitting in the chair Julius had slept in, and she permanently held on to the side of the bassinet, subconsciously guarding the missing babe. She wanted any connection she could have, however pointless.

Julius answered impatiently as the police machine-gun fired a rattle of questions at them. Anna's mind was operating slowly; she had entered a treacley world of cloggy thought. She knew it was the effect of shock, but she'd never experienced a shock as massive as this before. This was tragedy. All she knew was that her stomach was full of concrete, and her brain was on pause. Nothing made sense. Nothing mattered. She wasn't even properly in the room; she felt floaty and strange, as if she were watching the scene, not in it herself. She could've been forgiven for thinking she was drunk. Time around her was slurring; nothing was sharp. Everyone was yak-yakking. Especially Julius.

What were they all saying?

Why were they talking at all? There was nothing important or clever to say after they'd told the story the first time.

Why weren't the cops outside arresting every single woman in the street to see if they had Florence? They needed to search every house in London. They needed to bring every single baby in the world to her, so that she could see if it was Florence.

Why were they still talking?

'Right, sir, I think we have all the facts as they stand,' said DI Thripshaw, 'I think we have apprehended the situation to our best abilities thus far. We are presently conducting an initial search of the hospital, but to be honest, we're closing the door after the cows have gone home, clearly . . . It's less than hopeless . . . to be honest . . . '

Constable Debbie Cheese was looking at the ground. She'd worked with Thripshaw for three years now, and it didn't get any better. In her opinion, he was an adequate detective, but whenever he spoke, a swarm of confused word wasps came sizzing out of his mouth. He was insensitive and befuddled. He should never really have been allowed near live humans, especially not a grieving mother such as Anna. Debbie was standing right next to Anna and she decided to risk putting a comforting hand on Anna's shoulder. It might have been considered unprofessional, but no one else seemed to be being gentle near her. Anna felt it, and looked up at her briefly. She couldn't smile, even in pathetic gratitude, which she most certainly felt — there were simply no smiles available in Anna's top drawer of stock reactions. She was empty. The constable saw only a haunted face, pleading for help.

Julius ploughed on, 'Surely we need to sort out some kind of press conference? Make a public plea? Quick as?'

'Yes, Mr Lindon-Clarke. That is being set up as we speak, which is why we pacifically requested you remain *in situ*, for all intensive purposes. We have to set it up according to due process or it's proven to be next to useless, so please calm down and trust us on this. We're not making it up on the fly, y'know. This ain't my first rodeo . . .'

Julius's knuckles were itching. His desire to make physical contact with DI Thripshaw's potato face was powerful, especially since he had brought his punch-worthy mush so very close, in an attempt to calm Julius down. He was having the opposite effect. Julius liked to be in charge; he liked it when people snapped to it. This maddening fool was a huge challenge, but he was their only hope at this point.

'Please remain calm. No point beating a dead

91

horse . . . ' Thripshaw kept stumbling on. 'We need to be uber-careful we choose the right tact here.'

'Please . . . '

The room went quiet as they all turned to Anna, who was attempting to speak, but very quietly, which was all the volume she could summon.

'Please find Florence. Please,' she whispered urgently, using all the breath she had. 'She's gone.'

'Of course, Mrs Lindon-Clarke. We will,' assured Constable Debbie, who was the only genuinely composed person in the room.

'We will come and collect you when we're all set up and hunky-dory. There's a room downstairs we can utilize . . . ' said Thripshaw as he shuffled awkwardly in his concrete boots out of the room, his head firmly between his tail.

'Would you like me to stay with you for a moment?' offered Constable Debbie.

'No, no. I'm wanting to . . . be quiet now . . . with Jules . . . until you're ready,' Anna told her, and so she respectfully retreated, ushering anyone else other than Julius out of the room.

Julius was fuming and kept bellowing at various people on his treasured Nokia. He called his lawyer friend, Piers; he called another contact high up in police echelons in Manchester to see if he could mobilize anything quicker from there, only to find out that Manchester is Manchester and nothing to do with the Met. He called a couple of Westminster front-bench bods he knew. He repeated the tale of woe to each and every one, with the emphasis on how shocking and painful this all was FOR HIM. He hardly turned back from the window as Anna watched him react to the situation. It occurred to her that his main thrust was fury at the lack of speedy action, not shock at the fact that Florence was missing. He seemed to have absorbed that awful, unthinkable information quite quickly and was swiftly moving on to tactics. He wanted to place himself at the helm of the operations ship; he needed to be captain. This was MASSIVE and his compulsion was to be in charge. He was almost slavering at the immensity of the opportunity. It was a chance to be masterful.

Anna observed him as he noisily talked to person after important person with hardly a break for air, in his element, striding up and down in front of the window. She was saddened to see that he was regularly pausing to check his reflection in the glass. It was as if Julius wanted to reassure himself that he looked as heroic as he felt. On and on and on he went, blaming everyone he could think of. From the midwives to the police. Julius was at his maximum testosterone level, a loud bull.

A loud vain bull.

She was suddenly reminded of a time, years before, when she'd been crying about the loss of a dear friend. She'd noticed that he also started to cry. For a second she was touched, until she noticed him move to the mirror above their fireplace to check out his own crying face. To see if it was impressive. Anna remembered how she'd felt chunks of respect for him crumble away. She felt the same again now.

Anna sat still and didn't know who to be. She had been a mother for a fleeting moment, the very thing she'd wanted to be so desperately for so long. Was she still a mother? Was that over now? If you don't have your baby with you, are you still her mother? Maybe she's the mother to nothing now? Had it actually even happened?

Anna knew in her deepest heart that what had happened was real, but what HAD actually happened? Whatever it was had happened when she was fast asleep. She KNEW it was her fault. Yes, she knew that for absolute sure; it had to be, didn't it? If somehow, somehow, somehow that little baby girl could be returned to her, she would 100 per cent promise never to fall asleep ever again. Even Julius's back to her and his seeming refusal to look her in the eye confirmed to her that this mess was all down to her. There was no one else it could be. She had clearly fallen spectacularly at the very first hurdle in the perfect-mother race.

Perhaps she was being punished by some kind of cruel God? She didn't even really believe in God, but she was definitely prepared to believe in Satan if this was what could happen to a good person like her. She dared to believe that she was a good person. Wasn't she? She knew Julius wasn't. Not really. Not 'good'. Not kind or thoughtful or selfless or anything like that. She had come to realize that when his time came, one day, to be weighed in the balance, he would be found severely wanting.

But Julius was probably going to be the key to finding Florence. He was the one with the contacts and the power, of sorts, and he would be the effective one in front of the camera in a minute . . .

Oh God. She was going to have to endure that.

To think that only a few hours before she had been considering what kind of make-up to put on for their big announcement . . . now she was wondering if she could face it at all.

What would she say?

What, actually, did she feel? Was it nothing? She closed her eyes. She could see Florence's flawless little new face looking up at her, just as she had last seen her. Anna was astonished by how utterly beautiful she was. Unsurpassably lovely. Anna couldn't believe they had made such a sublime little human.

Anna wasn't a sentimental person. She didn't care for all that guff about babies being little miracles and the suchlike, but it had all become utterly authentic when she held Florence in her arms. She had longed for that baby skin on her skin, and the reality of it had surpassed anything she'd imagined. The giant need she'd felt was finally met, and Anna's unspoken promises, heart to tiny heart, were the greatest oaths she'd ever made.

Now she was gone, and Anna's world had stopped. People seemed to be moving about in it, but it was all senseless until she was reunited with her tot. Where was she?

Where was she?

She had to be somewhere.

In a crazy desperate moment, Anna stood up and walked to the window near Julius, who moved away to keep his space free of her. Anna pressed her face against the window as hard as she could.

It was warm. It was a winter day but the persistent daytime sunshine was peeping into their sad room, hell bent on cheering her up, but incapable of doing so.

She pressed even harder against the glass in the hope that she might break through it and be able to more easily look straight down into the streets directly below, where, of course, she would see someone moving along carrying Florence. She would see it and she would swoop down and she would pluck up that baby like a giant mother eagle and she would bring her back to her rightful place with Anna and Julius. Tears started to well up in Anna's eyes. She wanted her baby very badly. She pulled back from the window, and she realized that her breasts had joined in with the crying. She was lactating.

Isaac's Big Decision

As Quiet Isaac clomped into Hope's flat, he couldn't wait to drop all the cumbersome bags off his shoulders and out of his hands on to her kitchen floor with a thump. She had clearly done the same, as her bag was wide open on the table. He could see her nightie inside, on top of a crumpled pile of clothes, and her soft washbag stuffed down the side. Once he had offloaded, he walked straight to the sink and took a glass from the cupboard above and turned on the cold tap. He was parched. Then he heard it again. Unmistakeably this time. A baby's gurgle . . .

Isaac put down his glass and followed the sound up the hallway to the small living room at the front of the house. When he entered the room, he simply couldn't understand what he was looking at. Hope was sitting in the big chair in the corner with Minnie in her arms. She had somehow smuggled the poor dead baby home from the hospital and was holding her so tenderly, looking straight at Isaac with pleading, tearful eyes.

Then Isaac gradually realized that the baby was wriggling, moving her arms and kicking her legs out. And she was making contented happy sucky noises, because she was latched on to Hope's right breast, and she was feeding.

Isaac was convinced he was hallucinating. In his total confusion, he decided he must be seeing something he WISHED was true rather than anything

97

that was real. Like a mirage, just as nomads in the desert see an oasis of palm trees and cool fountains on the hazy horizon because they are so very thirsty. So Isaac was surely conjuring up the sight he would most wish to see in all the world, his girl and his daughter together, happy and healthy, just as it was supposed to be, just as he thought it WOULD be when they left this flat together yesterday to go to the hospital.

He stood rooted to the floor, waiting for the chimera to dissolve and for real life to kick back in. His eyes locked on to the lovely baby. If it was going to be fleeting, he wanted to cherish the memory of her as long as possible. He was afraid to move for fear of causing her to disappear. If this was a dream, he wanted to be right in it.

Hope broke the moment. 'Isaac. Come close and see her, she's amazing . . .'

The illusion didn't shatter. Hope spoke, the baby cooed and still they remained, as tangible as any real thing could possibly be.

But how COULD it be . . . ?

It just couldn't. He'd held the lifeless child in his arms; he knew she'd gone. He'd brought Hope home in the car. There was no baby. The baby seat was in his boot because it was so singularly unused. What was going on?

Isaac felt as though he hadn't blinked for years. His eyes were dry and scratchy and his knees had somehow locked, rooting him to the spot where he stood. He felt himself shaking.

Hope tried again: 'Don't be scared, come here . . .'

Isaac followed her direction and edged closer

98

slowly. The baby was in a cosy pink Babygro and was wearing the yellow and pink stripey hat Hope had valiantly knitted. Her face was turned towards Hope's body while she was happily suckling away, but he could see her bonny brown cheeks pulsing with each gulp, and her big eyes darting about, trying to see EVERYTHING. He could see a shock of straightish black hair peeping out from under the beloved hat, and he could see her miraculous, busy little hands reaching up and grasping at Hope's breast. She was a contented little soul. Isaac was silenced. He couldn't speak. He had no words appropriate for this moment. He lowered himself on to the sofa next to her. He realized his mouth was agape, and probably had been for a good five minutes. He was parched and had been deep-breathing since he saw her. That glass of water he abandoned in the kitchen was a distant memory.

At long long last, after a million confused years, he summoned some words, 'What's happening, Bubs? How is . . . Who . . . ' They weren't the most eloquent words he'd ever uttered, but then again, he was in a nightmare, and his broken heart was thumping in his chest.

'OK. Now, listen,' Hope attempted to answer him, 'I need to tell you something, and I need you to stay calm. Isaac, do you hear me . . . ?'

'Yes. Yes. I'm calm,' he replied. He wasn't. Far from it.

'OK. Today was the day our baby died.'

'Yes.'

'And today was the day God gave me back my baby.'

99

'Gave back? I don't understand . . . is this . . . ?'

'She isn't our Minnie. But she is Minnie. Now.'

'Hope. Where did this baby come from?' He held his breath; he felt clammy. His dread was heavy.

'She wanted me, Isaac. She reached up to me. And no one was watching out for her. No one. She was awake, and . . . she was hungry . . . and no one was noticing . . . '

'Did you take her, Hope?'

'She needed me, Isaac.'

'Did you take her? From the hospital?'

Hope paused. She didn't like this question. It sounded aggressive and criminal, and she knew for sure that she was neither. Isaac's gaze was penetrating. He was going nowhere until he had the answer, but the answer could mean the end. Hope absolutely HAD to be honest. She knew that.

'Yes,' she whispered, her voice so small.

'Pardon?'

'Yes!' Louder this time. 'Don't say it, Isaac.'

'This. Baby. Must. Go. Back.' He made it clear.

'No.'

'Now, Hope.'

'No. No. No. Please listen. I know she wants to be here with us. I know it.'

'She needs to be with her mother, Hope.'

'She is . . . with her mother.'

'No.'

'Yes, Isaac. Listen. Please listen. It went wrong at the hospital. I know it did. I don't wish anything bad on those poor people, but the wrong baby . . . died. Minnie wasn't supposed to. I know it sounds crazy . . . '

'Yes, Hope, it does.'

'I know, I know, but look at what happened. She reached out to me, she knew I would be her mum, and honestly, hear me out, from the second I picked her up, I gave her a choice, I told her, heart to heart, if you are my daughter, if you want to be mine, then . . .' Hope started to cry very quietly; she was telling her raw painful truth, and it was so hard. '. . . if you want to be mine, then you must stay quiet, my own little darling, you must shush, not a peep.'

'I see,' he said, gently stroking Hope's arm, pitying her in her desperate delusion.

'And she . . . she . . . she didn't, she didn't make a sound, she stayed quiet. No babies do that — they can't. It's Minnie, Isaac, it's her, and she wanted to come home with us. She beckoned me. It's Minnie.'

'It can't be. She can't be . . .' Now Isaac was faltering. The longing for a baby and the terrible, unbearable memory of the tiny dead mite conspired to make this tangible wriggling opportunity staring him in the face so very tempting.

Hope saw the crack. It was make or break.

'She didn't make a sound, did she? You didn't know she was there in the bag all the way home. Seriously, even by then, if she'd wanted to go back, if she'd cried out, or anything, I promise you, I would've asked you to turn around. But she didn't. She trusts us, she needs us, she's asking you to be her dad . . .'

Baby Minnie, for that's who she now was, was full and finished with Hope's milk, so she slurpily detached from Hope's nipple and looked around.

Hope decided to chance it. She handed the baby over to Isaac, gathering up a batik cloth throw she had on the back of the chair and hugging it around Minnie while she was in his strong arms, to keep her snuggly warm.

He looked down at Minnie looking back up at him, and all the euphoria he had hoped for but was so cruelly denied to him came gushing over him in a flood of dopamine. Minnie was seeing him, seeing her father, that's what Quiet Isaac saw reflected back in her wonderful deep dark eyes. He saw himself, a worthy father, and his desire to be so was immense. He was ready, he had been ever since the pregnancy test, he was like a coiled spring, waiting to hurtle into dad-action the second it was required. It was required NOW. This morning he had tipped into a dark place of no hope, but now he was seeing light in the exquisite face of this little daughter girl.

A daughter.

His daughter.

Oh, it was so painfully tangible. He was touching the very chance. Yet, deep in his being, he knew all of it was forbidden, he couldn't, he shouldn't, allow it. He looked up into Hope's beautiful pleading face; she was begging him to say yes, to keep the baby, to accept Minnie, to share the secret.

How could he deny her? He only ever wanted to make her happy, to fix her, to please her. That's where his joy and his purpose lay. Here she was, asking him the most momentous question ever. How could he say no?

Yet he KNEW KNEW KNEW he should.

There was right and there was wrong.

He'd been raised well. He knew the difference. Poor Hope was in hell and he desperately wanted to rescue her. It was a powerful need in him, to be her hero. And now, he also wanted to be the hero for this little girl.

At exactly that key, precipitous moment, there was a slamming of a car door outside.

There were many cars in their street. There were many car doors. There were many slammings. It was nothing unusual, but for some reason, both Hope and Quiet Isaac stopped in their tracks, dead still for a dreaded moment, then Hope jumped up to go to the window and look out.

'It's the police!' she cried. 'Oh Jesus . . . '

In that critical moment, Quiet Isaac made his big decision. He jumped off the precipice. Without a word, he stood up with the swaddled baby still in his arms. He left the front room and raced down the hall into the kitchen, out of the door on to the fire escape and fled down the metal steps, across the yard and out through the back gate into the alley beyond. He was gone like a fox at sunrise.

Hope was still buttoning up her blouse when the door-bell rang. She was in shock. Where had Isaac gone? For a moment she was rooted to the spot, uncertain of what to do.

Then, suddenly and surely, she knew exactly what to do. She took a crucial deep breath and left her flat, down the communal stairs to the front door where she could see the unmistakeable outline of police officers through the glass. She opened it.

'Hello, Ms Parker? I'm Police Constable

Cheese. Deborah. This is Constable Taylor. May we come in?'

'Er, yes, of course. Is everything all right? Nothing's happened to Isaac, has it?' Hope was alarmed. Not really alarmed. Cleverly fake alarmed. She was thinking fast.

'Let's just go inside, shall we?' Debbie tried to be comforting as she and her colleague followed Hope back into the hallway, past the annoying bike and up the stairs to her flat.

Hope stopped halfway up and turned around. 'Please tell me if he's OK. I can't bear it. This has been the worst day of my life — please tell me if it just got even worser . . . it can't . . . ' She slumped against the wall. She noted with interest that she actually DID feel a bit wobbly. Perhaps it was the stitches, perhaps it was the stress, but it wasn't taking much skill to fake it. Debbie Cheese took her arm and guided her on up.

'Don't worry, come on,' she reassured her.

Once in the flat, Hope went into the kitchen straight away, mindful to keep them away from the front room where Minnie last was, just in case they might somehow know. Would they smell her? Surely not. But still. Hope's heart was beating fast; she knew she had to keep her wits about her.

The bag which had contained the concealed Minnie was still open on the table. Hope saw Debbie glance into it. Hope sat down at the tiny table, and immediately stood up again.

'Do you want a cup of tea? Or something? Or . . . I don't know what . . . ?' Hope offered, confused.

'No, no, thank you,' said Debbie. 'We just want

104

to ask you a few questions. There was an incident at the hospital this morning and you might have some information for us, or might have noticed something . . . ?'

'So, Isaac is safe?'

'Sorry, who is Isaac?'

'He's my . . . boyfriend. OK, that's fine, so long as he's OK, it's not about him.'

'Where is he at the moment, then?'

'He . . . drove me home and now he's gone out to get some . . . things . . . and he's taken some of the . . . baby stuff . . . to the charity shop . . . I just didn't want it here, I can't look at it . . . ' For a brief moment, Hope dipped back into the feelings she had been having in the early hours of that morning when she realized Minnie was gone. Since then, her heart had been on a roller coaster, but she could still remember where it started, with the tiny limp body. She conjured the picture in her mind and she started to weep for it all.

Constable Debbie immediately sympathized: 'Ms Parker, we know you experienced a trauma this morning, and I'm sorry to have to ask you these questions, but there's a life at stake here . . . '

'What's happened?' Hope enquired snottily through her waterfall of true tears.

'A baby has been snatched from a room on the same ward where you were. Perhaps you could just fill me in on everything you saw when you left earlier . . . And if it's all right with you, Constable Taylor will have a quick look around . . . ?'

'Yes, of course, go ahead,' Hope replied with confidence. 'God, how terrible . . . poor parents . . . I know how that feels . . . to lose a . . . '

105

Her voice faltered and trailed off.

While Debbie carefully questioned Hope, and wrote everything down in a special little notebook, Constable Taylor had a thorough poke around the flat. He would find nothing suspicious; Hope knew that. After all, the baby had only been there for a short time. There was no evidence of her.

Unbeknownst to Hope, and luckily for her, that very morning a family of Romanians had been visiting a new mother on the same floor. It was a big group, loud and unruly, and very happy to see their new addition.

Also luckily for Hope, the inherent prejudice of some of the Met police meant that the focus of the investigation was on this group of gypsy people. Inspector Thripshaw was convinced they were guilty of kidnapping Florence. All of his energies were there; he had only sent Debbie to talk to Hope as a matter of formality, process and straightforward elimination. There was no strong suspicion; the police were mopping up every single avenue as quickly as they could before moving on to hone in on the Romanians, who had gone now, and were spread far and wide around the city, as was their wont. These two facts meant that Debbie Cheese was already on a losing wicket with Hope.

Debbie was a solid police officer, however, and observant at all times, so she scanned everywhere as she spoke to Hope and she was on high alert for any clue Hope might reveal. The fact was there were no real clues; even the bag Florence had been carried in was seemingly perfectly normal and contained ordinary overnight stuff. Now, IF

Debbie had decided to give that bag to a forensics team, she MIGHT'VE had a whole other DNA story . . . but she didn't. She immediately warmed to and trusted Hope like everybody who met her, and she knew that Hope had been through an unthinkably terrible time losing her baby that very morning, so the last thing she wanted to do was add to that dreadful burden if she didn't have to.

Hope gave an apparently full account of leaving the hospital after saying goodbye to Fatu, and travelling easily and innocently down to the car park where Isaac was waiting. There were car park attendants on the exit gates who would verify any story, Debbie reminded her, which only served to relax Hope since she absolutely knew that they would not have seen anything suspicious.

'Thank you for your help, Ms Parker.' Kind Debbie, solidly inhabiting her uniform, wrapped up her questioning as she flicked shut her little black book. 'And do feel free to call us if you think you remember anything at all, however small or insignificant, especially if it struck you as unusual. It may help us to put a picture together . . . '

Constable Taylor had, meanwhile, looked in every room, in every cupboard and drawer; he'd even been down the fire escape where Isaac had fled with Minnie minutes before and he'd checked the yard, the bins, the old shed. Of course, he found absolutely nothing. He even poked his head into the dusty loft space. As he walked back into the kitchen, he gave Constable Debbie the nod that it was all checked, all clear, which she took as their cue to leave.

107

'Will you be all right here on your own?' she asked Hope.

'Um, yes. Isaac will be back shortly, I'm sure. He won't want to be long. We're going to make soup and we have some people to call . . . Some of the family don't even know yet . . . I can't think of the right words . . .'

Constable Debbie reached out and touched Hope's hand.

She might've been a police officer, but she was still a human, and a female one at that, who could empathize with Hope's tangible sorrow. When their eyes met, the sad Hope that Debbie saw wasn't a fabrication. Hope genuinely was a woman who had, not more than a few hours before, experienced a despair that was hardly bearable. That was the part of Hope which Debbie connected with. Hope knew it too, and didn't mind that Debbie's good heart was baited in such a way, because it was the truth. A truth. Not the whole truth, obviously.

So it was that Constable Debbie Cheese left Hope's flat convinced she had conducted a thorough check and consequently eliminated her from any ongoing investigation.

Hope had never quite made it on to a list of suspects, and she certainly wouldn't now.

Hope was off the hook.

It had been an Oscar-worthy performance.

She closed the door behind the police officers as they clumped down the poorly constructed stairs with the threadbare carpet. She rushed to the front room and, from behind the blind, watched them get in their car and go. She exhaled slowly.

Now . . .
Where was Isaac with her daughter?
Where was her daughter Minnie?

109

The Press

Julius wished he had better clothes with him. He was tempted to get his secretary to pop to their house on her way to the hospital to pick up his tailored Paul Smith deep purple double-breasted suit, but changed his mind when, on second thoughts (which he rarely had), he remembered it was really a knock-'em-dead party suit. Shame, he thought, this might turn out to be a huge audience. Yep. Massive. But the purple is wrong for this. Better to look a bit dishevelled actually. More authentic. Yeah . . .

With that thought, he pulled his shirt out of his trousers and undid a couple more buttons. He'd been in these same clothes since last night and he wasn't the most fragrant he'd ever been. Still, more power to his elbow: it was definitely a credible look, and never before had Julius needed to appear as credible as at this very moment.

Anna had somehow dragged herself into the fresher clothes she had the foresight to pack, imagining there might have been a photo with them all together for Julius to hand to his PR team. They would've been standing on the front steps of the hospital, maybe even including a key midwife, perhaps Irish Sarah, in aesthetically pleasing ascending height order, and Anna would have had little Florence in her arms. For that purpose, she'd packed a seasonally jolly red jumper and well-cut Joseph trousers.

110

It all felt completely incongruous now. Down-right wrong, in fact, but Anna was in an altered state, and she was operating like a robot. Anything she did or said felt as if someone else was remote-controlling her. She answered questions, she washed, she dressed, she packed up ready to leave, all as instructed by the kind folks around her, all as if her head wasn't a bucket full of screams.

Anna had agreed to take part in the sizeable press announcement DI Thripshaw had arranged. She knew it gave her the best chance of getting Florence back. But as she was packing up her bag, she had no idea what she was going to say. She found herself unpacking the bag and packing it again three times. She realized that she was doing this in order to double-check that she hadn't somehow forgotten she'd put Florence in there, somewhere at the bottom of the bag. She even looked in the zip-up inner side pockets. She found herself genuinely searching and half expecting to find the baby curled up there so that she could turn to them and pronounce, 'Oh, there you are! Sorry, everyone, I totally forgot I'd already packed her away nice and safe. She's snuggled in here, look at her, little hamster, all scrunched up . . . !' and they would all laugh and do those big thank-God-for-that relieved eyes, and everyone would want to hold her so much, and she'd get tired and cry with her shakey bottom lip out and no one would mind in the least . . .

'Anna, darling, we need to make a move. Follow me, and listen, I'll do the talking, OK?' Clearly, Julius regarded himself as hugely considerate as he passively bullied her into keeping quiet. Clearly, he had convinced himself that he was by far the better person for the job of confronting the press. And clearly, to an extent, that was true: he was indeed experienced, owing to his job. But Anna was actually the perfect person to speak to them. Because SHE WAS THE MOTHER.

In a haze of half-awareness, she took his hand and followed him along the corridor and into the lift and along another corridor and into the ante-room. Through the door they could see a long table with microphones set up in front of a row of cameras, with various grumpy journalists waiting. This was after all 1 January; most of them were nursing very sore heads, and they really REALLY didn't want to be here. Not even for the kidnapping of Julius Albert Lindon-Clarke's brand-new baby. On any other day, they would've cravenly devoured this opportunity, but today, they didn't like their jobs. At all.

In the anteroom, DI Thripshaw briefed Anna and Julius on how he planned the conference to go.

'Mr and Mrs Lindon-Clarke, we are all set up now. I'm not going to lie to you, this will be no walk in the cake, but if you follow my leader, I will kick off the preceedings, and then I will hand over to you — '

'To me,' Julius interjected quickly. He truly didn't want Thripshaw to say much, since he appeared to put his foot in his mouth virtually every time he opened it.

'Certainly, yes,' Thripshaw agreed. 'It's best to keep it short, to the point, and heartfelt. Be your-selves and don't be afraid to let them know how you really feel. It's best to be fully honest. Now obviously there are a few of the tabloids out there, proper wolves in cheap clothing, but I will handle any off-pissed remarks. Either I will jump in or, if you give me the nod, Mr Lindon-Clarke, I will give them a shot across the bowels, don't worry. Now then, are we ready?'

With all confidence vastly reduced to virtually zero, the doleful group trooped in and sat in a sombre row with DI Thripshaw at one end, then Anna and Julius, then two other police officers who had been specifically targeting the Romanian community as part of a five-year investigation called Operation Roma.

Thripshaw took the lead. 'Good morning, ladies and gentlemen — mainly gentlemen I see — and welcome to two thousand with a thud. As you may be aware, we are here to investigate the snatching of a newborn baby girl early this morning from this very hospital. Mr Lindon-Clarke, the father, will speak first, and I would ask you to be sensitive, please, folks: Mrs Lindon-Clarke here has been through a hedge backwards this morning, as I'm sure you will appreciate — all of us know the extent of the bondage between a mother and child is huge. Mr Lindon-Clarke . . . ?'

Julius resisted rolling his eyes and pulled the microphone towards him on the table. For the first time since Florence had gone missing, he reached out to Anna and put his big hand on hers. She was already in a strange numb place where nothing made sense, and this unusual action compounded the surreality of it all.

He started to speak; there was a tremble in his

113

voice. Was it real? 'My wife and I are understandably devastated at the loss of our precious first-born daughter, Florence — of course we are — and we are relying on this city's magnificent police force to find her. We have every faith that, with the help of the morally upright citizens we know are out there, we will get that vital lead we need, and we will bring little Florence home . . . '

Anna watched him speak. She knew he was certainly doing that because his mouth was moving, but she had very little idea what he was saying. It suddenly struck her that she wanted, more than anything, more than ever, to be dead. Then, at least, all expectation of feeling would cease, and she could sink into a seabed of gloopy thick sorrow without being watched or judged, which is what she felt was happening. She was concentrating hard on trying to breathe. It wasn't easy because her lungs and throat had calcified with shock.

'This tragedy only serves to highlight an issue we have been discussing for almost a decade now,' Julius continued, 'which is the obvious lack of security in hospitals. I have long been an advocate of CCTV on EVERY corridor, in EVERY lift and certainly in all reception areas and car parks.'

This was news to Julius's longstanding PA, who leant against the wall as she reeled with the sophistry.

'Perhaps if such a system had been in place in this very hospital on this very morning, my own daughter wouldn't be missing right now. It's time to put this matter back at the top of the agenda . . . '

Anna watched on as Julius slid comfortably into

his familiar political territory, using this prime but inappropriate opportunity to bang a pet drum.

Even DI Thripshaw could see this wasn't good, and he interrupted Julius: 'Yes, thank you, Mr Lindon-Clarke. Perhaps Mrs Lindon-Clarke would like to second that emulsion with her own words . . . ?'

'No,' said Julius, irritated by the intervention just as he was preparing to take flight.

Thripshaw could see that the journos were glazing over while Julius was speaking, and that was the last thing he wanted. He needed this to be impactful. He needed to make sure a heart and soul was seen by the cameras. Neither was present in Julius.

'Yes,' he said firmly, 'I think so . . . Mrs Lindon-Clarke?' He indicated for Anna to take the microphone. She didn't move, so Thripshaw pushed it towards her, and gestured that the floor was hers.

Anna looked down at her hands, which she noticed were clenched tight, whitening the knuckles; then she looked at the microphone and up at the waiting journalists, poised with their notebooks and pens . . . She slowly leant forward, and spoke quietly.

'Someone has ripped my heart out of me. Please give her back . . . or I can't live. Don't hurt her, don't hurt my heart . . . please . . . ' And with that, Anna could no longer stem the tide of torment she was holding back. Speaking out and admitting how she felt, putting her anguish into the air like that, burst the dam. She put her hands to her face to hide the tears that came gushing out of her, but the force of her suppressed despair was too powerful to stop. In any other circumstance, she would have been mortified to be blubbing so openly in public. She was famously emotionally restrained. Not this sad morning, 1 January 2000, the day her life fell apart. On this day, she had nothing to lose. She'd already lost it.

As Julius went to put his arm around her, she batted him away as if he were fire she was fending off. She didn't want to feel the burn of his touch, or anyone's touch unless it was Florence. She longed for the beautiful soft flesh on flesh with her, the flesh of her flesh. She wanted it so badly that she physically hurt.

Julius was embarrassed that his effort to comfort his wife had been so publicly rebuffed. The journalists were definitely scribbling now, and he could feel the zooms of the cameras. This was tabloid gold. Their relationship laid bare with such intimate awkwardness at this extraordinary moment.

Anna was barely able to stand when she was ushered out of the room by the two policemen and Julius.

DI Thripshaw wound it up very quickly. 'We'll leave it at that. As you can clearly see, this has been a complete tragedy for this poor family, so if anyone has ANY information, we'd be grateful to hear from you. We're not operating under any aspersions currently, but I can promise you we will not give up on this. I have given Mr and Mrs Lindon-Clarke my solemn vow that we will continue to hunt for the cruel people who took their daughter, and that search will persist until we're thick in the head. Thank you. Sorry there isn't

116

time for questions, my fault, I underestimated the fragility of Mrs Lindon-Clarke. As you witnessed, it's way too soon. Thank you.' And with that, he followed the others out of the door.

Once in the anteroom, Julius furiously berated DI Thripshaw. 'What d'you think you're doing? How dare you cut me short like that?'

'It wasn't helping. Leave it at that,' replied Thripshaw. 'Perhaps you could . . . ?' He nodded towards Anna.

This annoyed Julius even further. Not only had the dolt ruined Julius's big moment, but he had leapfrogged over the bigger issues to highlight Julius's lack of empathy. How gauche, on both counts. And how annoyingly perceptive. Julius had to concede, especially with so many people standing around, so he went to his wife, who was doubled over and trembling, and he took her in his arms.

'C'm'ere, my love, come on now. We'll sort this out somehow. Someone somewhere knows where she is. We've just got to find her, that's all. Which we will. Come on,' he reassured her. Anna clung to him. He may have been wreckage, but he seemed to be floating.

Turds do. Don't they? Turds and sweetcorn.

Surprisingly, Julius found this approach useful. Anna seemed to respond. She had certainly calmed down a bit, and it gave him a status in the hellish scenario. He could possibly even be a bit of a hero if he played his cards right. He decided that he would endeavour to support her as much as he could, yes, but he also pledged to himself that he wasn't going to let this opportunity slip

117

away. It was bloody awful. Someone had taken his daughter, but at the same time, and for the first time ever, he had the ear of the nation. He would surely be an utter fool if he didn't maximize the opportunity. It was a win–win. Hopefully, they would get Florence back which would . . . be great . . . and make Anna happy, and also, he'd be able to head up the campaign to change the face of security in government-funded buildings. He would start with this, hospitals, because it was pertinent and he had the personal slant going for him now . . . Imagine, though, if he could extend the scheme to schools and, of course, prisons? Imagine if, oh, perhaps the initiative might in future even be referred to as 'Clarke's Law'?

Or something like that . . . ?

Isaac's Second Decision

It was early evening and the winter sun was leaving at a lick in order to honour her commitments in other warmer parts of the world. Hope was pacing around inside the flat, up and down the corridor from the front of the flat to the back. In the front she checked the street from her living room. Nothing. She rushed down the corridor.

In the back, she checked the yard from her kitchen.

Nothing.

Where was Isaac? Minnie would surely be hungry again by now. Was she warm enough? Where were they? She felt a rumbling panic rising in her belly. Surely he wouldn't run off completely with Florence? Would he? For a brief second she engaged with that thought, but found it too unpalatable to dwell on. She couldn't cope with two losses; she was barely managing one. No, no, no. She daren't even consider it for real.

Why didn't Isaac have a mobile phone? Why did he resist it so strongly? Besides the fact that he couldn't really afford one, he claimed that he simply wouldn't use it. His parents called once a week on the landline in reception at his halls. He regularly saw Hope. That was it for him; he could communicate with those he cared most about and didn't desire anything further. He also had regular conversations with Hope about the fact that, as an engineer, he was pretty sure the technology would change drastically, and he advised her to hang fire until mobiles were cheaper and better. He said it would be soon, and when the phones were more affordable, he would buy her one, maybe for her twenty-first birthday? For Hope, the anticipation and dreaming about it was almost better than any present itself. She was twenty. She'd had to grow up pretty quickly at home when she was younger so when she could choose, Hope fiercely protected her right to be immature and downright gleeful.

That was all right when it came to presents and romance and fashion. It wasn't all right when it came to parenthood. She and Isaac had crossed the Rubicon into maturity right at the moment they made a baby. It was in this responsible frame of mind that she was fretting about Isaac and Minnie. Not for a moment could Hope stop to consider that the blonde woman asleep in the maternity suite that morning might be experiencing a thousand times the horror of her own worry.

Hope was anxiously peering up and down the street from the bay window in her living room when she heard the kitchen door handle go. She raced down the passage to find Isaac holding Minnie in his arms; she was wrapped up in his coat for extra warmth against the cold evening.

'Thank God. Here, give her to me.' Hope took the baby from him, and she was shocked to feel how stone cold Isaac was in only his shirt. With Minnie still in her arms, she rushed to the bedroom and yanked the duvet from the bed and brought it back into the kitchen where she wrapped it around him as well as she could with one hand. She manoeuvred him to sit at the narrow breakfast bar. It wasn't easy; he was frozen. Hope went straight to the kettle and put it on, while she expertly plopped a teabag into a mug single-handed. She might have been carrying an infant for years; it seemed second nature.

Quiet Isaac was unnervingly quiet. Hope didn't push it. She made him tea and let him warm up without a word passing between them. She sat opposite him and unravelled the baby from the coat and the batik throw. Minnie was such a little star, she gurgled at Hope and quickly latched on when Hope once again offered her breast, which was swollen and ready. The only sound was that of Isaac slurping his sweet tea and Minnie slurping her mother's milk. Somehow, in the undoubtedly traumatic atmosphere, these three people were breathing calm oxygen. There was something about the energy of the baby that slowed them both down to her rhythm. Her little heartbeat was their main concern; she mattered the most and they could console themselves with the knowledge that she at least was content. For now.

Halfway through his body-thawing mug of tea, it was Isaac who spoke first. 'I went back.'

'Back where?' she said.

'To the hospital.'

She gasped, gathering herself, and stayed silent in fear while she waited to hear his story.

'I knew it was the right thing to do. Perhaps the parents were still there. I thought I could make it all right. All right for everyone. I walked into the front hall bit, where the reception is, where all the seats are? I sat there for a minute. I thought I could leave her there. Someone would see her and take

121

care of her; she wouldn't be on her own for long. It's the best place. Then nobody would notice me, no one would blame you and they would have their child back. It would be right again . . . and I would come back here and we would eat soup and we would be OK . . . ' He stopped talking. Hope waited. And waited . . . until she could tell he was ready.

'So . . . what happened . . . ?'

'A lady came and sat down next to me. She had a baby too, in a pram. I think they were Indian, or something . . . She said hello to the baby first and asked me her name. Minnie, I said. She told me her little girl was called Aisha. She didn't ask my name. She mainly spoke to Minnie who . . . was so quiet. The lady said she was such a good girl, so happy and calm . . . like her daddy. For a moment, I was wondering what he might be like, her daddy, who she was going to be back with soon . . . and then I thought . . . she means me. The lady thinks I'm her daddy. Course she does. I'm sitting there, holding her, looking after her. Who else would do that except her father? Who loves her, whatever happens? Her father. Who will always put her first, above all? Her father. That's me.'

There was a catch in his voice. He was trying hard to keep it together. This was the most difficult challenge he'd faced yet in his young life.

Hope held her breath. He was so very nearly there, where she wanted him to be, where Minnie was their daughter with no further debate, where it was over and they could get on with living. Where it was all normal. He was standing right on the edge of that . . .

122

Minnie suckled contentedly.

Suck. Suck. Suck. She moaned quiet little baby moans of gratification. The most calming sound in the world.

Isaac watched Minnie, so at home on her mother's breast. Belonging there. He longed for this image of the three of them to be how it would always be, how it rightly should be.

He continued, 'In that moment, sitting there, she assumed I was a father. She knew it as a fact; she didn't question it for a second. They all did. Anyone who put eyes on me today saw me with my daughter. Saw a good dad. And that's what I could be. What I am, when she's here. I can't be, if she's gone. She's . . . gone. Minnie is gone . . . '

Hope saw him slipping back into the early-morning chaos of that day. She couldn't let that happen, or all would be lost.

'Isaac, look at me. Here we are, look, here she is. She's safe. It's gonna be OK, babe . . . You did the right thing . . . '

'No, Hope, I didn't. I sat there for ages, looking at her, knowing what I had to do. You don't know how much I wanted this. All of us together. You happy. Her happy. She was looking at me, she's innocent, only I could make the decision for her. It was all down to me. I even stood up and put her down on the seat behind me, and I moved away, started to go. I couldn't. I couldn't. I was responsible for her. I was the only person who knew where she was, how she was . . . '

'Who she was. Who she IS,' Hope chimed in.

'I know who she is, Bubs, and I know who you want her to be. Right then, at the hospital,

I decided that those people upstairs had already had her taken away, they're dealing with that, I know it must be hard but . . . you would have to deal with her . . . with a baby being taken again, twice, if I left her there right then. I know you. I know how . . . heartbroken you were this morning and how quickly mended she made you. I love you, Hope, I do, I know how beautiful your heart is, how pure. How lucky any child would be to have you as a mummy. I'm in your team. I'm loyal. I'm loyal. I'm a loyal man . . . '

'Yes, Isaac, you are, and that's why I love you.' Hope affirmed it. She spoke the truth. And there's nothing like a truth, even a half-truth, to underpin a whole lie, however big. Somehow a lie settles better on a righteous foundation. It's like the clotted cream on top of the jam on top of the scone.

It sits well.

It's easier to eat.

With his truth rumbling about as the bedrock for his justification, Isaac had made another big decision.

'From the minute I went back out of the hospital doors, that was it. I'm in. No one stopped me. I carried her back here, all the way, walking home. To you. This is where she needs to be. You two need to be together. I see that. It didn't start right, but it's come right.' Isaac's conviction was veneer thin but getting thicker every minute. He told himself that he'd somehow behaved honourably. Both of them were slightly mad that day. Yet they were in tune. Working together, they seemed to have got away with it. 'Til that point, at least.

But Isaac had more to say. 'I'm glad you're

happy, Hope. You ARE happy, aren't you?' he asked, genuinely seeking the answer. He wanted to conquer her suffering, whatever the cost to his own moral record. He was most definitely 'in', and in deep. He'd never felt more of a foreigner before. This step away from his well-trodden, principled and honest path was uncomfortable, but he knew this was his decision. She was looking to him. For surety. For reassurety.

'Isaac, this is everything. EVERYTHING. All I need for my life, OUR lives, to be good and meaningful is in this room. We are going to live right, I promise you. Minnie will know what it is to be safe and to be loved. She's going to know that her life can be anything she wants it to be. She's gonna fly, Isaac, really fly high.'

Hope watched as Isaac stood up, shook off the duvet, and moved to the sink where he put his teacup down.

'Well. Now. That's good. Very good. Her life will be a good one. Yes. I just want you to know some things, Bubs . . .'

He turned to her, and for some reason, Hope felt a tug on the plug in the bottom of her heart.

'You see, from the first minute I met you, Miss Hope, I knew you would change me, and you have. At first I thought, Hey, I'm young, I don't want to feel this deep, no way. I'm here in England for an adventure. I didn't know you were my adventure. You are my all. Light, dark, laughs, worry, future, dance, sing, cry, love. All of it. Is you. Like no one else. I have found a home for my heart in you. You get me. You love me.'

'I do,' she whispered, suddenly feeling like a

very small girl in a vast cathedral. Their air was swirling, changing direction . . . tug tug on the plug . . .

'I know you do, and it's given me strength to do things, to be less afraid. Truly. I thank you for that, I do. I was afraid today, this morning, when . . . it all went wrong, but then I looked at you, and I took my strength from you and then I could do anything. So I did. I brought this blessing back to you. It's all for you, Hope. My Hope. You have been my Hope.'

'Have been'? Past tense? Hope gulped. No, please.

Tug tug.

'I want you to have everything you want and deserve, and I pray that now you have?'

She nodded, tentatively.

Tug.

'Good. Then I've done what I needed to, but listen hard to me, my darlin' one. I cannot be any further part of this. I won't be able to do it. I can't see Minnie's eyes looking at me every day, knowing what I know, and not telling her. I cannot lie to her.'

Tug, the plug was out, and Hope felt her heart's lifeblood draining away.

'What are you saying . . . ?'

'I'm saying I have to go. Don't worry, I will always keep this hidden. I will never speak about it. I will keep your secret, but I won't keep hers, that's between you and her and God. If I don't see her, I don't have to tell her. It's up to you if you do.'

'No. Please. Is this a choice? You or her?'

'No. The choice is made. I go back to S'Leone.

126

Tomorrow probably.'

'What about your studies?'

'I will say it's family reasons. It's the truth. They'll understand. It's only one more term; I can do it remotely from home. I'll still graduate. But not here.'

'Is there anything I can say to stop you? Tell me what I can say, please, Isaac!' Hope started to weep quietly.

'There's nothing, Bubs. I've done a wrong thing and now I'm going to do a right thing. As right as I can. I know I will forever stand in need of mercy and forgiveness. I can live with that, knowing she is safe with you, and you are happy.'

Hope stood up with the baby still attached to her, and she went over to him. She knew he was a man of his word and that he would go, without doubt. He was solemn and firm.

She put her free arm around him, and he put his arms around both of them. The last time they would be together like this, a family. Minnie would miss out on so much, not having this remarkable, fine man in her life, Hope thought, and this was on her.

Isaac pulled away, and Hope saw his wet face and his trembling mouth. He attempted to say something, but it was difficult for him.

'I will send money for her . . . whenever I can,' he burbled as he climbed into his coat, his head hanging down to avoid eye contact. He stopped to touch the baby's head one last time, and he moved towards the door.

'Isaac,' Hope said. He stopped, his back to her. 'My Quiet Isaac. I don't know a better person.'

127

She saw him take a huge breath in, the last where he would share the same air with them, his beloveds.

He opened the door, slipped through, and was gone.

Hope stared at the door.

It was over.

This day, where she had lost and gained and lost again, so very much.

Eighteen Years Later

Minnie could not get comfortable. Every which way she tried to sit on the sofa, it wasn't right. She could feel that her heart was beating fast, too fast, but it had done so regularly in these past few weeks as her pregnancy progressed. She was told to expect it, that it would get more difficult. She was told to seriously rest, and that was what she was trying to do.

Lee was trying to do anything he could to help without letting her know that he was nervous. Lee told jokes when he was nervous, so Minnie knew anyway. He brought her milky coffee and kissed her gently. 'All right, Mrs Mummy?'

'Lee, put your pants on, for godssake!'

'Whassya prob, girl?' He started strutting up and down in front of her, throwing his best Jagger moves to distract her.

'Look 'pon your hero lover man baby daddy and salivate yourself. How built and fertile am I? Poppin' off the babies, pam pam!'

'Stop it! I don't wanna laugh, it hurts.'

'Have you ever witnessed such a giant knob?' he asked, pointing at his distinctly ordinary one.

'Yeah,' Minnie said, pointing at the whole of him.

'Shut it, slag.' Lee deployed his best cockney gangster voice.

'Seriously, Twat, put your pants on.'

'Just trying to give you something else to think

about.'

'I know.'

'Fancy goin' to the footie? Or I could take you up Asda's. Buy some ciders? Have a fight?'

She punched his arm. He laughed, and she saw his face exactly the way it looked when she'd first met him the year before . . .

He was working on a building site then, near her home, and they both used to have breakfast in the same café.

Her on the way to school.

Him on the way to work.

She in grey uniform.

He in dusty plaster-splattered sweats and big steel-toed boots.

He had a beard and a shaved head. She found out later he did it to come out in sympathy with his sister who was losing hers. Chemo. So he shaved hers and she shaved his. It was damn cold in the winter so he wore a beanie hat outside. His sister had embroidered the word 'TWAT' on the front of it, and he wore it unapologetically, with pride, for her, anytime he was outdoors.

When Minnie met him, however, he was inside the steamy café with his work buddies. First of all, she noticed that he seemed to have his head on upside down, and then she noticed that all of them were having a huge fry-up, except him. He was having porridge with fruit scattered on top. He had definitely clocked her as she came in: she was unmissable with her mop of orange curls and her glossy kissy mouth. He took as many quick peeks at her as he dared without either Minnie or his own mates noticing. So he thought. He was mistaken on that one. Minnie was forensic when it came to boys. She was used to unwanted attention. It was impossible to be as individual and distinctive a person as she was without drawing focus. She didn't desire the attention, but equally she wasn't prepared to forgo her style simply to avoid silly comments.

On the day she saw him in the café, she was in her drab uniform, yes, but as always, Minnie found ways to customize it, all the while staying JUST inside the school rules.

The rules stipulated a uniform skirt; they didn't say you couldn't embroider it with giant red roses all around the hem.

The rules stipulated a grey blazer; they didn't say you couldn't have a bunch of real flowers, whatever you can find that morning, sticking out of your pocket. The rules said to wear hair 'up'; they didn't say up where or how; they didn't say that you couldn't braid it with red ribbon and twist it until the orange curls became an exploded profusion of a Mohican like an overstuffed pot of marigolds.

Minnie went to school as if she were the love child of Coco the Clown and Frida Kahlo.

There was no missing her.

And he didn't.

But, like her, he was, in actuality, the littlest bit shy, so he would never have made the first move, for all the bravado his tattooed arms and shaved head seemed to indicate.

Luckily, she had her earphones in, listening to Lady Gaga telling her she was 'Born This Way', and she didn't hear his friend behind her, telling her she'd dropped a five-pound note on the floor

131

from her pocket as she was getting her purse out of her silver rucksack to pay for her cinnamon swirl Danish and hot chocolate, so Lee had to touch her arm in her field of vision to get her attention. She jumped abruptly when she felt his touch, as if electricity were volting through her. She wasn't wrong. There was certainly something . . .

She removed her earphones, and for the first time she heard him speak, this sorta bashful, cheeky-Charlie, baldy beardy-weirdy she'd already had a sneaky side-eye at.

He smiled. 'Hey. Sorry. You dropped a Lady Godiva.'

'Sorry?'

'Fiver. This . . . ' He handed it back to her.

'Oh, sorry. Yeah. Thanks. Duh.'

'You won't need it . . . ' he said, pocketing the note as she reached to get it.

'Hey! Yes, I will . . . '

'Nope, I'm getting your breakfast today, Curls. What is it to be? Side of pig? With chips? Or endangered fruit from exotic countries?'

She instantly liked his vibe, especially since he could hardly bring himself to look her in the eye when he spoke to her. He was a curious mix. Not the run-of-the-mill loud-mouth she ordinarily dealt with in here. He was different, in a really good way.

She left the café with four cinnamon swirls in her bag and a large hot chocolate to boot. He pushed her fiver back into her hand as she was leaving. She grinned and thanked him. Only later, when she unscrunched it, did she see that he'd written his number on it, with 'TWAT' next to it lest she forget who he was. She wasn't going to forget him. Ever.

That was over a year before. She was just seventeen then. He was nineteen.

Now she was eighteen and Curls was having Twat's baby.

Lee whispered, 'I know what would help to get this bean moving...They DO say... y'know ... C'mon, foxy lady, you're looking mighty fine today and you know you want to ...' He was snuggling into her neck.

She giggled. 'You must be joking! Get off. The docs told me I had to stay still and quiet as poss. Besides, you ain't coming to paradise ever again, boy. Look what happens!'

'Your loss. Coulda made it twins, last minute.'

'Shut it.'

Lee wandered off to resume his PlayStation game, reassured that Minnie was OK. Well, as OK as a very uncomfortable, very pregnant girl with an underlying heart condition could be.

Minnie watched his bare pink bum as he strode off. She loved the sight of his long strong legs, his manly form.

She reached down into her silver rucksack and, puffing from the effort, took out her notebook. She liked paper and she liked different coloured fine-tipped felt pens. She drew, she wrote poetry, she copied down quotes and she wrote letters. Sometimes she wrote letters to fictional people, but mostly she wrote to real people. She had never yet actually posted one of her letters, but just writing them gave Minnie an outlet for her humour, her flights of fancy, her joys and her rages. She had shelves of these notebooks, always the same make,

'CD Notebook, 7mm ruled, MADE IN JAPAN', lined up in neat ranks in her bedroom, here in the Bristol flat she'd always shared with her mum. The notebooks were intensely private. She might have occasionally shown her mum the odd picture she'd drawn, or a funny quote, but otherwise it was all for her eyes alone, so she let rip in those pages. She often stayed up late at night filling up endless notebooks rather than sleeping. She'd been known to fall asleep on her desk at school because she was shattered. She had never fallen asleep in English though. She would fall asleep in useless classes like Maths or Chemistry. Or Politics. Pointless lessons, where words or drawings didn't seem to matter. She liked the patterns that formulas made in Maths, but not enough to keep her awake.

Most of her friends were forever looking at their tiny phone screens, but not Minnie.

'Cha, put that daftness down for a second and look at mi face, eh?'

Minnie preferred everything to be outward, flowing from her own imagination on to the page. She was a sender rather than a receiver. A creator. Originator.

Minnie had never taken a selfie in her life.

She didn't want to be the focus of any attention.

She didn't need to see photos to know what she looked like.

She looked like Minnie.

Minnie with the broad open face, huge dark brown eyes and skin the colour of a perfect new acorn. She had a high forehead with a button-broad nose which was covered with currant-bun freckles. She had a wide, full mouth with what her mother called 'enviably even teeth' and 'lips that everyone wants to kiss'. Her hair was a bit of a trademark, a veritable fountain of reddish-brown curls, which gave zero tosses about tidiness.

In a moment of crazy abandonment, Minnie had asked her mum to bleach the top part of her hair from her ears up, like a wild Mohican. It took hours to lift her natural colour out, but she had a topknot of pure yellow straw until she added the bright orange dye on top. When it was dry, it fell down over the dark hair like a creamy curly topping on a carrot cake. When they saw the result mother and daughter ran around the room, clapping with glee, they loved it so much.

But that was all way before she knew she was pregnant, before she knew . . . everything.

When she was Minnie Parker, no question.

When she knew who she was.

Not like now.

Minnie stroked her tight belly, took a deep breath in an effort to steady her erratically thudding heart, and she strained to write:

Dear Mum,
Bean is so ready to be born. It isn't time yet, but I'm about to burst, and I'm getting too tired too quick, so she better come soon.
I say 'she'. I don't know. I told them not to tell me. The nurse said, 'Oh what a lovely healthy-looking little . . . ' and I started to do lalalala really loudly so I didn't hear what came next. Lee was laughing so hard he did that snorting thing, then he joined in with the lalala and so did the nurse and know what? — Bean

was jumping about inside. I reckon she was giving it the full lalala too. I call her 'she' because that's my normal. Girl power, eh, Mum?

Oh God, how much did we love the Spice Girls?!

So, this is the <u>soundtrack to My Weird Life</u>, OK?

Spice Girls on a daily basis — you
The Specials and Bob Marley on a daily
basis — Grandad Zak
Madonna — Nanna Doris
Gaga — me
Rihanna — me
Kate Tempest — me
Katy Perry — you & me
Pink — you
Green Day — you and me
Beyoncé — you and me
Adele — you and me
Cardi B — me
Skepta — Lee
Best Best Best Thing right now: Janelle Monáe —
    there are no pretenders to this kween's throne.

Btw, talking about Girl Power, you able to catch up with the news? On #MeToo? That American film producer is done, guy!

Ever seen a man look more like a predator than him? No. I saw the first girl who blew the whistle, Rose something, in an interview. Her face, Mum.

    she'll never be all right
    she has to haul the hate around

136

she's packing disgust
worst of all, it's mainly for herself
she loathes what she did
   what he did
and what he did made her loathe herself
i can't even forgive him . . . how could she?
there's no way out for her
except a tiny crack of light
where all her sisters are
where i am
where you are
saying come on Rose
tell it all
put him away
but telling means
Rose has to set fire to herself
so we can all keep warm
and safe
she's not Rose
she's Joan

So that got me thinking about how some people sacrifice everything so that other people can live better.

and that's you, mama
the judge decided THEY were the victims
and me
but I know what you did
i know how you lugged your secret about
all on your own
to protect me
worried and guilty and heavy
you sacrificed your honesty

and for an honest person, the <u>most</u> honest
that was a huge forfeit
with a huge price
but when you come home
Bean will be here
i will tell her all about you
she will know you
my mum
her grandma
look at what you did to be a mum
how much you wanted it
how lucky am i?
to be so longed for
but today — i am understanding something
in a way I couldn't 'til now
i will be a mum soon
and like you did
i feel her moving about inside
i know
that if Bean died now
i would be out of my mind
she mustn't die
she must live
or i will die
i already love her too much
i'm scared, mum
what if — i have your same genes and it's
   an inherited thing?
then
i remember
because i do forget
that
I DON'T HAVE YOUR GENES
i have hers

the 'victim's' genes
and SHE DID have a living baby
so . . .
at this exact moment
however much i love you
and i do
i have to say
i'm glad she was my mum

there

said it

PLEASE PLEASE understand
it's just about Bean
right now i want the best chance for her
I want everything to go right
i know you will get it, mum
because you get me.

i wish you were here
not just for me
for you
and for Bean

she's getting ready, mum
she's got to be strong
i can hear you
telling me it will be OK
come on, Minnie Moo
come on, Bean
come on, life
i love you, mama
for EVERYTHING you are

i can see all the memories in my mind:
i am in your arms
i am three and i fell over when I tried
*   to walk in your best red weekend wedges*
you picked me up
magic-kissed it better
kissed the hurt arm
and the hurt pride
told them to stop laughing
you knew that was my worst hurt
told them i was an extraordinary ray
didn't obey the ordinary laws of refraction
shone in my own unique way
i was a style pioneer
artists like me should be encouraged
*   to go our own way*
*   to wear a mum's best red weekend wedges*
takes skill
balance
dash
better to fall off 'em
than never to wear 'em
you put me back in 'em
i did a whole circuit of that front room
left them all eatin' my badass stylish shit

please let me be even half the mother
you are
because you are A LOT
you are EVERYTHING

Suddenly, Minnie felt a sharp pain in her chest.
Deep down in there, where her heart was hurting the most, it was starting to give up. Literally.

Minnie's heart couldn't take any more. Of anything. The engine was too knackered to cope.

'Lee!' she called out.

He came running.

'Yes, bae?'

'I don't feel right.'

'OK, sit tight, I'll get some water . . . '

'No, Lee, get the ambulance. Please. Quick.'

As she spoke, she dropped the notebook and collapsed into his arms.

The letter to her darlin' mum Hope, in custody, would have to be finished later.

Back Then: Hope

Hope looked up at the flat for the last time. She was feeling nostalgic. It'd been a big part of her London life, and the place where Minnie was made. She had pushed past the stoner downstairs' annoying bike for the last time, she'd strapped Minnie into her car seat in Isaac's old car that he'd left behind, and she was heading home to Bristol.

Hope had very little to take with her. Her bed and sofa and TV had gone ahead in a van driven by one of her uncles. Even Minnie herself didn't involve much actual 'stuff'. A Moses basket and a bag with all her bottles, nappies and a change of Babygro for the journey. She was just over a month old now and still very tiny, but she was a hungry baby so Hope was feeding her half formula, half breast.

There had been a couple of moments when Hope wished she'd been able to get advice from a neonatal or a paediatric nurse, but of course, she couldn't. Minnie had a temperature but Hope calmly dealt with it. Minnie had a strange rash on her neck: Hope dealt with it. Minnie was waking up hungry in the night: Hope dealt with it by substituting formula for some feeds. It was going relatively well despite zero support, but Hope knew that, in the long term, the answer was to return to Bristol. She needed her wider family wrapped around her if she was going to raise Minnie right. Hope had missed her little sister Glory when they were apart. So that was the first call she made when she decided to go.

'Hi, G. So. Sitting down? I'm coming home! Yeah, yay, right!

Me 'n' the baby. No. He's . . . er . . . gone. I'll tell you when I see you. And I can meet the gorgeous Ky at last, check him out, see if he's suitable BF material. He's got to pass the sista test. That's who you are, girl. My sista. I've missed you so much. Get yer arms ready for incoming love . . . '

Glory had been the hardest to leave; she was only sixteen when Hope headed up to London, leaving her at home to cope with Doris and Zak and all the nonsense of their debilitating using habits; but Hope had taught her well. Shown her by example how to withdraw when the two of them were in a state, how to wait until their many melancholic, substance-induced storms had passed, before stepping in to care for them in the quieter calms afterwards. Hope sent some of her wages home, to an account only Glory could access, to make sure they all had some nutritious food and warm clothes, etc. Between the two sisters, they cared very well for their beloved, flawed parents. Yet however much Hope knew Glory had coped, she still always felt the nagging guilt that, as the older sister, she had abandoned her. In that way this was a good day. Hope was going to be back in town to take charge.

She'd given her notice at work. No one was that surprised; they knew she'd suffered a tragic stillbirth. She did it all on the phone and apologized for not going in personally to say her goodbyes, but they all understood.

143

Hope went to register the stillbirth. It wasn't easy.

First of all, she had no one to look after Minnie. She couldn't ask anyone. How could she, without alerting the wrong folk? She even considered, for one mad moment, asking Mr Downstairs Stoner to have her for an hour while she dashed to the registrar's office, but she couldn't do it. He was off his face most of the time, which was very useful for not noticing a baby upstairs, but not good for looking after one.

Eventually, Hope knew she had to take a huge risk, one she never would otherwise. She drove to the registrar's office at just the right time in the early afternoon, when she knew Minnie would fall asleep, replete and drowsy after her lunchtime feed. She put Minnie in her Moses basket in the back seat and lightly covered her over with a blanket and a coat on top. She propped it all up so that nothing could fall directly on to her, and she locked the doors quietly. It hurt her heart to do it, but she had no option. She thought about asking another mother to keep an eye on her, but knew it would arouse suspicion — why would anyone do that rather than taking their baby into the room with them ... unless something was amiss? No, she couldn't do that.

And what if the registrar saw her with a baby?

And what if the woman she entrusted Minnie with was a certifiable murdering lunatic?

NO. NO. NO.

This was the only way.

She checked through the window that the heap of clothes was in place. She reassured herself that

144

no one would want to break in to this old banger and that the heap seemed innocuous, and she walked away briskly, looking back all the time.

As she entered the reception area, Hope went straight to the receptionist, grateful that there was no queue, and said,

'I'm sorry, but my name is Hope Parker — well, no, I'm not sorry about that, but I need to know if the appointments are on time? It's just that . . . I have an elderly mother waiting for me . . . ?'

'OK, Mrs Parker — '

'Miss.'

'Miss Parker, I'll call you as soon as possible.'

'Thank you.'

'Take a seat.'

Hope looked around. There were very few people waiting, thankfully. It must be a slow time for births, deaths and marriages. Maybe the human race was on a general go-slow when it came to matters of life?

She wasn't.

She wanted to get this done and get straight back to Minnie. She sat down next to an older man whose face told a story of unimaginable loss. He looked haunted and was clutching a brown envelope. Hope couldn't engage with him, she knew it would draw her into an emotional pit she couldn't enter. On the far side of the room was a woman in her early thirties with two toddlers and an infant in a pram. Thankfully the toddlers were a welcome distraction from the gloom that orbited the old man. The only other couple were cuddled up in the corner facing the other way, clearly not wanting to be there.

But Hope's thoughts were with Minnie in the car. Why wasn't there a window in there, from which she could keep the car in sight? Stupid room. Stupid ill-thought-out room. It was almost as if they didn't WANT mothers with stolen babies who were secretly stashed in the car to be able to keep an eye on them . . . or something . . .

She was shocked out of her agitated reverie when the receptionist called out, 'Miss Parker? Room Two, please.'

Hope walked up the corridor, knocked on No. 2 and went in.

A friendly woman welcomed her and gestured that she should sit in the blue pleather chair across from her desk. 'Hello, Miss Parker, I'm Susan Meagre . . . You on your own today?'

'Yes, miss. Is that OK?'

'Of course. I was just . . . probably . . . hoping you might have some support at this difficult time?'

Difficult time?

In the chaos of the previous few days, Hope had all but forgotten the real reason she'd come here, she was hitherto simply fulfilling a necessary formality.

'Oh. Yes. No, I'm OK, thank you. Just want to get this over . . .'

'Yes, of course. Now then, you are what's called the primary informant, so of course you can register on your own, but I need to ask you if you would like to have the father's details entered? If so, I'm afraid he would need to be here.'

'No. Thank you. That . . . won't be the case today.'

146

'Right.'

'He's ... gone ... home to ... another country.' Hope told as much of the truth as she could manage.

'I see. Do you have the documents with you from the hospital?'

Hope handed over the envelope Fatu had given her and she watched as the registrar opened it and started to fill in the details in her big important book.

Hope gave her name and her London address.

She watched as Susan Meagre filled in Minnie's name and in a box marked 'Cause of Death' she wrote 'Unknown'.

Yes. Unknown.

In a box marked 'Details of Father', she put lines through the boxes. Obliterated.

Also unknown, in effect.

Hope's heart hurt to think that anyone might suppose Isaac didn't care, because he so passionately did. For the first time since she left the hospital, Hope thought about Minnie. The first Minnie.

Her daughter.

She pictured her so clearly. She remembered every detail of her little sweet sleeping face.

'Are you all right?'

Hope looked up at kind Susan Meagre, and she crumpled. Susan came around the table and put her arms around the trembling Hope.

'I know. It must be awful. You've been so brave. God bless little Minnie ... '

Little Minnie? Yes, she must get back to her immediately; she might have woken by now.

147

Hope took the certificate Susan gave her and, after thanking her profusely, raced back to her car to find little Minnie safely still fast asleep. As usual, being the best behaved little soul so that her mummy could get her to where she needed to be: in Bristol, where, hopefully, no one would ask any further questions because they were all expecting Hope home, bringing her brand-new daughter, little Minnie.

So Hope took that one last glance up at the flat. She propped up Isaac's picture of Captain Paul Cuffee that she'd brought with them in the car. She wanted to see it so she put it between the gearstick and the dashboard. She put the car into first gear.

She mouthed, 'Thank you, Isaac.'

And she pulled away.

She was going home.

With Minnie laid to rest.

With Minnie right beside her.

And with Isaac in her heart.

All of them free now.

But.

All of them chained to the truth.

And each other.

Minnie's 1st Birthday: Isaac

Watching his family sitting together around the simple wooden table on the porch of his house made Isaac feel waves of contentment. That he could at last provide something for those who had supported him for so long was a source of great pride.

He had only had his real full-time job for a few months, but with his new degree finally in his arsenal, he could earn properly, he could move out of his parents' home and he could afford the rent on this little one-storey wooden house near the port in Freetown.

He wanted to be near the harbour. His close friends didn't understand why he'd choose to be near all the mayhem, the clatter of harbourside commerce, the smells of fishing and fuel, but Isaac had a singular reason, nothing he needed to share necessarily, but something that helped to ease his burden. He felt close to his purpose here, in the shadow of his long-time hero. Thoughts of Captain Cuffee arriving on this soil, bringing his first cargo of thirty-eight freed slaves back to Africa from America, with all the optimistic hope of a new life in Sierra Leone, often played on his mind, especially when he was struggling with difficult, hidden feelings about everything he had left behind in England a year ago.

It might be New Year's Day, but Isaac's guilt was growing old and big and familiar. He liked the notion that Hope might just occasionally be looking at the picture of Cuffee.

He had left it by accident in his haste to go, but he was glad that he had, because, after all, it was Cuffee who had brought his mother's ancestors to this place two hundred years ago, and it was the blood of those ancestors that ran through Minnie's veins . . . when she was alive and kicking inside Hope. Not so the case with the new Minnie. Although he had no biological connection to her whatsoever, he WAS and IS most certainly connected, he knew that for sure.

Fastened forever to her with a big fat fib as the glue.

'Hey, where you gone?' Efiba nudged him gently, jerking him into the present.

'Huh? Ah, you know me . . . ' he replied.

'Yes, sir, I do.' She giggled. 'Mr Dreamer, floatin' off all the time. Well, now is no time for daydreams, there's Puff Puff to put on the table. Priorities.'

'Yes, yes, I know and Momma has made the caramel sauce.'

'From the secret recipe she'd have to kill me if she told me . . . ' Efiba giggled again and Isaac knew she was joking and not joking. It was true that his mother guarded the recipe for the sauce she spread on the sweet dough balls. It was a family treasure and until Efiba was family, that's how it would stay.

He watched her. She was wiping beads of sweat from her temples and her neck with a cotton cloth she'd retrieved from the freezer. It was the only way to stay cool in the blistering African heat. He

150

found her graceful movements to be so lovely.

Isaac was indeed inching towards asking Efiba to please marry him. She would be such a kind, beautiful, thoughtful wife, and she loved him very much. She showed him in so many ways, every day.

She spooned up behind him and held him close every single morning when they woke up together.

She knew how much he liked his minty tea to start his day, and she brought it in his favourite old tin cup.

She understood that he needed to be quiet.

She paid homage to his parents by respecting their family traditions, however different they were to her own, and she laughed at their jokes and teasing.

She didn't question him too much; she noticed how tense he became under scrutiny.

She thanked him often for all his kindnesses.

She supported him.

She knew him.

She sensed when he slipped into sadness, and she would whisper, 'Remember, I am your life jacket anytime you need to wear me,' in his ear.

She woke him gently when he whimpered in his sleep sometimes, like a dog dreaming of running.

She let him be. Just be.

And Quiet Isaac appreciated all of her. Even the parts of herself she was so harsh about.

'My forehead is big as a moon.'

'I'm as short as a twelve-year-old kid.'

'I don't know anything much, I'm not clever.'

'I stink.'

Her regular dialogue was a litany of self-deprecating criticism. It was easy to reassure her when she was down on herself because Isaac genuinely admired her and didn't see her in any light other than a bright, shiny, positive one.

Something was holding him back from proposing, though.

Something he couldn't explain to her, especially not today, on New Year's Day, Minnie's birthday. That's where his thoughts were . . . all around little secret Minnie. Where his heart so often was.

Isaac leant over to Efiba and kissed her gently on the cheek. 'Let's get the desserts out, come on, before Momma turns murderous . . . '

★ ★ ★

It was much later, when the family had gone, and Efiba, full of delicious lunch, was snoozing on their bed, that Isaac sat down to write the letter he'd been constructing in his head all year. Hope had given him a PO box number and they had agreed not to communicate any other way: it was too risky. Isaac hadn't written yet, he was so unsure what to say, but today was the day.

He was sitting at the table they'd all gathered around at lunchtime. It was cooler now the sun was disappearing. He placed his outdoor petrol-lamp near the pad of lined paper, and he sat back in the rattan chair with his arms behind his head. He looked up at the sky he could see over the tin roofs of the houses further down the hill, and above the busy industrial landscape of the harbour. He took a deep deep breath. He blew out. He wondered for a moment if that same air would ever have the momentum to whirl its way up up up across northern Africa, across Portugal, over the Bay of Biscay, across the pointy bit of France, over Guernsey and Jersey, all the way to Bristol to Minnie, who might just be in the middle of a big baby yawn unknowingly taking in a gulp of African dad-air. Could that happen?

He would so love a connection with her — anything to let her know that he cared. He felt heartbroken that she might grow up believing he had abandoned her easily. Nothing he'd ever done or would ever do was more difficult. This letter might at least go some way to letting her know.

If . . .

Hope let her see it . . .

Would Hope let her see it when she could read?

Would Hope ever let her see it? Would she read it to her?

Regardless, Isaac would write it, and in that moment he resolved to write to Minnie on her birthday every year.

He picked up his Biro and, in his scrawly writing, he started.

Dear Daughter,
I am your father, and I love you. You need to
know that as a fact.
One day, I will tell you the story of how I met
you, and how much your mama and I wanted
you, and maybe then you will understand how
the situation came to be.
For now though, you are one year old today
and I am thinking about you. I bet you've
changed so much. I hope your eyes are as bright
as they were. When I close my eyes, I see yours

153

so clearly, looking directly at me, straight at me, just like you did. You were so quiet and interested in everything. I only knew you for a few hours, but they were honestly the most beautiful hours of my life so far, little one. We ran up the road together with you inside my jacket. I felt your little heartbeat next to mine, and you dribbled all down my shirt 'til it was straight wet and I didn't mind at all. Even though that was my best shirt — your mama bought it for my birthday. From Marks and Spencer. Posh.

I am a long way from you on your birthday, but trust me, little Minnie, I don't forget you. I still feel your heartbeat.

I keep you close that way.

In my thoughts.

Your loving father XX

He folded the letter twice. He put two green banknotes inside the fold. He placed it in the envelope, he sealed it, he addressed it, and he kissed it. He would post it quietly in the morning. He'd send some Africa to Bristol.

Isaac stood and stretched his arms up. Then he walked back inside, back into his present life, and back to Efiba.

154

Florence's 1st Birthday: Julius

Julius stood in front of the long mirror. His natural home. He was much slimmer than this time last year, thanks to a strict regime of steamed broccoli, an attractive, sexually generous Danish personal trainer, and a renewed alliance with his own narcissism. The pounds had dropped off. So much so that rumours had circulated concerning his health, which of course Julius relished. He didn't mind the hunger: it kept him keen. He needed to be as sharp as possible right now. He had an arduous career voyage ahead, if all went according to plan. It was going to be 'an extended and tricky process of personal change and self-development'. Or so he said in all of the literature he issued concerning himself, all the while being extremely careful never to mention his ultimate goal. However, all those who needed to know knew that Julius Albert Lindon-Clarke wanted to be the first black Prime Minister. He was stealthily ensuring that each step moved him further along that yellow brick road to his own Oz, and the top job in the country. Wizard.

Today was important for lots of reasons. It was Florence's first birthday, and the perfect time to remind the public what happened, to jog their memories, and hopefully restart the search. Anna agreed to stay at home this time, whilst he reignited the appeal for any information about the baby which could be useful. The police would no longer be involved unless there were to be a new lead; they'd 'exhausted all avenues', they'd regretfully told Anna and Julius.

Julius was in no way exhausted. He was racing to reacquaint everyone with the situation. He and his team had worked hard all year to make sure little Florence remained in everyone's thoughts. Certainly the campaign was costly, both financially and emotionally. Anna was drained: she had appeared on every breakfast/ mid-morning/afternoon/early-evening TV programme that would have her. Sometimes she was alone. Sometimes Julius accompanied her. They took the advice of the PR company they'd employed to guide them at every turn on . . .

what to wear
what to say
when to say it

Julius had decided to be with Anna when the coverage was 'serious', when it was a journalistic news-type programme. He made it clear she was best to do it alone when she would be talking to Lorraine or the Loose Women. He had little interest in those, despite the fact that the viewing figures might be miles higher. However much he wanted to find Florence, and he truly did, he knew how key it was to incorporate all this publicity into his ultimate goal. He didn't wish for this to have happened, but since it had, he was determined to use every opportunity to let the public know him and trust him more. Allow them to believe in him.

Julius decided he didn't want a re-run of the

156

clumsy TV appeal they did on the day Florence disappeared. He had hardly spoken that day, and he'd found the police that were involved hugely irritating and incompetent.

Their year had been grim. He had hoped that Anna would emerge from her shock and sadness sooner, to be honest, to find some of the old fire in her belly, but she had remained fuggy, as if someone had buried her in the sand on the beach. Her head was visible, she was speaking, but her entire spirit was underground somewhere. She did a good impersonation of Anna when it was vital that she communicate — in front of cameras or to a journalist, for instance. She was beautiful, and perfectly eloquent. She told her remarkable story with confidence, poise and heart. She really did look and sound like Anna, but Julius knew the truth was she was absent from that public husk.

As far as Julius was concerned, and that's all that mattered, today was vital in his effort to have 'Clarke's Law' rolled out across the nation. CCTV would be standard in every maternity ward in every hospital across the entire nation. At last. His assistant beckoned him, he took a deep breath, adjusted his brave purple tie, and went to face the cameras.

157

Florence's 1st Birthday: Anna

The day had a very different feeling for Anna. She stood in the corridor outside the Brunel Suite at the Crawford Hotel in Marylebone. She was shaking and sweating. She'd felt considerably wobbly all morning, anticipating this terrible moment, but this was it, the point of no return. On several occasions throughout the day, she had decided to ignore all her better instincts and let everything just be, the way she was used to. It would be easier like that, to simply ignore all the red flags and let life limp on imperfectly, but something had shifted within her.

It was no coincidence that it was Florence's birthday today.

Something about the stark reality of that gave her courage. She slipped the plastic key into the slot . . . and watched the little light above it clunk from red to green. She heard the bolt slide in the door, she pushed it, and it opened into the suite where she knew Julius was inside with his lover.

The whole wretched year and everything awful about it had propelled her to this moment. Her year of guilt. ABOUT EVERYTHING.

Of course, a year ago everyone's New Year had been interrupted and spoiled, and of course, Anna felt guilty about that. She had told and retold the short story of what had happened as far as she knew it. She heard herself endlessly repeat: 'They must've snuck in when we were asleep . . .' And the culpability stung her more each time she said it.

How the hell could anyone be so asleep that they don't notice someone stealing their new baby? Especially if it was a group of people — the Romanians, which the police had implied was the most likely. How could several people enter that room silently, pick up a silent infant silently and then silently exit with not a soul clocking them? How could Julius have been as fast asleep as she was? She was tired, she deserved to be . . . she'd just given birth. BUT. YES.

She had been fast asleep.

That's all she knew.

She was a bad mother, that much was indisputable, as far as she was concerned, however much her family and friends kept reassuring her otherwise. In that very reassurance, she sensed a huge dollop of the judgement she feared and which she so readily heaped upon herself. Especially from her mother.

'Darling, you did everything a new mummy is supposed to do and then you were exhausted and you slept. You are supposed to sleep, otherwise you will have no strength for what's ahead, for . . . motherhood.'

She had been saying stuff, the right sort of stuff. It would APPEAR to have no subtext as she spoke it, she was using motherly, comforting words and tone, yet all Anna heard was: 'you were exhausted', which was a massive fail (as she saw it) and 'you slept', which was worse. It was Latin for 'you were negligent'. It wasn't Latin; it was mumspeak.

The awful thing about knowing your family so

well is that you read them and know intuitively when they are faking it. Anna's 'Ma' was half-mother, half-weapon, and Anna's childhood had been a masterclass in building personal armour in order to protect herself against the constant barrage of judgemental batterings Ma unleashed with little to no warning. The whole family had learnt how to walk on eggshells around her. No attacks were ever physical, all were emotional, and supremely bruising, so even in a rare moment like that, where Ma didn't seem to be overtly punishing her — in fact, quite the opposite — that's precisely how it felt to Anna. Ma would never be able to comfort her, because Anna didn't believe the sympathy was authentic. Ma was the queen of blame. Everything bad that happened was someone else's fault. Everything good that happened was her doing. It made the rules simple, at least. It was tidy. And terrifying.

It was so sad because Anna couldn't trust any kindness coming from Ma, and it compounded her already behemoth-sized guilt. That day, the ultimate proof had been when Ma said publicly, 'Do you need a cuddle?' It was an Exocet missile of strangeness that exploded inside Anna. It was a performance Ma was giving, and it was impossible to stop it. Even Pa sat quietly behind her, rolling his eyes, knowing he was powerless in the face of her sheer fakery. This was how Ma convinced unfamiliars that she was thoughtful, motherly. She imitated the sweetness of others she'd witnessed, without any real, genuine feelings. She was an emotional chameleon.

The fake sympathy had made Anna cringe.

She was weary and had none of her usual filters operating, and zero strength, so in response to her mother's offer, she found herself saying, 'Um, I don't think so, no, not after thirty-five years, ta.'

And that was it. She had lit the fuse. BAM! Pa quickly bundled Ma out and home to Surrey, leaving Julius open-mouthed at Anna's unusual audacity. They could hear Ma's irritated burblings as she was being packed into the car outside. Anna closed her eyes and exhaled. That had been a long time coming. Right then, she couldn't give a flying toss; she didn't want to handle any further drama. It was already at topple-level, and it was time to speak up.

Anna ordinarily preferred a quiet life. That's why she'd remained with Julius. She didn't want the noise of the inevitable rows she would surely have to have if she took issue with all of his many shortcomings. It was easier, quieter, to support him in his career, but keep her own head down. However, when necessary, Anna could stand tall, because Anna most certainly had a backbone. She had had to push on through her shyness and her anxiety this whole year in order to keep the search for Florence alive. She might have doubted herself fairly often, but she WOULD be heard.

So. Now. Entering this hotel room, Anna's opinion would be heard, and her resolve would not fail her. She was a year mightier, equipped with a simmering rage, and ready to confront difficult stuff.

As she stood just inside the door, she could hear the sound of them both laughing in that silly way that is so butt-clenchingly humiliating, unless you are one of the couple wound up in the gooey giddiness of it all, the game of giggle and flatter and coy that we all play when a relationship is fresh and exciting and we're pretending to be irresistible and cute. It had been an age since she'd made those noises with him. She couldn't imagine ever doing it again; it would be unthinkably mortifying.

Did she really want to see what she saw next? No. Did she need to? Yes. She knew that, unless she laid eyes on him in this very moment, he would fabricate endless lies to disprove it, as per usual. He was slippery as hell.

The curtains were closed, and daylight was seeping into the room around the edges of them. There was just enough glow to see the rude sight of a naked girl's back and bottom as she jiggled about preposterously on top of a prone and gormless Julius. For a short, cringing moment, they didn't realize Anna was there. All three shared the same fuggy adulterous air. Anna had tried to avoid thinking about images like this when she was suspicious of his fidelity in the past, but here it was, right in front of her, confirming all of her tortured imaginings.

It was worse, actually, because this was so very crude. Whenever she dared to think about any scene between Julius and his lover it would be candlelit and romantically perfect. This was much more sordid. A beige bore of a suite, with a creepy musky aroma. Nothing in there was the perfect she'd imagined, including the people, although she had to concede that the young woman seemed bendy — yes, more flexible, definitely, than

Anna — and she had small wings tattooed on her back. That was an unwelcome intimacy Anna would never forget. She knew instantly that, just as she'd guessed, this was the 'personal trainer', the liberal Dane she'd been told about. The person Julius generously attributed his weight loss to . . . no lie there.

'Boo,' Anna said. Softly.

The Dane screamed and quickly clambered off Julius, grabbing the duvet around her as she scrambled to the furthest reaches of the bed, just as Julius also tried to grab part of the duvet to cover himself. It struck Anna as ludicrous — whom was he shy in front of? Both women were familiar with his nethers.

Unfortunately.

'For Christ's sake, Anna!' he yelled. 'What are you doing here?'

'Visiting?'

The Dane was mumbling 'Oh my God' repeatedly. Julius stumbled off the bed, and losing his tiny tug of war with the Dane over ownership of the duvet, he compromised by covering his rapidly wilting penis with his hands, like a footballer between the penalty and the net.

'Look, this isn't me . . . isn't the me you know . . . ' he blurted.

'Right,' said Anna. 'Looks like you . . . but sort of redder . . . ?'

'No, you know what I mean. I'm not this man.'

'Yes, I think you are.'

'But I don't want to be, Anna. This means nothing . . . '

'Rude,' replied Anna, indicating the Dane and,

163

ironically, feeling sorry for her having to hear him dismiss her so readily.

As the Dane rose from the bed, gathering some clothes and making a swift beeline to the bathroom, Anna might have empathized more if she hadn't muttered '. . . in *our* room', in a frustrated way, as if this was putting her out somehow.

'In *my* life!' Anna responded to her back as the angel wings speeded up her exit.

'Anna, please, don't think anything of this . . . '

'Put your Y-fronts on, Julius, do us all a favour.' As she took up a senatorial position in a beige armchair in the 'seating' part of the suite, Anna felt decisive. She wasn't going to move until there was some sort of resolution.

She realized that her heart was beating very fast, and her breaths were shallow, but she was determined to remain calm. This was her ambush and she needed to own it.

Julius clambered into his Calvin Kleins and a hotel dressing gown and sat down opposite her, repeatedly rubbing his face vigorously, as if that would rid him of the shame. She could see he was thinking fast, his mind racing through all the possible consequences of this hideous situation.

'Please, darling . . . ' was his first après-pants attempt at conciliation.

'I'm not your darling any more, Julius. You don't get others to bounce around on top of you if you have a genuine darling . . . you just don't.'

'This is just a silly moment, Anna. You know what I'm like — I'm a sucker for some flattery and that's what she did . . . '

'Right. She flattered you?'

'Yes. Told me . . . stuff . . . '

'Like how clever and handsome you are?'

'Yes. No. You know the kind of stuff . . . '

'I don't, Julius. I really don't know what someone would have to say to make you think, Oh
right, yeah, what I ought to do next is put this in
you and risk my whole marriage . . . '

'Stop it, Anna, that's unnecessary.'

'Please don't lecture me about what's unneces-
sary. It's our missing daughter's first birthday, and
I thought you were busy making sure we find her.
All THIS is what's unnecessary, frankly.'

'I've been an idiot. I admit that.'

'Aww, well done,' Anna responded patroniz-
ingly, 'some culpability, finally.'

'She . . . she . . . ' He was fumbling about trying
to find a new home for all his blame.

'She what . . . ? What did SHE do . . . ?'

'She . . . wore white trousers. Tight white trousers.'

That floored Anna. She looked at him aghast.

The Dane heard this last feeble comment on
her way back out of the bathroom, wearing said
white leggings. 'What?' she spluttered.

'Come and sit down, please. We need to sort this
out.' Anna gestured to the only other seat available, which was on the small sofa, meaning the
Dane had to shoogle up close to the panted and
ridiculous Julius. She compromised and perched
on the arm of the sofa reluctantly. Anna had fully
expected her to take flight and escape, but there
was something about Anna's reasonable tone that
encouraged the other woman to stay. For now.

Anna found herself distracted by the white

165

trousers. What was it about them that he found so irresistible? She very much didn't want to be thinking about them at all, but couldn't avert her eyes from them. The Dane had great legs — was it that? Anna, with all her insecurities, did at least know that she herself had a couple of fine pins. It occurred to her that she didn't in fact own a pair of white trousers herself. Maybe she needed to rectify that? Why didn't she have any white trousers? Could it be that they looked a bit . . . cheap . . . trashy, even? Why was she thinking that? The Dane was neither, quite the opposite, but . . . the white trousers . . . sort of were. Is THAT what he liked about them?

Stop fixating on the white trousers!

Anna felt like a headmistress opposite two naughty children in her office. It was clear that it was for her to chair this strange moment, although, in truth, it ought to be different. By rights, they should be begging her forgiveness.

'Please can you open the curtains, Julius.' Anna deliberately used his full, formal name.

He meekly complied, but as he rose and went over to the window, his dressing gown flapped open and up, at which point Anna noticed that in the hurry he'd put his pants on back to front. The pee gusset was on his arse.

His considerably smaller arse. Anna had the surprising sudden realization that she had preferred him when his arse was more considerable, that this over-exercised and dieted reduced arse was boney and ageing . . . and vaguely feminine.

Stop fixating on the arse!

Anna had a fleeting, collusive eye-lock with the

Dane where she could have sworn she detected a shared embarrassment about the pitiful sight of this twat with his literal knickers in a literal twist . . .

'So, listen, we need to be grown up about this. Julius, do you love . . . her?' Anna ventured into dangerous territory with zero hesitation.

He was stumped. The lids were off all his boxes, and everything he had hitherto compartmentalized was mingling in a way he'd never intended. She knew that this was an impossible question for the adulterer to answer. He was so unfamiliar with speaking the truth. It would stick in his craw.

'Well . . . ?' said the Dane, impatiently.

'Umm. I love YOU, Anna,' he said quietly.

'Pardon?' Anna had heard him perfectly well, but wanted him to have to repeat it louder.

'You heard me,' he said with a tinge of irritation.

Anna stayed silent. Boomingly silent. He was forced to speak. Eventually . . .

'I love you, Anna.'

'Only me?'

'Jesus, why are you making this so hard?'

'GUESS!' she retorted.

And waited.

'YES. Only you,' he whispered as he hung his head.

'So, are you saying that you want to pursue a relationship with . . . her . . . or are you saying this . . . affair or whatever it is, will cease? Please, please, answer honestly,' said Anna.

All this time the Dane was following the conversation very closely, alternating between Anna

167

and Julius as if she were watching tennis. Now she stared right at him, while he averted his gaze.

'I want to save our marriage. I don't want to be this man any more, but you must understand all the stress with Florence has been — '

Anna snapped. Her eyes were ablaze. 'DON'T bring her into this. Don't you dare sully her with this. Don't speak her name in this shitty room, or I will end you, I swear, right now.' She recovered her composure as quickly as she had lost it, and continued: 'So am I to understand that you are prepared to live a faithful life with only me as your lover from now on? Please answer honestly.'

'Yes. Yes, I am.'

At this point the Dane wanted to have *her* say. 'Mrs Lindon-Clarke — '

'Do call me Anna. We've shared the same dick, after all.'

'OK, Anna. I want you to know that none of this was personal . . . '

'Oh, it's personal, believe me.'

The Dane pressed on bravely. 'I want you to know that *he* approached *me*. Seriously. I didn't really even fancy him. I want you to know that.'

'Charming,' mumbled the injured adulterer, adding a childish, 'You didn't resist much.'

The Dane continued unabated. 'I mean, I feel a bit odd now because the way he's being here now is not how he is being with me. I s'pose that's obvious, but he told me stuff . . . '

Julius was panicking. Shush, please. Come on. Stop it. The dam was about to burst.

It did.

'Listen, Joojoo . . . ' the Dane continued.

168

(JOOJOO?! Anna felt physically sick.)

'This whole scene is utter shit, but the woman deserves the truth.'

(THE WOMAN??! Anna felt physically sick.)

'He told me that it was pretty much over between you two ever since your daughter . . . was pinched.'

(PINCHED??!? Anna felt physically sick.)

'That you stopped loving him, or having the sex with him or even holding him. He said he felt unloved and unwanted . . .'

(UNLOVED??!! Anna felt physically sick.)

'He cried when we were in the gym, and I . . . cuddled him.'

(CUDDLED??!!! Anna felt physically sick.)

'And he said that even that slight touch was like rain in the desert . . .'

(Anna felt physically sick.)

Julius attempted to stop her. 'That's enough.'

'No, let her finish, she's only telling *her* truth.'

The Dane picked up the baton. 'He told me that he'd never done anything like this before.'

(Physically sick.)

Julius put his head in his hands. Even he, with all his brazen denial, couldn't look Anna in the face on this particular front.

'Oh. God. So that's not true then . . . ?' The krone had finally dropped for the Dane.

Julius mumbled something incoherent into his hand facemask.

The Dane continued, 'Right. Oh God. Should have known. He told me he didn't feel guilty because you guys were getting a divorce anyway, and a man has needs . . .'

169

(Sick.)

'. . . and that I had saved him.'

(BLEUUUUGH.)

'OK, I'm going to stop you there,' Anna interrupted quickly before she actually heaved up her breakfast porridge all over both of them. 'You need to know a couple of things. First of all, Julius's arrested emotional development is pretty much that of a fourteen-year-old. How old are you?'

'I'm twenty-six actually.'

'Yes, so that is too young even for you. Believe me. 'Joojoo' is a particularly alarming case of chronic juvenility, but the rule of thumb with men is usually to gauge them at about a third of their actual human age. Just a tip for future transgressions. Or simply for the future. Secondly, I have to tell you that you're not the only one. I'm sorry if that doesn't help to make you feel special, but he's been a very busy chap for a long time, although he promised me it would stop. He says he hates himself for it. Clearly, he's prepared to loathe himself by now, so FYI, if I were you, I'd get myself checked for any kind of STD since, as we all know, he doesn't 'like' to put a hat on it. I have regular checks, ever since I lost the trust, and the reason I do that is because, contrary to the stonking lies he's told you, we do, of course, have sex. Fairly regularly actually, although admittedly it's less lovemaking and more habit recently, but . . . because of that fairly frequent practice, I am currently pregnant.'

'Anna, darling!' Julius blurted out. 'Pregnant?'

'Not your darling. Your wife.' Anna speedily rebutted the untimely hug he was approaching to give her; she stood up sharpish and started towards the door.

Then she turned back to the Dane. 'I'm sorry for you that you're mixed up in all this. For what it's worth, I don't blame you as much — he's a skilled manipulator. He's a politician, after all. Did he tell you that I don't 'understand' him . . . ?'

'Yes, he did.'

'Hmm. Disappointing.'

With that, Anna swept out of the room. She resolved that the future would be different after this.

Minnie's 1st Birthday: Hope

Minnie burst out laughing when Hope carried in the caterpillar birthday cake with the single candle on the top. Hope knew it wasn't the cake that set her off, or the candle, it was the bad singing and clapping. There was nothing little Minnie liked more than music and dancing. And clapping. Hope pretty much always had some kind of music on in their little garden flat. The radio went on when they woke up and went off when Hope went to bed. She even had an old cassette player of her dad's to put at the bottom of Minnie's cot to lull her to sleep. All the cassettes she used were her dad's old Bob Marley and UB40 and the Specials and Jimmy Cliff ones. Minnie would call out for Hope to come in and turn the tape over to the B side if she hadn't fallen asleep by the end of the A side. Recently, she was even attempting to do it herself although, with her chubby little one-year-old fingers, she wasn't quite dextrous enough just yet. If a whole side of any cassette had played and Minnie didn't cry out for more, Hope knew for sure she'd nodded off.

During the day, Minnie would haul herself up against any chair or table to stand up and wobble about precariously like a Weeble at the first bar of any music. She was already a definite person in her own right; she was longing to be independent, even if her little legs weren't willing as yet; she was a determined little mite. She behaved as if it were a nuisance that she should have to learn anything — she wanted to already know it. She wanted to be in the growing-up fast lane. Some-times she was impatient and tetchy with it, but Hope was one of life's supreme soothers. She knew the value of it; she'd done it for herself and her sister forever, so it was second nature to be a calmer, and she knew exactly how to placate a grumpy Minnie. No problem. A privilege, in fact.

Minnie's lovely open face had become even lovelier. She had flawless skin and huge dark eyes and a comical row of four front teeth emerging from her lower gum. There were none on the top thus far, which made her ready smiles hilar-ious: she looked like an old hillbilly hick from the sticks.

She didn't fully know why, but people would laugh when she smiled, so she smiled a lot. And they would laugh more. And on it went. Big laughs from silly little things.

There were a dozen or so folk crammed into Hope and Minnie's small flat to celebrate this important day. Her sister Glory was there with her partner Ky and their brand-new baby girl they'd decided to call Princess, all wrapped up and held tightly like the very precious princessy thing she was. Hope remembered when she'd likewise held Minnie so tightly and carefully when she was as new. The need to protect and cherish was very strong in both sisters. They were instinctively motherly.

A couple of uncles and their partners and kids were there too. They had all been fantastic sup-ports for Hope when she arrived back in Bristol with Minnie a year before. They felt sorry for

Hope that her supposed 'boyfriend' had high-tailed it back to Africa, leaving her to raise their daughter alone. He didn't seem to care at all: he ran off, sent no money and made no contact, and they would berate him in support of Hope, calling him a 'dyam hidiot' and a 'wase o' space'. Hope had to let this be. They didn't know the truth and they couldn't, but each of their barbs at him was a harpoon in her. Darling, kind, upright Isaac — unknown and maligned.

Everyone was a bit worse for wear after their New Year celebrations the night before, but they wanted to be there for little Minnie, whom they'd all taken entirely to their hearts. They'd clucked around her all year commenting on how like her mother she looked. Only the first time this was mentioned had it occurred to Hope that it was a strange thing to say. She'd had a brief moment then, where she looked closely at Minnie's features, at her faultless skin, at her mop of cinnamon curls, at her huge expressive eyes, at her chunky-lunky toes and fingers, and she remembered the big snoring black man with his chin on his chest in that maternity suite and the dark blonde hair strewn across the face of the slumbering mother.

Mother?

No, no, no. Don't think about that. HOPE is Minnie's mother. She'd vanquished all those threatening thoughts, and consigned them to a deep, hard-to-reach place behind the back of her memory, marked 'unremembered'. From then on, she easily accepted all comments made about Minnie's physicality and personality as a kind of vicarious flattery, and it wasn't hard to acknowledge that yes, Minnie really was so very like her.

And her dad, of course.

But mainly HER.

And with each compliment or remark she accepted about their similarity, the sediment of denial incrementally forming firmly on top of the truth gained another weighty layer.

'One, two, three . . . blow!' said Hope, clapping and smiling along next to Minnie, who was utterly unaware of what was expected with the candle, so Hope blew it out for her and she squeaked with delight.

One person who was clearly struggling to enjoy the party was Doris, Hope's mother. Glory had her arm around her and Hope noticed that she was making brave attempts to smile, but she seemed pitifully sad. No wonder — it had been a hell of a year. She'd gained two grandchildren, lost a husband and started a serious attempt to conquer her relationship with vodka. She was feeling hugely wobbly.

'Let's have some music! Your choice, Uncle Devon! Something to kick us off into a fantastic New Year, eh?' said Hope optimistically as she delegated the job of jollying up the party to her uncles.

Then: 'Cut up the cake, G, I'll sit with Mum for a minute,' she said as she took Doris's arm, 'and, Ky, can you keep an eye on Minnie?'

'Sure,' replied Ky as he lifted Minnie out of her high chair and into the clamouring arms of her several young cousins who loved to pretend that Minnie was their baby.

Hope led her mum to the sofa and sat next to

her. 'You OK, Mum?'

'Yes. No problem,' replied Doris.

'Lies. Mum, it's OK not to feel OK, OK?' she comforted her mother, putting her arm around her, noting just how scrawny she'd become under the clever camouflage of one of her big woolly jumpers. Winter allowed Doris to wear layers of loose warm clothes to hide her bony body. Until someone touched her like this.

They both knew Hope was noticing. Hope wanted to reassure Doris. 'You're not alone, Mum, and you never will be. Not as long as I have breath in my body — and Glory's the same — and we're bringing more kids into the family by the minute, so, honestly, you've got loads of us ...'

'I know, darlin', I truly know. I jus' not sure how much strength I have in m'blood for all dis.'

'For a party?'

'For life.'

That floored Hope. Her mum had been battered by a tough year, but Hope had never heard her sound so defeated. She needed to say the right thing.

'Mum, listen to me ...' Hope started, but noticed that Doris's head was drooping. 'Mum, please look at me. Please,' she tried to encourage her.

Doris raised her face towards Hope. All the skin on her skull seemed to be tired of holding on tight, and had given up, just as Doris had in this moment. She had lost her way and her sorry eyes told Hope that. Even in her worst drunkenness, Doris had always had a flare in her eyes. She had a purpose: to get to a bottle; and once she had, she was content for a while until her purpose rose up to consume her again. It was a dreadful cycle, but it was a structure of sorts. All habits are. The familiar, however destructive, is better than the new. Even in her haziness, Doris had always loved her girls. She hadn't always remembered about them, but they were in her heart. And, unbelievably, Doris had kept her cleaning job; somehow she muddled through and no one ever reported her because everyone loved her, and because her hours were night-time hours, and Doris was skilled at scuttling about, getting her job done without being spied on, often without being really noticed at all, it was easy to camouflage her sozzled state.

All of that had changed in the summer when Zak died and Doris suddenly had a dark hole at the centre of her already unsteady world. Part of the reason Doris had numbed herself with lots of alcohol for so long was that she knew Zak would never reach old bones. How could he when he polluted his body so regularly with such a potent poison? Doris needed the booze to help her avoid thinking such unthinkable thoughts. When they were both in their Elysium, nothing else mattered, and nothing bad was ever going to happen, so that's what they both chose. Their habits were benign. No one else had to witness them once Hope had moved out and subsequently away. Glory had been propelled into the arms of Ky by a need to escape the stupor of her parents' home. She'd left them to it, and they muddled on in their interdependent fug, oblivious.

When Hope had arrived back in Bristol with her new baby, she knew she couldn't live with them, it would be catastrophic, so she moved into her little garden flat and laid down some rules. 'OK, guys, listen up. I want you to have time with Minnie, she's your first grandchild, I know that. BUT. It has to be here, at mine, and the deal is you both HAVE to be sober. Seriously. Or you ain't coming in. Got it?'

So, Doris and Zak had visited every morning around 10a.m. for about an hour, tops. That's when they could keep their promise and, to their credit, they never broke it. Hope was sorry that she couldn't rely on her mum and dad for babysitting or for any support outside this one daily hour, but, for Minnie's sake, she recognized what a giant effort it was for them both to stick to the agreement, and they all chugged on, doing their best within it.

Zak had seemed relatively steady as summer approached. If you'd seen him, you would have thought he was a lethargic sixty-seven-year-old. He wasn't. He was forty-seven, with a stealthy blood clot pumping its way around his body, waiting for him to be inert enough for it to invade his lungs. The mixture of that lethal clot and his whole respiratory drive shutting down while he gouched out meant, on that fateful night, that his body simply forgot to breathe.

Forgot to fight the clot.

Forgot to fight.

Forgot he was loved. Forgot his wife. Forgot his kids.

Forgot to live.

He simply stopped dead, and when Doris woke from her inebriated slumber, he was cold and slumped next to her on their sofa, with his 'horse' box of gear and accoutrements on the table in front of him. She took him in her arms and rocked him, gently encouraging him to wake up, for two hours before she called anyone. She called Hope first, of course.

'Umm, Daddy's asleep, Hope. I cyan wake 'im. He's really really sleepin'. I think you should come,' she said and put the phone down.

Hope knew. She'd been awaiting this phone call since she could remember. In some awful, truthful way, it was a relief.

The funeral was small and sad and full of loud music, just as he would've wanted. Some of his old band members were there. Two were already dead, and the ones who turned up could've been. All but one of them appeared to be husks of people, as ravaged by their various substance-use as Zak had been. Somehow, when musicians are at the funerals of their chums' untimely deaths, it's a sorrier sight, as if they uniquely should remain forever young or forever rebellious or forever glamorous, as if they owe us that. We want them stuck in amber and ageless. We don't want to see them as haggard spectres gathered in gloomy groups, smoking vapes and wearing black coats from the back of the wardrobe which hang loosely on their diminished bodies, awkwardly not knowing what to say. People who don't talk much because they prefer to play, having to find some words.

Clumsy or not, they all found kind words for Doris, whom they loved very much. They also found hip flasks of courage-giving brandy that

179

they shared with her, which wasn't Hope's favourite sight of the day. Sandwiching their mother between them, Hope and Glory walked Doris up the aisle at the grim crematorium and sat in the front row, Zak's four girls together, including little Minnie who sat on Hope's lap and was sheer sunlight on a very dark day.

As far as Minnie was concerned, this was a fantastic play date. There was music, so that meant fun. However much the celebrant tried to keep the ceremony focused and serious, Minnie's delighted squeals and clapping hands couldn't fail to lift everyone's spirits. When a happy child laughs, everyone laughs. A ripple effect. Minnie had been an oasis of joy for Zak, so it was fitting that she was at the centre of that day, uniting them all, when everyone present wanted to remember the best of him. There was plenty of wonderful about Zak to celebrate . . .

. . . and that's what Hope wanted to remind her mum of now, on this day, while Minnie was enjoying her birthday.

'Mum . . .' Hope took her mother's face in her hands, the face she'd looked into and loved her whole life, the face that was now the tiredest it had ever been. 'I know you miss him, we all do, but you do times a million. He was your true love — you always said that — and he still is. No one can ever take that from you. That's yours forever, isn't it? The love doesn't die, does it, Mum? You still love Nanna Bev and she's gone, but . . . you said she lives in you. And that's what I think about Dad; he lives in me and Glory and Minnie and you — and in Princess too now. The best of him. We won't forget him, ever ever ever.'

'Well, no, that's right,' Doris agreed slowly. 'Mind you, there's some bits we don't mind forgetting, eh?' She even managed half a smile.

'Yes, Mum. True dat, but listen to me now . . . Dad was Dad. He wasn't that greedy drug. It stole him from us sometimes, but he was still there, wasn't he? I refuse to let that bloody gear nick all my good memories of my dad, and you mustn't either, otherwise it'll be like that's all he was. Dad was a poet, and a clown, and a mechanic, and a drummer. His whole life was about different beats, and smack was just one of them. Let's please remember ALL the drumbeats, yeah? Otherwise it's not proper music, is it?'

'No, no, you speak sense,' Doris admitted, taking comfort from everything her clever daughter was saying, allowing herself the salve of the soothing words.

'And y'know the best thing of all, Mum? He's free from it now, and so are you. Free from the grip of it. Like Mark at the rehab place told you: you don't have to go looking for places to hide from it now. You don't need to drink to ignore it, because it ain't there no more . . . '

'I know, I know, but it hard, y'know. I still want to. I want to so bad, just to not feel it . . . ' Doris was feeling the weakness.

'But, Mum, we need you. Me 'n' Glory 'n' Minnie 'n' Princess. We need you more than ever now, to be our mum, coz we've lost our dad . . . our lovely dad . . . ' And with this, Hope started to well up.

Now it was time for Doris to mum-up. She took Hope in her arms and cradled her, saying, 'It'll be OK. I'm doin' well. I'm doin' m'best. I'm here, Hope, I'm your mum. Always your mum . . . and their nanna . . . No more of that. C'mon now, hush, dry your eyes. Let's stop this nonsense. There's a party!'

Glory came to them with slices of the caterpillar cake, and saw her mum and sister crying together, and she knew that Hope had, once again, been the soother, just as she had been for her all those years before. Hope was the glue that would keep this family tight. Thank God for Hope.

'Cake!' said Glory.

'Yes, come on, Mum, let's dance, let's bring some of Dad's beats to this yard . . . ' said Hope as she held the clapping, happy Minnie aloft. 'The beat goes on!'

Anna

The next day, after spending the night in a hotel, Anna went to see her doctor in the afternoon. She wanted to go before she saw Julius again. She didn't want him to dissuade her.

The receptionist told her there were no appointments but that they could possibly fit her in the next morning. Anna decided to turn up there and resolutely sit in the waiting room until he found a slot to see her. They knew Anna well at the swanky practice in Notting Hill; she'd been a pretty regular attendee during this last difficult year and they all liked her very much. She hadn't behaved like this before, so Nicola, the head receptionist, knew this was serious.

'Happy New Year,' and, 'Would you like a drink, Mrs Lindon-Clarke?'

'No, thank you. I'm fine.' Anna wasn't fine.

'We've got a lovely new coffee machine. Makes macchiatos 'n' everything. 'S amazing?'

'No, thanks. Really fine.' She wasn't. A short pause, then . . .

'Cortados? Piccolos?' Nicola was tenacious.

'Er, no, ta.'

'Hilly whites?'

'Lillywhites . . . ?'

'No, sorry, HILLY WHITES!' Nicola laughed. 'It's a flat white, but with peaked froth?'

'Try to forgive me, but I seriously don't recognize any of the words you're using . . . ' Anna did her polite best to shut Nicola down before she was forced to gouge her eyes out with a car key. Which she was utterly prepared to do, to make the noise stop. She remembered in the nick of time that Nicola was unaware that she, Anna, had just found out, only a few hours ago, that her husband was indeed the phoney she had long suspected, and a lying cunt, so she took a deep breath instead of killing her, and decided to be merciful. 'Sorry. Just . . . umm . . . don't need anything, thanks. Other than to see Martin. Soon as. Ta.'

'Yes. I know. We're on it, Mrs Lindon-Clarke.'

'Thank you.' Anna resumed her calm and pretended to read awful magazines again, all the while making sure her presence was felt. Ten minutes later, after some muffled interaction on the internal phone, an appointment miraculously opened up and Nicola directed her into Martin's room.

Anna apologized profusely for barging in. He was reassuring, as always, and she might have wept when he sat opposite her and pulled his chair closer to genuinely ask her what he could do to help. It took all of her limited resilience not to collapse into his arms sobbing, but that would simply not have done.

'Oh God, Martin . . . I . . . just . . . He . . . God . . . It's just —'

'Slow down, Anna. And inhale. And exhale. Great. Breathing helps. Don't want you to die. Bad for my ol' reputation.' He smiled at her, and she instantly appreciated everything she liked about him.

184

Understanding face
Big clean hands
Tattersall check shirt
Picture of his two small daughters on his desk
Capable calm green corduroy trousers
Softly spoken

Anna could never work out if she felt such a connection with him because he was a fantastic GP, or perhaps he felt sorry for her, or . . . maybe he was just a tiny bit in love with her . . . ?

As she drew breath to explain, she had a sudden panoramic flashback of everything this kind man had heard and understood and helped her with in the last awful year.

He had tended to her après-birth wounds, both internal and external. He'd carefully monitored the sleeping problems which plagued her for months afterwards. He'd guided her away from the serious sleeping pills she needed initially, towards more organic, herbal remedies, and eventually to camomile tea, which was all she used right now. He'd praised her and warned her in just the right measures. She trusted him. He helped and listened when she cruelly suffered various unexpected bouts of postnatal depression which knocked her for six. How and why would she have to suffer a serious depression to do with having a baby when she had no baby? As if her devastating sadness at the loss of Florence wasn't enough to bear, for God's sake. That in itself was a pain so sharp and deep, she wondered on occasion if she might bleed to death from it. Bleed out sorrow blood 'til she was no more, 'til the grief consumed her.

She had told Martin about this horror, and he was marvellous. He reminded her that she HAD to remain strong and fit and alive for when Florence returned, and that it could be any minute. He had that sort of conviction. He was so sure, and she caught his hope.

She heeded him, and it saved her.

He prescribed her the tiniest doses of anti-depressants to help her cope.

He insisted on seeing her regularly every week to make sure she was managing.

He encouraged her to talk, to say everything she was feeling, and he never once made her feel as if she had to hurry out of his room.

He gently dissuaded her from having the cosmetic surgery procedures she was considering when she misguidedly thought that if she could maintain her young face, her husband might not be as unfaithful as she suspected he was.

Anna was at her lowest when her mindset was like this, and Martin knew it would pass, so he guided her well away from making terrible choices at vulnerable moments.

He also took her bloods and did the various HIV/STD tests she repeatedly requested as a result of her intuition about Julius.

(He conducted Julius's regular tests too, but of course he didn't speak to her about those.)

Most importantly, in his effort to see her through the shock of what had happened with Florence, he tried to instil in her the importance of imagining her future, and wanting it. He remained optimistic about Florence returning, but he also

186

sensitively introduced the idea of another child when the time was right. He suggested that she prepare her body, while her mind and heart were still bruised, and he knew that would in turn help to heal her mind and heart.

He gave her folic acid and calcium to take.

He told her to quit smoking if she could, and he suggested walking everywhere for exercise and to clear her head and to give her days some structure.

Anna had followed his advice, however wretched she had felt, and consequently felt physically better than she had for years. One of the awful by-products of looking better was that her husband started paying her attention again. She noticed that Julius was, of course, sticking to his exercise regimen. He clearly liked the way his body was shaping up. He was more toned and much leaner than he'd been for a long time . . . and of course, he was packing in tons more exercise than the formal programme proposed, with all his extra-curricular exertions with the Dane, so he felt tip-top.

Anna had noticed that, along with his galling self-love, Julius's confidence had increased a hundred fold. He was already arrogant enough, but this new confidence pushed him into new realms of fuckwittery. He obviously felt mighty. He wanted to have plenty of sex. Including with his lucky wife, who was, like him, also looking 'mighty fine'.

Back in this bright room at the surgery, Anna felt safe with Martin. He knew and understood much and he wouldn't judge her. Or would he on this occasion? It was going to be so hard to say what she had to.

'Martin, you know better than almost anyone, this whole year has been awful . . . '

'I know. Yes,' his deep voice reassured her.

'And I think that it's changed me. I'm just not in the same place any more in here.' Anna pointed at her head, and continued, 'I've tried really hard to . . . get back on track. I think I'm pretty much there physically . . . '

'Yes, you've achieved so much, Anna.'

'Yes, thanks, but . . . so much of all the rest of it, of my life, just means nothing now. Don't worry, Martin, I'm not going to top myself or anything like that . . . but something happened yesterday . . . with Jules . . . I found him with . . . well, I'm sure you can guess . . . '

'Oh God. Sorry, Anna, that's awful.'

'And it was Florence's first birthday, and all I can think is that I'm glad she didn't have to have him as a dad. It's so awful. He doesn't deserve her. He doesn't deserve any kid . . . '

'Steady, Anna. You're probably still in a bit of shock.'

'I'm not shocked. Listen, I've known for ages what he's like, I just ignore it, deny it, because when I think about it, I take it so personally. I feel shit, because I'm not enough, and I feel shit because I'm getting older, and I feel shit because I fell asleep and I didn't keep her safe . . . ' Anna fell silent as she let the heavy truth of all that sit in her.

Martin kept the silence with her.

She eventually took several big breaths and spoke again:

188

'I just know I have to face stuff now, even if I AM a little bit crazy at the moment. It's almost like I needed to get to this bit to know what to do next. I don't suddenly know everything that's right to do, it's not like a movie moment or anything . . . I don't know how we, me and him, could possibly go forward from this. We can't, really. But I do know that it's completely wrong to bring anyone else into this equation. I'm not going to give anyone else Jules as a father, and until the day, the moment, the second that I find her, I can't think about anyone or anything else. I can't have this baby, Martin, I just can't.'

'Anna . . .'

'Please don't persuade me otherwise. You so easily could, I want it very much, but I know, utterly, that it's wrong. I need to find her, not replace her.'

'I understand that, Anna. You must be aware of the fact that time is not on your side here. This pregnancy, like the last one, took some doing,' said Martin.

'Yes. But I was a different person then. I'm not going to pretend any more. Not after yesterday. I can't raise a child with Jules. He is a child.'

'Anna . . .' he said softly, and put his hand on hers.

'Please, Martin, please help me. I've decided. I only found out a couple of days ago. It's hardly started to grow. Please, please. I need to do it before it breaks my heart. Please.'

'OK, Anna, OK. Don't worry. We can organize everything. Could you get to a clinic tonight, for the procedure tomorrow if I can arrange it?'

'Yes,' she whispered, and with that, her already broken heart shattered into a billion painful pieces.

★ ★ ★

A few weeks later, the Honourable Claire Hartley, senior partner at Hartley Tod family law firm, sat as still as a sitting statue, staring unwaveringly at her opponent. She was neatly put together.

Armani suit — blue
Armani blouse — crisp white
Shoes — Manolo Blahnik, black
Bag — Aspinal's, black
Jewellery — Hancocks of Burlington Arcade, chunky and old

She barely bothered to hide her disdain as the men faffed about with piles of paper on the shiny conference table.

'Right, I think that's about it. We have everything we need for our side, how about you, Claire?' said Piers the Wife Slayer.

Anna had nicknamed him that after the first official meeting she and Claire had with him and Julius. Claire had warned her about Piers's savage reputation in the divorce courts, but Anna couldn't believe he would be so blood-thirsty with her, considering he'd been the best man at their wedding all those years ago. He'd been in their lives for so long; he'd stayed in their home whenever his own relationships broke down, which was often. Anna had come to know him as a friend, albeit Julius's

190

friend, but still, she'd done the wifely thing many times, and offered her husband's best mate every kind of support she could muster when he was in most need. Anna had even put him into pyjamas and into bed in their spare room when he was sobbingly, vomitingly, hopelessly drunk. She'd wiped his privileged, posh-Chelsea, good-looking but also very unattractive face with a flannel, and he'd whispered 'Thank you, Nanny' as he dropped off. Surely, then, he wouldn't be going for her throat at this critical moment, as the two lawyers were preparing the case to go to court?

Claire had warned Anna not to underestimate the power of male loyalty, and this particular bromance was long, strong and chock-full of testosterone. No way was Piers going to let his certain knowledge of (*a*) Julius's repeated and unregretted adulteries, or (*b*) Anna's continued attempts to bring their relationship back in line, or (*c*) Anna's ongoing pain about her lost child and her consequent depression, exasperation and increasing reliance on sleeping pills, get in his way. Except the sleeping pills part. He'd already let Claire know in no uncertain terms that if Anna didn't toe the line by allowing this divorce to be discreet and much in Julius's favour, protecting his image at all times, then he might be 'forced' to reveal information like that about Anna. Claire had advised her client to fight them like rabid dogs to gain the ground she so justly felt Anna ought to occupy, but after lots of reflection and debate, Anna instructed Claire to capitulate, so that she could have a quiet life. Her desire was to sink into the background of his landscape, and to eventually exit it altogether. They would always be linked by the very fact of Florence's abduction, and the consequent very public and strategic effort to improve security in all maternity wards in her name. Or rather, more accurately, in Julius's name. In ambitious Julius's important name.

For years, Anna had watched as Julius's attempts to run for the BIG job in government were thwarted at every turn, often by his own hubris. His mistaken belief that the more the public got to know him, the more they would like him, had been his ultimate downfall. Much as his party desperately wanted a man of colour to aim for and achieve greatness, it doesn't matter what colour you are (even if that very fact might be to your advantage in times of growing diversity, especially in a party where there is precious little, where there's a shocking paucity of different skin), it just doesn't count for anything if you are essentially a king tosspot. The British might be known for valuing the odd buffoon, but Julius's narcissism and snobbery had ultimately rendered him intolerable, unelectable and rejected. He still had a backbench presence, but his voice was seldom heard in any potent or memorable way.

Anna had spent her entire married life with him trying to gently nudge him away from all the false idols he worshipped. She'd known he had political ambitions from the start, and she had respected that, especially since he claimed he genuinely wanted to effect change for the good. But then . . . he became swept up in his need for success. He put everything else second, apart from his libido, of course, which he had somehow conveniently worked into his narrative of himself as an alpha male. Anna was tired of it. His mind wasn't attractive, his body wasn't attractive and his morals were positively abhorrent.

So desperate was she to divorce him that she told Claire repeatedly to agree to pretty much all of his demands so that she might the sooner be free. She was content to sign any non-disclosure agreements. The way she saw it, those documents meant she agreed not to reveal what a fake he was. By dint of logic, that also meant she didn't feel obliged, conversely, to declare how 'real' or 'honourable' he was either. EVER. In fact, her plan was to keep her lips sealed about him. So, Anna caved in and let him have all the trappings, the art, the house, the pension, even the vintage soft-top Mercedes he bought for her but which he really bought for him. None of that mattered. She would rent her own flat.

'Yes,' replied Claire now on behalf of Anna, 'I think you have everything you need, Piers. Literally EVERYTHING and more. I should just like to add something my client has not instructed me to say, but I'd like to, whilst we are all in the comparative safety of this room. You are mighty lucky, Mr Lindon-Clarke, that my client appears not to have a malicious bone in her body, because your clear culpability in the gradual corrosion of this marriage is indisputable. For my money, you are an ocean-going wanker, and everyone knows it. Now, I think that's our business concluded. Let's hope the judge looks favourably on this absurd sham of an agreement, and the whole tawdry business can come to a swift conclusion with a decree absolute issued within the next six weeks? Then, perhaps, my client will be able to search for a loving, functional and authentic human, one with an actual beating heart, to spend her valuable time with. Are we done, gentlemen?' With that, Claire started to pack away her files, ready to leave.

Piers whispered in Julius's ear, 'Well, got off lightly there!' as he, too, started to pack away so that they might all vacate the neutral meeting room and be done with it.

Anna looked across the big polished table at Julius, who had pulled out his phone in a gesture of affected boredom as Claire had started to speak. Truculent as ever. He was avoiding her gaze, as he typically did when a truth was stinging him. As always, Anna felt a fleeting sympathy for him. Not for any of his awful decisions or behaviour, but for the pathetic wretch he'd become.

The Julius she'd fallen for was at least a substantial person; this husk of a man in front of her was not. She was racking her brains to remember the things she once loved about him. What were they?

Anna had loved that he confided in her back then, that he told her about the bullying he'd experienced at school, about the lack of a father in his life, and the scars that both of those unfairnesses left on him, as well as his actual scars from his childhood heart surgery. Anna had always felt that he was somehow emotionally stunted, stuck at a juvenile stage of his life, since he didn't seem to be very mature or warm-hearted. All the time she loved him, she had defended his actions to herself in this forgiving way. When the love dripped and

194

finally dwindled away, the creeping surety that he was, in fact, a psychopath dawned on her. At the least, he was a sociopath, but he ticked more of the psychopath boxes. Sort of psychopath light.

Here today, though, she didn't need to go to her default setting of forgiveness. The only real abiding affection she had for him was to do with the fact that they'd made Florence together, and she was beautiful, but she wasn't here any more and neither was their love.

The lawyers both left the room, and as Anna walked around the table, heading for the door, he took her hand as she passed by. He pulled her gently down towards his face. For a horrific moment, she thought he was going to attempt to kiss her, but he didn't.

He said, 'I saw you looking at me. I still do it for you, don't I?'

Yep, a psychopath, for sure. He couldn't have been more insensitive. Or wrong.

'Bye, Julius. I hope you find someone to love you as much as you love you. I couldn't.'

Anna swept out of the door, leaving all her feelings of inadequacy and doubt in his lap.

Minnie Grows Up

When Minnie was ONE, she fixated on one word and applied it to everything. The word was 'Wawa'. Hope was wawa. Nanna Doris was wawa. Food was wawa. All animals were wawa. Her body parts were wawa. She sounded like an ambulance on an emergency call. She once stuffed a small bead from a broken necklace of Hope's in her mouth, and swallowed it before Hope could fish it out. Hope rushed her to A & E, where she was told there was nothing to do but wait for it to pop out the other end. When it did, and Hope showed it in her nappy to an amazed Minnie, she pointed at her bumhole and said, 'Wawa.' From then on, all bums were wawas in that small family.

When Minnie was TWO, she could walk and even run a little, and she loved fetching things for Hope. One day, Hope was in the front room with a cup of tea watching TV, and, feeling extra lazy, she thought she'd utilize Minnie's new skills.

'Minnie Moo! Can you get the sugar for Mummy's tea please from the kitchen? Mummy has two sugars in tea, one . . . two, there's a good girl.'

Minnie listened carefully and waddled off to the kitchen; she reappeared and placed one grain of sugar in Hope's tea; then she repeated it, back to the kitchen for another grain, so that Mummy had the right number of sugars.

When Minnie was THREE, she loved climbing, and if Hope lost her anywhere in the flat, it was a surety that she'd be on top of a wardrobe, or dangerously high up a tree in the garden. She loved being taller than she actually was, so would strut about in Hope's heeled shoes, which is why she fell when she was walking around in Hope's red weekend wedges. To soothe her injured pride, Hope took Minnie to the charity shop and they bought two more pairs of high-heeled shoes, this time in as small a size as they could find, so that Minnie could strut around in them whenever she liked. One pair were ballroom-dancing-type shoes in silver, very fancy, and the other pair were old-lady beige comfies with a tiny heel. Minnie loved them so much that she slept in them on alternate nights.

When Minnie was FOUR, Nanna Doris gave her a yellow tricycle for her birthday and she hammered around the park on it, forcing Hope to run to keep up with her. She made up a song she sang over and over: 'My yellow bike, it's a trike, it's got spikes, and I like . . . it.'

She started primary school in September, and spent more time with Nanna Doris while Hope took a couple of part-time cleaning jobs. By then, Hope could finally begin to trust her mum, rely on her again. Hope was nervous when she first suggested some regular childcare to Doris, but she had to take the ultimate trust plunge at some point, and Doris had been sober for three years. Doris and Minnie had a very special bond. Minnie was allowed more Haribos than Hope would approve of and to stay up later than at home — their secret.

Minnie liked school a lot, and already enjoyed

learning letters and how to spell her name. She mixed up some words, of course. Hope laughed so loud when Minnie came home at Christmas, after they'd done the nativity, and told her emphatically that she'd spent the morning telling the 'big story of cheeses . . . '

When Minnie was FIVE, she proudly told everyone her full name and address. Because she could. She chatted to anyone she met. Once, when Hope took her into a public toilet and they were dutifully washing their hands afterwards, a middle-aged woman came out of the next cubicle, and Minnie said, 'Well done, good girl,' to her as she approached the sink.

When Minnie was SIX, she could dress herself and was starting to form her own style. She would add little flourishes, a bow here, a hairclip there, and she'd borrow a scarf from Hope and wear it as a belt. She noticed when other people wore interesting clothes; she was observant about things of beauty. On the way into school one day, she suddenly stood stock still, yanking Hope's hand back and looking up; and she said, 'Stop, Mummy, I have to get my eyes full of sky coz I won't see it again 'til playtime . . . '

When Minnie was SEVEN, she was very much in love with her group of friends, especially with a little chap in her class called Majeet who wore a navy-blue turban. He was clever and liked words, just like her. The junior school had a prize-giving each year, to encourage the children to be confident enough to walk across the stage. Of course, they structured it so that each child received a prize for something, however arbitrary. One time, they gave a book voucher to Danny Eccles for 'Using His Handkerchief Regularly'. He was delighted. This year, the legitimate prize for 'Best Reader' went to Minnie. Hope and Doris were there, bursting with pride, as she walked across the stage to collect it from the headmistress. Halfway over, however, Minnie stopped and turned to the audience, and said, in a very nervous, wobbly voice, 'I can't have this nice prize without saying thank you to Majeet. He reads with me, and it's for him too. Thank you, Majeet. There he is, that's him.' She pointed at him and everyone clapped, and then she continued on to the headmistress. Minnie's little heart was giant.

When she was EIGHT, Minnie started to be grumpy occasionally and she would lose her temper over unlikely things and stomp off like a teen. Hope tried to clamp down on this bratty behaviour by encouraging her to manage her temper and stay calm. Hope completely recognized herself in eight-year-old Minnie when she took her to one of Doris's Pentecostal church services one Sunday. The service was loud and boisterous with lots of wonderful singing, and when the preacher was going at it full pelt with the fire and brimstone, several of the older ladies in the front pews started in with the garbled 'speaking in tongues' and Minnie suddenly stood on the seat of her pew several rows back and said in a strong, authoritative voice, 'Carpet-level calm, please, people!' and sat back down again, mission accomplished. Hope wanted to die a thousand deaths.

When Minnie was NINE, she had a few bouts with ill health; she was extra tired sometimes and short of breath.

Hope waited to see if it would pass, assuming she had some kind of infection. Hope lived in fear that Minnie might ever be ill, because the doctor's would be the riskiest place, with the questions they might ask about her genetic background, so Hope was pleased when it seemed to pass. Perhaps it was because she felt under the weather that Minnie started to fixate on how bodies work and she became anxious about Hope or herself possibly getting sick . . . or worse. Minnie asked lots of questions about dead Grandad Zak that were hard for Hope to answer, but she did, as honestly as she could. Hope tried to alleviate Minnie's worries by reassuring her that nothing bad was going to happen, and even if it did, someone would come to help . . .

'What if you got poorly?' Minnie asked.

'If I was just lying on the floor?' Hope replied.

'Yes, if I couldn't wake you up, like Nanna Doris couldn't wake him up?'

'Well, OK, you would call 999 on the phone, tell them our address, which you are very good at knowing, and then you would wait . . . '

'Would you still be asleep on the floor?'

'Er, maybe, yes.'

'So . . . I could eat all the biscuits until the people came . . . ?'

Minnie was going to be OK.

When Minnie was TEN, she started to ask more about her father. She knew he was called Isaac and that he lived in Africa. Hope was longing to tell her all the beautiful things about him: his courage, his kindness, his eye with a flash of green lightning in it; but she only told her tiny fragments, for fear she would want to find him and that wasn't the promise she'd made to Isaac. Minnie often asked questions about her father when she was in the front of the car with Hope. That way, she could say difficult stuff without having to look at her; it made things easier. Hope answered as best she could whilst she navigated annoying traffic all the way to Nanna Doris's house.

When they walked in, Nanna said, 'Did you have a good journey?'

And Minnie replied, 'Yeah. Mum saw a lot of people on the way called twat.'

When Minnie was ELEVEN, she and her cousin Princess started a vigorous campaign to be allowed to have their ears pierced. Neither Hope nor Glory wanted this to happen so young, but the determined girls conspired to persuade their mothers by drawing pictures of themselves with multiple piercings all over their faces, noses, lips, eyelids, claiming that this was what they really wanted and that they would both definitely go ahead and get this done, exactly as in the pictures, as soon as they were legally allowed to at sixteen, UNLESS they were permitted to have the smaller, simpler dainty ones now with parental permission. It was business. It was a formidable transaction. It was blackmail. And it worked. Both of the cousins had their ears pierced and tiny studs placed there whilst the holes formed. They shook hands on the way out of the shop. Canny. Teamwork.

When Minnie was TWELVE, Hope bought her a kitten. Minnie named it CAT. She was a rescue cat from the Cats Protection League, and was very thin when she arrived.

Minnie was devoted to Cat, who slept on her bed and adored her. One morning, Minnie woke up to find that Cat had brought a tiny baby mouse in from the garden. Far from trying to kill or eat it though, Cat was nursing it, protecting it. Minnie researched how to feed a pinkie mouse, and so she religiously fed it watered-down kitten formula from a pipette until it grew. She named it MOUSE and, ironically, Cat and Mouse became inseparable. Hope found the whole situation difficult. A mouse, an actual rodent, being welcome inside the flat . . . ? She was pretty much appalled, but Minnie was insistent that these two strange bedfellows were her very best friends, and she pleaded with Hope to let them be. Again, Hope acquiesced. Of course she did.

When Minnie was THIRTEEN, she owned one cat and between one to thirty mice at any time. She was beginning to flex her independence muscles and would have wild mood swings. She spent too much time in her bedroom alone (except for creatures) and Hope would find endless notebooks full of dark stories about lost love, death and vampires. Sexy vampires, of course. She became morose and monosyllabic. Her skin had also broken out in spots and, because she'd had flawless skin since she was a baby, this came as a huge blow. In an effort to help, Hope tried to introduce more fruit and vegetables into Minnie's diet, much to her dismay. Minnie only liked Coco Pops for breakfast; nothing else would do. One morning, before school, Hope prepared a fruit salad for her instead. She arranged it in the shape of a rainbow on the plate, using different fruit to form the coloured arches, raspberries, then mango cubes, then kiwi, then blueberries, then melon, then strawberries as the top arch. She was pretty pleased with herself. Minnie walked into the kitchen rubbing her eyes and yawning. She stopped still when she saw the fruity platter.

'Um. Excuse me. What the actual . . . ?' she said.

'I thought we could share it. Y'know, maybe start a health kick together?' her mum replied hopefully. After all, this expensive fruit had put a big dent in Hope's shopping budget.

Minnie blinked a lot, as if in total shock, then grabbed her school bag and coat and flounced out, shouting back over her shoulder, 'Thanks for ruining my whole bloody life!'

When she returned that same evening, she was contrite to a degree, and told Hope, 'Look, sorry, right? But the thing is, I love you and I would never kill you or anything, but please never cause me trauma like that again.'

It was a year before Minnie ate fruit. Not because she didn't like it, but because her pride prevented her.

When Minnie was FOURTEEN, she wrote rap songs about sexism and being a girl, which she performed to her mirror. Very, very occasionally, she would run a couple of rhymes past her mum, or practise them with Princess; other wise, it was a private activity. She also waged a war of loathing against her own body. She disliked so many things about herself: her forehead, her thighs, her feet, her growing breasts, her fingers and on and on. Hope noticed this slide into low self-esteem and

203

decided to step in.

She knocked on the bathroom door one evening when Minnie was in the bath, and asked her to come and join her when she got out. Minnie trudged into Hope's bedroom in her PJs with a towel around her wet hair. Hope invited her to stand in front of the full-length mirror alongside her. Hope was in her PJs too. Minnie was reluctant until Hope gently persuaded her with, 'Please. For me . . .'

Minnie stood next to her mother and looked in the mirror.

Hope said, 'What do you see?'

'A lump. Look at me. God. Stupid fat lump.'

'Well, OK, that's NOT what I see, but OK, it's your body, you see it as you see it, you are the only one that has a right to it, no one else does. BUT . . . can I just ask you: if someone on the bus called Princess a stupid fat lump, what would you think of them?'

There was silence for a moment . . .

'Bully.'

'Yeah, a bully. You seem to be prepared to bully yourself about your own body. So can I ask you, just for a couple of weeks, to try and stop that? And maybe, Minnie Moo, if you can't exactly love yourself yet, maybe you could at least not hate yourself, eh? Maybe you could try to be a bit tolerant and at the very least be kind to Minnie? Be a bit more gentle? Maybe think about the fact that she might feel a bit raw sometimes and need some understanding? Be a good friend to her, to you, just as you would for Princess. You deserve that at least, surely?'

Hope held her breath. Had she pushed it too far?

Minnie squirmed a bit, but then muttered, 'Yeah. S'pose so.'

'Thanks. Wanna know what I see, out of interest?'

'No.'

'Well. I'm going to tell you. I see a strong-minded, unique, interesting, talented, mighty young woman with a huge heart, who's a bit confused about who she is, and while she's trying to find out, which takes time, she's a bit anxious, and that fearful bit of her makes her unkind to herself. But y'know what? Even THAT is lovely, because it shows me you're not at all conceited. Can't bear conceited people.'

Minnie raised the ghost of a smile. Hope felt confident enough to continue.

'And, by the way, as it happens, what I also see is BEAUTY. Solid beauty. Twenty-four carat. But then, I see a lot of me in you, so I would say that, wouldn't I?'

Minnie laughed. 'Shut up, Mum.'

Hope went on, 'Seriously, li'l darlin', what YOU are is an extraordinary ray, and that is a ray which doesn't obey the ordinary laws of refraction. It's different.' She whispered: 'And better! I learnt it in school, I've never forgotten it, and now I'm looking right at it. My own extraordinary ray. Yes, thank you, Lordy Lord!'

Minnie's eyes were welling up, and Hope saw it. Perhaps her sentiments had landed in Minnie's heart after all.

Hope finished it with, 'So, we're agreed, yeah?

You ain't gonna beat yourself up any more, right? In fact, why don't you just leave that to me . . . ?'

With that, she grabbed Minnie and pulled her down on to the bed and they wrestled and giggled and shouted 'WAWA' until they were drained.

When Minnie was FIFTEEN, she got a Saturday job working on a market stall selling clothes. Her uncle knew the woman who owned the stall, Bibi, and she agreed to give Minnie five pounds per hour, cash in hand. On top of selling the gear, Minnie offered to customize some of the denim jackets. Bibi was hesitant at first. She thought it would ruin the jackets, and that altering them was just silly, unnecessary additions, but when Minnie bought one of the jackets and customized it for herself, wore it on the stall and had tons of praise and interest in it, Bibi saw the value. She gave Minnie one to do at first and Minnie embroidered the pockets and lapels with tattoo designs of hearts and anchors.

It sold for four times the price within an hour of being on a hanger. So Bibi gave Minnie a free rein and some float to buy the appliqué and beads and various other bits 'n' bobs she needed to do her best work. They came to a deal where Minnie would get five pounds for every jacket sold.

Minnie started to make some decent money. She spent it on notebooks, pens, make-up, take aways and, for a while, on cigarettes, which she was trying desperately hard to like, partly because she'd met a canny boy called Callum who worked full-time on the market with his dad on their fruit and veg stall, and he smoked. He tasted of tobacco when he stole kisses from her in the café on their breaks. She didn't like it, so she decided to smoke too, to see if that negated the stale taste. It didn't. She told Callum they'd be better as mates. Minnie knew what she liked.

When Minnie was SIXTEEN, she asked Hope to dye the top two-thirds of her hair bright blondey orange. Hope thought it was a great idea and they did it in the kitchen after looking at lots of 'bleaching afro hair' videos on You-Tube. Hope wrote a jokey disclaimer for Minnie to sign, which stated, 'My mum has no idea what she's doing. I have agreed to let her bleach my hair. If it all falls out, it's my fault.' It didn't fall out, it stank of bleach for a while, but it looked amazing. The first time Cat sauntered into the bedroom unaware, and saw the crazy hair, she arched her back, hissed at Minnie, and pelted back out.

Hope and Minnie were a team, and like all teams who love each other, when they fell out, it was brutal, personal and bruising. On one occasion, after a flaming set-to which started off about emptying the washing machine when it was finished, rather than leaving her clothes in there, sodden and forgotten for two days until they were so stinky the entire cycle had to start again, the row escalated quickly into a fiery mess which culminated in Minnie shouting, 'God! You are so controlling. No wonder my bloody father, whoever he is, decided that running off to another continent would be preferable to being anywhere near you!'

This floored Hope, who sat down quietly to let it sink in. The sting of it hung in the silent air for a horrible few moments. Eventually Minnie plodded back into the room, eyes wide as she scanned her mother's face, afraid to gauge the damage.

'Sorry, Mum. Didn't mean that. Seriously, I was just, like, fewmin' . . . sorry,' and she rushed to Hope and hugged her hard.

'It's OK, Min, it's OK. You didn't mean it.'

When Minnie was SEVENTEEN, everything in her life changed. On her way to school one morning she went into the café and met Twat and came out with four cinnamon swirls, a hot chocolate and his number on a fiver. She was nervous to call it in the beginning — what if she'd misjudged him and he genuinely was a twat? She looked at the number on and off for three days and then Princess dared her to call it, so she did.

'Hi, um, Twat? It's me, Curls . . . '

'Hey, the Cinnamon Swirl Queen. I'm so glad you called. I didn't think you would.'

'Yeah. You're lucky. I felt like scraping the barrel today, so you were the first person who came to mind.'

* * *

The relationship started with banter and terrible jokes, and the banter never stopped, the jokes got worse, and Minnie loved it. He said things like: 'What's the difference between mashed potatoes and pea soup? Anyone can mash potatoes . . . haha.' He was relentless, and she always laughed. The two of them understood each other very well and very quickly. She felt sheltered by him, and free to be the confident, nervous, loud,

208

quiet, happy, morose, baffling mixture of a real person she was. He was similar in that he was not quite what he seemed. Cheeky, yes, but like Minnie, he was an interior person, who just happened to present with a bit of flash.

Lee's mum and dad were loud, over-confident people who enjoyed showing off on their 'fully loaded', 'more than just a motorcycle' Honda GL1800 Goldwing, on which they toured around Bristol and the South-West seeking out fairs and county shows where they could display the bike and meet up with other owners. For reasons beyond Lee's ken, both his mum and his dad chose to play the part of hardened bikers when they indulged in this hobby, so they had a full wardrobe of bikers' leathers, vests, boots, neckerchiefs and sunglasses, which they would wear when attending. They LOVED being in character, pretending to be hard as hell, which Lee felt was in total contrast to the transport, basically a sofa on wheels, the most comfy and expansive motorbike imaginable. Not a throbbing hog, more a giant marshmallow in a trolley.

Lee had very quickly realized that their passion for the bike and the dressing-up wasn't to be mocked. In fact, they were singularly humourless about it, so he left them to it, and they left him and his younger sister to it on most weekends when they blat-blatted off on their far-too-regular thrill-seeking jaunts. Relieved to see them rattle off down the road, the siblings were left to their own devices, and formed a strong bond because of it, with Lee always keeping an eye out for his sis, and constantly making her laugh with his silly jokes, 'Sometimes, y'know, I just tuck my knees up to my chest and sort of tip forward — it's just how I roll. Haha.'

This was the loving Lee that Minnie fell for, and because she completely opened her seventeen-year-old heart to him and knew she could trust him, she decided after six months or so that she really wanted to sleep with him. She told Hope that she loved Lee, and Hope wasted no time in getting her to the nurse for advice about contraception. Minnie was offered an implant or birth-control pills. She made the wrong choice. For her. Minnie totally forgot who she was and somehow believed that she would remember to take a pill every day. She didn't and in September, she missed her period. She didn't worry too much, the whole contraception lark was new to her body and she suspected that it might take a while to settle in, probably agitating her normal rhythms. When she missed her second period, she told Lee and he went and bought a pregnancy test.

She peed.

They sat together on the floor of her bedroom with their backs against the bed. Lee said, 'Look, whatever happens, right, we're together with this, OK? Curls? OK?'

Minnie had tears rolling down her face. She was very quiet. She knew before she even looked, she knew. She whispered, 'What have we done? Seriously, what have we done?'

'We've fallen in love, that's all, and that ain't gonna change, whatever this says. Trust me.'

'This is the bit where my dad legged it — when

there was me.'

'Min, look at me. I ain't going nowhere.'

And they sat transfixed, long after the second line bled through, confirming their suspicions.

'What's the percentage it's right . . . ?' Lee piped up eventually.

Minnie reached for the packet and read the side. 'Ninety-nine per cent.'

'Right,' he said. 'Wanna do it again to check for that cheeky one per cent?'

'No,' she said, 'it's right. I know it's right. God!'

'C'mere, baby-mummy.' He took her in his arms and held her very tight. She was trembling. 'Honestly, Curls, you're going to have to accept that I'm here forever, OK? It's happening, and I'm here . . . I've got a job, we can do this,' he reassured her.

'What about school? I'm doing my A levels next year.'

'Do 'em the year after. It's OK, really, you'll only miss a year . . . You DO want to have it, don't you? You're not thinking . . . ?' Lee sat back, suddenly letting this awful thought dawn on him.

She instantly bounced it back: 'No! No! God, really? No.'

'Oh, good.' He blew out a long breath. 'I wouldn't cope with that. Not . . . y'know, something we've done together like this. Not something — I mean — some *one*. Christ . . . ' He was starting to process the hugeness of it.

'I wonder if it's a boy or a girl?' Minnie said.

'So long as it's a baby, I don't care.'

'Shut up, Lee. What else could it bloody be?'

'Well, y'know, an alien. Have you been cheating

211

on me with an extra-terrestrial? Or, y'know, a lep-
rechaun, or a hobbit or an orc . . . ?'

'Stop it, Twat, you twat, honestly . . . '

'Do you even want to KNOW if it's a boy or
girl?'

'No. Maybe not. Just if it's OK, I s'pose.'

'So give it a name that goes for either for now,'
he suggested.

'Yeah. How about BEAN?'

'Yes! That's good. YES. Bean.' They both
laughed.

'Yeah,' he said.

'Yeah,' she said. They went quiet together.

'You'd better tell your mum . . . '

'Yeah. Shit. Yeah. Wait 'til eight o'clock.'

'Why?'

'She's watching *Easties*. She loves that.'

'OK.'

Lee leant over and kissed her belly through her
top. 'Hello, Bean. I'm . . . er . . . yer dad.'

Hope Decides

Hope was curled up on the sofa, Cat was curled up next to her and Mouse was curled up next to Cat. It was a cosy scene of Beatrix Potter proportions and strangeness. Hope liked evenings like this, when everyone was gathered in. She couldn't ever settle happily until she knew her beloveds were safe. She rattled through all of them in her Rolodex mind: Doris at bingo with friends, not drinking, lovely. Glory and Ky househunting and fretting about Princess's exams, which Princess wasn't fretting about. Minnie in her room with Lee, probably on the PlayStation. Yep, all accounted for, so thoughtful Hope could eat a bowl of pasta and put her feet up in front of her favourite soap on the telly.

This was Hope's regular MO. Putting absolutely everyone else first. To anyone else, Hope was a benevolent soul, a loving mother and a generous relative. Hope harboured a different opinion of herself, of course.

Only she carried the truth, and it was present in her very bones. It was a hefty weight. She longed to unburden herself of it all, especially as the heaviness seemed to increase incrementally rather than fade. She was carrying an internal deposit box of a lie which kept being added to, not with feathers but with bricks. It was a cruel parasite that chomped away at her conscience, and gored her with its ugly horns. She hurt a lot. She was a

213

walking bruise that no one else could see.

Hope had never considered a new relationship. How could she? She would have been bound to embark on that journey with secret, lethal luggage, as she could never tell the truth about Minnie. And she genuinely didn't want to risk bringing any other child into the world, in case the same unthinkable horror happened again. She thanked God for the blessing that was Minnie every day; she didn't want to push it, be greedy.

And she loved someone else.

Every single night, she thought of Isaac as she tried to sleep. He was the one person she could share it all with, and probably the one person who would understand and even possibly forgive her. Yet she had made a promise never to contact him, to let him go and have his lighter life, free of all this bulky guilt. In her abundantly true heart, she hoped he'd found all the happiness he deserved. She didn't want to interrupt that but, boy, did she long for him as the other half of her, as her confidant and her love.

The one thing Hope never did was watch television on 1 January. She didn't want to see any appeals about Florence. All of that uncomfortable history was kept at arm's length. Or in a cupboard.

In a box, in a box, in a box at the back of her wardrobe were seventeen letters from Africa. From Isaac. Hope collected them from the PO box in early January each year, and diligently stored them all together, unopened, for one day . . .

It was the only contact from him. His birthday letters to his daughter. Hope wondered every year whether or not he would've remembered or even wanted to continue. She longed to read them so much. She thought about what he might be saying to Minnie. Would he be telling her about his life? Would he be asking about hers? Would he be telling her how much he still loved her? Would he be taking a huge risk and telling her all about what happened? The letters sat in the nest of boxes and they waited, one of them for each of Hope's seventeen years, until one day . . . this day.

Hope's soap opera finished, and she was having a much-enjoyed stretch when Minnie and Lee walked in from the bedroom. She could see that Minnie had been crying. 'Hey. What's up, Min?'

'Umm, Mum, can I talk to you? Can we talk to you . . . ?'

'Always.' Hope lifted the remote, turned the TV off and patted the sofa next to her.

'Right,' started Minnie, trying not to cry again, 'well, God, I can't believe this, it's actually happening . . . '

'You're worrying me now . . . ' Hope put her hand to her mouth. Minnie grabbed her hand and held it firmly in hers.

'I'm not completely sure how this has happened, to be honest — '

'Aren't you?' Lee chipped in. 'You'd better go back to school then!'

'Shut up, Twat! No, I mean, of course I know how it happened, it's just I thought we were being dead careful.'

'Oh God.' Hope felt her stomach lurch.

'Mum, listen, it'll be OK, won't it? It's just, me 'n' Lee are . . . God . . . we're having a baby.'

Hope's mouth was agape, and it remained so for

215

far too long. Her wide-open eyes were locked on her daughter. A kaleidoscope of memories flashed through Hope's mind.

The dead baby in her arms.

The taken baby in her bag.

Isaac's beautiful sad face.

Her birthdays.

Standing in front of the mirror together.

Braiding her hair.

In her uniform on her first day of school.

Her face, her music, her big wide laugh.

Her hand in Lee's hand when she first brought him home.

And, now, her hand in his as she told her mum this huge news. Hope wanted to say something memorable and important, but instead uttered, 'Umm. OK. That's . . . big.'

'You OK with it?' Minnie enquired, worried.

'You are . . . so young, but I suppose that if you're planning to stick together through thick and thin, then it'll be all right . . .'

'Other than the fact that you've just said the most blatantly hypocritical thing I've ever heard, yes, we're planning to do this together. Well, I say plan, we only just found out. The only plan is to do the right thing, that's all I know,' Minnie said.

'I know it sounds hypocritical, hon, but the fact is, it's no picnic to raise a kid on your own. Even though you 'n' me have done it — together, just us — done it so well, I would wish for you to have an easier time, have tons of support. That's all, darlin'.'

'Enter the faithful boyfriend with a job and a big bag of commitment,' Lee interjected.

'Lee, you don't know how happy it makes me to hear you say that, you sound like . . . ' Hope was tempted to say Minnie's dad, but she stopped herself in the nick of time. '. . . such a decent dude. You ARE a lovely guy — I'm so glad she has you, glad THEY have you. Glad you all have each other, for God's sake! C'mere.' She reached out and hugged them both, whispering in Lee's ear, 'If you let her down, boy, you won't be makin' any more babies, trust me, you won't have the gear . . . ' which made Lee holler laughing.

'What? What!' asked Minnie.

'Nothing. It's your mum, she cracks me up,' said Lee.

Hope sat back, but still held on to Minnie's hand. 'I will always regret not giving you a father, li'l one, because you deserved that, and . . . a father missed out on someone truly amazing.' Hope was telling her truth as best she could.

'Thanks, Mum. I'm going to need your help with this. Y'know, what about A levels 'n' stuff . . . ?'

'Min, you can delay that, what's it called . . . defer it, that won't be a problem. But, hon, y'know there's something you are forgetting about . . . '

'Oh? What?' Minnie looked concerned.

'To do a little dance of joy! Come on! And you, Lee, it's all your bloody fault after all . . . ' And with that, Hope dragged them both up and they hollered and whooped and jumped about and laughed.

Minnie was puffing. 'God, I'd better be careful, hadn't I? Can a baby fall out?' she gasped when she sat down, shattered.

Hope joined her on the sofa. 'This is going to

change your lives, you know, you two, and you've hardly got started, but the great thing is that you'll have tons of energy for that little — '

'Bean,' Minnie interjected.

'You're calling the baby Bean? Who are you — Gwyneth Paltrow?'

'For now, 'til we find out exactly who she or he is. Yep, Bean.'

'You bonkers kids. Oh Min, this is going to be amazing. You realize that I will NEVER be called 'Granny', don't you? I'm only thirty-seven.'

'What, then?'

'Umm, something like Queenie or Momma or Grammy or just — Your Highness would do!' Hope announced.

'So it's gonna be all right?' said Minnie the mum.

'It's gonna be all right,' said Hope the mum's mum, 'and the reason I know that is because us guys can get through anything if we stick together. I don't know much, but I know that. We're the living evidence, right?'

'Yeah, 's right, true dat,' said Minnie as she walked to the kitchen. 'Wanna cuppa?'

'Yep. Always. Hey, Lee, you'd better tell your mum and dad too, eh? Make sure they know I'm gonna be the favourite grammy.'

Lee shuffled off to the bedroom to make the call. He wasn't sure how the news was going to be received, and he didn't want Minnie to overhear anything that might upset her. He knew his parents could be brusque, and they weren't particularly baby-loving; they weren't anything-loving really, apart from the beloved motorbike.

Minnie clattered about in the kitchen while Hope watched her every move, trying to process all this surprising new information. How was Minnie's life going to unfold now?

'Tell you what, Mum, I'm going to have to register properly at the doctor's now. I know you hate all that stuff, but seriously, I need to be under their care officially. Do you think you could have a look for my birth certificate, a proper look this time? Haven't you got a file or something . . . ? Or p'raps we can apply for a new one if you've lost that one . . . ' and on she prattled, while a seismic shift happened to the tectonic plates inside Hope.

For this was the moment she'd prayed might never come.

For so long, Hope had avoided taking Minnie anywhere that documents might be needed. She'd managed to convince the lady on reception at the local medical practice that she'd lost the red birth record book that she'd been given when Minnie was a newborn, so they issued her with another. It was relatively easy. No birth certificate was required, and she instantly had a kind of proof that was entirely convincing. A strong foundation on which to build a long-term lie.

It was astonishing how often that little red book with all her inoculations, and measure of height, weight and development, did the job of proof of identity. On the rare occasions Hope was asked for a birth certificate, she fudged it entirely, claiming it was lost and a new one was being applied for. Or she ignored the request. She couldn't believe how little it seemed to matter. She knew the day would come when it DID matter. Perhaps when

Minnie wanted a driving licence, or to get married, or to register for national insurance . . . ?

Hope knew a moment like this was coming, but life got in the way and distracted her from considering it too much. Plus, the thing about denial is that once you have made a conscious decision to let your mind split into two parts — your now, everyday life, and that other part that's too tricky to allow thinking time for — it's amazing just how easily you can normalize the crazy, secret stuff. It just sits there, being a heavy weight, yes, but an increasingly bearable, manageable heavy weight, so on you go, dealing with it, living with it, letting it be, letting it lie, letting it, letting . . .

Now, Minnie was slapping that letting across the face and waking it up. It's not letting lie any more, it's fighting to be known, this secret, it's surfacing, gradually emerging, up and up from the depths, longing for breath. Hope could physically feel it creeping out of her.

What? Here? Now?

This evening, when Minnie had just told her something so immense? Surely not right now, she thought, trying to submerge the huge inevitability, trying to push it down and back into its old familiar cave deep inside her. It wasn't going to go back, it was going to come up and out. It was stronger than her, this dreadful secret, and it was going to win, Hope knew that. She even knew why.

It was going to prevail, because it was, it *is* the TRUTH.

And the truth is king.

Hope listened to Minnie blethering on about midwives and babies and hospitals and babies

220

and babies. It was background noise but it was the soundtrack to a potent moment. Hope looked around the little flat from her place on the sofa. This was her normal, her happy, her safe place. This was where they'd raised each other, she and her beautiful daughter. Everything that really mattered to her was in this flat right now. In this exact moment. The minute before she told Minnie. Sat her down. Told her the whole story. Took her first honest breath for seventeen years.

Minnie's World Changes

Lee wandered back into the living room when he heard Minnie's raised voice. He came across a stand-off between mother and daughter. It looked serious. They often bickered, these two: that was their regular music. They could spar about anything — biscuits, telly, shoes, climate change — but it wasn't ever a real worry. They read each other; they knew the battle rules: no biting, no scratching, nothing personal or permanently damaging, no cruelty. All quarrels were quick to resolve. It was over soon and easily. It took time for Lee to understand the row drill; it was so very different to his own home life, where a fight was rare, serious and unforgiven. In Hope and Minnie's flat, you could say anything, and it wouldn't be held against you or regarded as an eternal stain.

This, however, looked, smelled and sounded like something entirely different, and it was. Minnie was standing up, eyes glued to Hope, arms aloft with her fingers splayed, in a gesture of complete WHAT THE FUCK.

'Sit down, Twat, you gotta hear this,' Minnie ordered him, eyes on fire.

He didn't argue. He sat. She continued, while Hope buried her head in her hands.

'So. Who do you think that is sitting right there?' She pointed at Hope.

'What d'you mean? You couple of absolute units,

whas-sup?' he said, starting to be concerned.

Minnie continued, breathless with shock and creeping rage, 'I'm being serious, bae, who is that woman, sitting there right in front of your very eyes?'

'Umm. It's your mum, innit?' answered Lee timidly.

'You see. That's what I thought. Yeah. That's my mum. Well. Thing is, no, WRONG! I mean, I can understand why you might think that, given the fact that she's been my mum since . . . well . . . for-fuckinevva . . . but turns out it's NOT my mum! It's some weird . . . imposter . . . pretending to be my mum. Pretending to be a mum at all!'

Minnie started to pace up and down the room, slapping her forehead in disbelief.

Lee looked at Hope, her head bowed, and back at Minnie.

'Stop it, Curls. What's going on?'

'Oh, nothin' much. Only my whole life has fallen apart.'

'Is this about the baby?' said Lee.

'Not our baby, no, although God knows who the GRAMMY is really gonna be. I guess it is about A baby, yes. Me. Baby me. This woman here has just told me that she took me from the hospital the day I was born. Took me from a different room. From different parents. My . . . real . . . parents. Just took me and brought me home. Like you might pick up a shell if you're at the seaside, and bring it home and show your family, and, like, everyone says, Oooh, nice shell, you've been on the beach, result.'

'No,' murmured Hope quietly.

223

'Except, instead, you picked up a baby, and brought it home, like, Hey everyone, look what I got in London! Get a T-shirt like everyone else — I'm not a souvenir.'

'Hang on,' interrupted Lee, standing up. He couldn't quite process what he was hearing. 'What do you actually mean? Is this right? Hope? Did you nick a baby back in the day? Did you nick her? Seriously, did you?'

Hope still hung her head. She wished he wasn't there. It was bad enough having to face the dreaded moment with Minnie, but this complicated things much more. Minnie didn't wait for an answer; she was in full flow.

'Nicked me. Just went in and stole me out of the cot. Bloody snatched me from right under their noses. Not yours to take. Know what you are, Mum? If I can still bloody call you that, whoever you are. YOU ARE A KIDNAPPER. That's what you actually actually are. Like in olden days 'n' stuff! Like pirates or something. What's your next crime going to be? Maybe you can sell my baby when it arrives?'

'Stop it, Min.' Hope looked up. 'It wasn't like that. If you can let me explain — '

'Nothing you can say can make this all right, Hope, nothing.' Minnie hurled Hope's name at her like a grenade. She had never before called her by her first name like this. Hope felt savaged by it, by her own name, by the sheer lack of mumness.

Minnie continued, 'I feel like absolutely everything is upside down. Everything I know, I don't know. Y'know, like, who am I then?

Who . . . am I from? Not from you, clearly, but, like, who are those people? My actual parents? Where are they? Have they been looking for me? Do they know I'm even alive? You don't just help yourself to a baby. Who does that? If I heard about it, I'd think it must be a nutter. I didn't know you were a nutter. I thought you were normal. I've trusted you my whole life. Who are you, actually? You're a steaming great liar, that's what.

I can't believe it.

I don't want to believe it.

Fuck, Lee, who am I?'

And she fell into his arms, sobbing.

'Calm down, Curls. Come on. You're in shock, I think. It's not good for you or the baby. Come and sit down,' he said, encouraging her.

She was dumbfounded, and she moved as if to sit, but stood upright again, clasping her head as each fresh question, each horrific new thought occurred to her. They were swirling and tumbling through her mind, like fast-flowing water, each more troubling than the last.

'What is my name?' Minnie demanded.

'Your name is Minnie,' Hope reassured her with tears in her eyes.

'Is it? Is that what they called me? Or what you called me?'

'That is your name.'

'Answer me, Hope! Be honest with me for the first time. Try it. Go on. What's my name?'

'Steady, Curls . . . ' Lee tried to placate her, but she was having none of it and turned to confront Hope. She moved closer and leant down so her angry face was uncomfortably close to Hope's,

225

and she hissed:

'What. Is. My. Name?

You owe me that, if you think I have any worth at all as a human being. I deserve to know my own name. My real name.'

Another grenade.

'They . . . called you . . . Florence.'

'FLORENCE? Oh my holy God. Florence. What, are they posh or something?' She turned to Lee and put her hand out. 'How d'you do, I'm Florence. Still want to have a baby with me? Even though I'm a total wanker?'

'Umm, yes. Please. Florence. I sort of like it, I've always had a soft spot for a bit of classy skirt.' He sniggered nervously.

'It's so not funny, Lee, you twat.'

'I know, I know,' he said. 'But you made it funny, to be fair.'

'This nightmare, it seems, is my actual life, what's happening here. Goes to prove that it's true, everything you do comes back to you in the end, doesn't it?' And with that, she flumped down on to the sofa with him. They sat in shocked silence together for a few moments, all three of them.

Hope had no idea what to say, and yet there was so much. She felt a warped kind of relief, but it was not anything she could appreciate. The weight of the actual untruth was lifted to a certain extent, but her horror was in the dawning realization that she'd dumped it all on Minnie at probably the worst possible time. So, where the agony of the kept secret had lived inside her, there was now a cold gaping hole, rapidly filling up with hot shame. Yes, everything comes back to you.

'I want to, um, tell you . . . ' Hope was faltering. '. . . how sorry I am.'

'Right,' said Minnie curtly.

Hope pushed on: 'But I can't, Min, because I'm not, I'm just not. If this hadn't happened, there wouldn't be you. Us.'

'OK,' said Minnie, 'does your heart not feel or something?'

'Oh, it feels, all right. It's broken right now.'

'And what about the heart of my mother? Do you think that's broken? How d'you think she has managed to live without her baby? After you tore her life apart? And now, you've done the same to me. Today, when I told you about MY baby? You certainly know how to brutally kill the joy. Gotta hand it to you. It's savage. This should've been beautiful.'

'I know,' said Hope.

'What the hell have you done?'

'I've loved you. And whatever you think of me, I always will.'

'Yeah, well . . . ' Minnie trailed off.

More silence. More shock. The tension in the room was sufficiently palpable to taste. Tin on the tongue.

Lee was the first to find it intolerable. 'Tea?' he offered, and escaped into the kitchen to complete what Minnie had started a few minutes ago, before her world collapsed.

Minnie was hurt. And furious. And insulted. Ordinarily, if she felt any of those awful feelings, she would rush to her mum to share it, but not this time. Realizing that fact only made her feel even more desolate. She was sitting in her home, where

227

she was usually safe and cherished, with the two people she loved the most in the whole world, carrying another person who would mean everything, yet she'd never felt so lonely. She felt abandoned by everything she'd thought she understood. Her relationship with her own world was tipped up on its axis, and had, in a flash, become nothing she knew. 'Who else knows about it? Does Nanna Doris know? Or Aunty Glory?' demanded Minnie.

'No one knows. I came home with you. They knew I was pregnant.'

'So they think, to this day, I am — I was that baby?'

'Yes. They've never questioned it.'

Minnie lashed out. 'You're such a liar. Like a queen liar, like the mother of all liars. Keeping it going this long, it's unbelievable.'

Hope doubted whether she should say what she felt compelled to say next, but there was no returning from this moment of truth. There was an inevitable pull towards it.

She'd only been consumed by an irresistible impulse as potent as this once before in her life. And that had led to this.

Despite the potential can of worms she might be opening, and contrary to her big promise which she'd faithfully upheld until this moment, Hope knew that full disclosure was her only option now. She HAD to tell Minnie the whole truth.

'Look, Min,' she started gulping, 'there is one other person who knows about what happened. Isaac. Your father.'

'The absent African? Huh! He's about as much

my dad as you are my mum! He's no bloody use to me.'

To Hope's ears, these words were the cruellest. She had made the decision all those years ago; she was the one who had abducted the baby, not Isaac. His only crime had been to protect Hope and to love her enough to keep the secret. For the good of everyone, he'd had to leave. His honour had been his sacrifice and his sin. So, it was hard to hear Minnie, whom he had wanted so much and whom he loved so much, be so very dismissive about him. Hope could even feel violent about the depth of her love and therefore her defensiveness. Those words of Minnie's stung, and Hope's instinct was to slap her, to slap that rudeness out of her mouth, but of course she would never do that. Hope had never once been physical with Minnie. Hope wouldn't hurt a fly, unless that fly was hurting her daughter. In this moment, while Minnie was indeed hurting, Hope knew what she had to do.

Hope stood up and went into her bedroom, and opened the wardrobe. She reached in for the box.

When she presented the box to Minnie on the sofa, she said, 'I'm sorry you think Isaac wasn't here for you these last seventeen years. When you open this, you'll see that he was. He's been here all along. I just couldn't tell you.'

Anna

The therapist's office was in a basement near Gloucester Avenue, but it was surprisingly light. Anna sat on a comfortable low sofa. Maddy, the systemic psychotherapist, sat across from her on a well-stuffed armchair. There was a coffee table between them with a large book of black and white landscape photos of Dartmoor and a box of tissues. Anna saw the tissues and resolved not to need them. She was determined that this session would be practical and useful, rather than emotional.

'So, OK, it was Grace who recommend that you come and see me?'

'Yes. She said you were a huge help. And Grace is . . . well . . . you know full well how resistant Grace would be to something like this.'

'Right. So, Anna, what can I do to help?'

'Good question. To be honest, I don't think, really, you can do anything, I just need to . . . say some things. To someone who isn't in my family.'

'Great reason to be here. Ready, steady, go.'

'Ummm. Right. God, hard to know where to start really. I suppose I should tell you straight off, that I have always wanted to kill my ex-husband.'

'He drives you nuts?'

'Well, yes, but that's the least of it. It's been a long time since we were married, but this feeling has been bubbling. Recently, I've actually fantasized about the different ways I could do it. Properly, really, actually do it. End him. And that gives me great pleasure. And satisfaction. And relief. I absolutely could do it. Any day now. I know it's wrong, but I am starting to think that whatever punishment would be worth it, so y'know, the benefit would outweigh the cost.'

'You strike me as someone who knows the difference between right and wrong?'

'Yes, of course. Absolutely. I've worked out where I could get a gun and I know the exact trajectory of the bullet that would finish him instantly. Most people think it's up through the roof of the mouth or side of the head, but a surprising amount of people survive those blasts. It's far, far better to shoot directly into the heart, assuming the person actually HAS a heart, that is. Pretty much guaranteed to work. And I like the metaphor.'

'Are you set on this?'

'I absolutely will not do it. I just needed someone to know that I really WANT to. That's all. Thanks. So, I'm probably finished then, I'll just make a move. Don't want to keep you. There are people in a genuine pickle needing your time, I'm sure.'

Anna stood up, looping her Hermès satchel over her arm.

'Sit down, Anna. There are fifty-five remaining minutes that I think could be useful . . . ? You will certainly pay for them, so you might as well use them.'

Anna thought for a moment, and then sat down again.

'Great. Anything else you think I should be aware of?'

231

'Let me think . . . Someone stole my baby seventeen years ago, and I haven't been able to live since. I'm here, I know that, I exist, I can see I'm conscious in the mirror, but I'm not living. I'm just waiting . . .'

'I see.'

The Box

Minnie waited until she heard the front door slam, then sat on the floor and looked at the box in front of her. Lee took a packet of crisps and a banana, and retreated to the bedroom so as to be near enough, but not in her space.

Minnie felt as though Hope had dumped her out to sea and here was a life raft bobbing on the horizon. In a strange way, she wanted to prolong the moment before she opened it, because she wasn't sure she would cope if whatever it contained was any kind of rejection. Hope had always, until now, given Minnie a bedrock of security with her unflinching love, but Minnie had nevertheless always sought the attention and approval she wasn't getting. Outwardly, and for her mum's benefit, she had pretended she couldn't give two figs about this Isaac bloke — after all, he had abandoned them both. In her true heart, though, Minnie had always longed to know him and to know why he left. Somewhere, in a blameful deep pit inside, she had questioned whether, perhaps, just maybe, it was because of her? Her logic was simple and difficult to refute.

Minnie believed that when a beautiful little new baby is put into your arms, you fell in perfect love entirely, and nothing nothing nothing would ever part you, unless a bus ran you down, or a bomb blew you up. So how could her own father, Isaac, who had made her, how could he have looked at

233

her and then decided to leave? Was she not good enough? Not pretty enough? Did she cry too much? Did she personify everything he feared? Was he ashamed of her? Why didn't he want her to meet all his family? Why didn't he take her with him? Why didn't he want Hope?

If, for some reason, the answers to all of these lifelong questions weren't in that box, Minnie would have to continue to blame herself, so she was nervous. Now that Hope had finally told her the dreadful truth, she was starting to unpick and gradually understand why Isaac might've gone. Minnie wasn't even his daughter — of course he would go. Perhaps he didn't know that Minnie wanted a father very much. So much, that the prospect of opening this box, which Hope had said was some kind of contact with him, was making her tremble and gulp.

As Minnie took a deep breath, she closed her eyes and repeated a quiet little mantra of 'It's OK, it's OK' to reassure herself that whatever was in there would make her happy. She didn't even want the happiness all for herself. She was aware that if she could be more content, maybe little Bean inside her would catch that. After the earthquake shock she must've shared with Bean earlier when Hope first told her the astounding story, surely she owed the baby something? Something calm and lovely? Oh, please let it be lovely.

Minnie lifted the lid off the plain brown box, and held her breath while she looked inside. To her surprise, there was another box, a black one, within. She lifted it out and prepared herself again. She took the lid off that box only to find another, a red one, this time.

'Oh, come on!' she whispered to herself. 'Bloody annoying.' And then, a bit too quickly, she ripped the lid off that inner, final box to see the treasure within. A small baby's hospital wristband, with 'Florence Lindon-Clarke 1– 1– 2000' printed on it. It was clear it had been cut off. Underneath that was a pile of airmail letters with African stamps on, all unopened. Seventeen of them. Minnie lifted the letters out very carefully, to see that under them, at the bottom of the box, was a small knitted hat in pink and yellow stripes. It was so teeny, almost as if it were actually for a doll.

Minnie marvelled at how small a baby's head actually is, and she had a fleeting moment of relief, considering her own imminent future. She put the hat down and gathered up the letters. They were in a stack, bound up with an old piece of red ribbon that Minnie felt she recognized, but wasn't sure where from. Some distant toy or Christmas wrapping maybe . . . ? She untied it and the letters splayed out on the carpet. They were in order of date, according to the postmarks. The stamps were colourful and not like any stamps she'd ever seen, not that she'd seen many.

The only time Minnie wrote a letter that had a stamp attached and was sent off was when Hope insisted she write proper thank yous for any presents she was given on her birthday or at Christmas. She wrote all the time, in her notebooks and diaries, and she did write letters, but not ones that she actually posted. These stamps appeared exotic. They had images of hornbills and snakes and famous explorers she'd never heard of, mostly dark-skinned ones. There were what looked like chess players and astronauts and trains and boats and even, in 2007, one of Diana, Princess of Wales, to commemorate the tenth anniversary of her death. The envelopes were so definitely not British, the paper was thin and in various pastel colours, with stripes around the edge to indicate they were for airmail. For a different country. Leaving Africa and coming to England. To Bristol. The writing on the address was the same on every envelope:

Miss Minnie Parker, c/o Hope Parker, and then the PO box in Bristol.

So, he had always put Hope in charge of these letters. She was the one who would decide when Minnie should have them, or even if she would EVER have them. Clearly, he respected Hope and, for a moment, in the midst of this awful anger, that chimed with Minnie. Hope was indeed respectworthy. Usually. Minnie took the first letter in her hand, and laid the others aside temporarily. She was shaky. She lifted it to her nose and sniffed it. The aroma was faint, but undeniably there, a woody, sweetly musky smell. Was it a bit of Africa or Isaac? Or was she imagining it? Wishing it? She looked once again at the handwriting on the envelope. Scrawly blue Biro, old-fashioned slightly curly cursive style. It looked friendly, inviting, not too formal.

She opened it carefully and took out the pages, and two unfamiliar green banknotes dropped out. African money. She opened up the pages to look.

It's just some writing, she thought, how can writing hurt me? But look at it. My father wrote each of those words himself. Held the pen and wrote those words. To me. Actually . . . is he my father? Who is he to me? Stepfather? Kidnap dad? Captor? Stop stop stop these horrible thoughts and read the letter.

And so she did. It was two pages. Two very thin pages, and as she read them, Minnie didn't blink once. She didn't want to miss a single second of Isaac.

It began 'Dear Daughter'. Already, she was welling up. Until now, there was only one other person in the whole world who called her this. She read on: 'I am your father, and I love you.' It made her gasp, out loud. A tiny sob. It was a bit *Star Wars*, but it was manna from heaven, and perfectly what Minnie needed to read and know and believe.

She ravenously fed on all of the letters, in order, one after the other, without any hesitation. There was money in every one. He'd written each one on her birthday, and as the seventeen years went by, in the lines of those letters, he drip-fed her both his life and all the support and encouragement she'd longed for. She read fast, and she very quickly adjusted to his handwriting style. She easily scanned the lines, cherry-picking key things to remember, the passages that stuck out.

When she was three:

I hope your birthday was good, and you got to eat too much cake, and maybe then you were a bit sick, so to feel better, you ate a bit more cake . . . ?

When she was five:

I want you to know that this year, I am going to marry Efiba, my girlfriend, because she is going to have our baby. I wish I could ask you to come, I wish I could know that you are OK with this, but I am just going to have to believe that you would understand. She doesn't know, can't know, that I already have a daughter. But I know, Minnie, and I never ever forget you. Know that.

When she was eight:

Elijah is very naughty. He could do with his older sis to keep him in check! I think of you every day when I look at him. I missed out on so much of you. I can imagine the lovely young girl you have grown into, because you were the most beautiful baby. I remember every single little thing about you. You are often in my dreams, but you're still a baby. I'd love to see a photo of you, but until I do, I'll paint my own pictures, and in all of them, you will be smiling.

When she was ten (with a stamp of Captain Paul Cuffee on the envelope):

This is a difficult thing I have to tell you, because maybe it will come to mean nothing to you, and if that's true, it's my fault, but I need to tell you that my mother, your grandmother, died a few weeks ago. You would have loved her and she would for sure have loved you, if

238

*life was different and you'd been able to meet
her. She was very ill with a serious cancer in
her belly, and she asked for the whole family to
come to her bedside. Efiba and Elijah and me
were all there, but it felt wrong to me. When we
were leaving, I knew it was goodbye, so I gave
her a kiss, and when I did, I told her about you
quietly in her ear. I said, 'Momma, you need
to know your first grandchild lives in England.
She's called Minnie and she's ten,' and I said
sorry for not telling her before. She was very
weak but she squeezed my hand and nodded. So
she knew, Minnie. She knew before she left us.
I am trying to remember that 'Those who die in
grace go no further from us than God. And God
is very near.'*

When she was thirteen:

*This Christmas, I was talking with friends, and
one of the wives said that her father had a big
effect on her self-worth. This has worried me,
because it's probably true. Dear Minnie, I pray
you don't suffer anything just because I'm not
there. I know your mum will always teach you
to walk proud with your head high, like my
mum taught me. But what can a dad teach?
Maybe this. Be yourself, be kind, be polite, be
on time, be brave and fight like a girl because
the girls I know are strong! Don't be grateful
for too little, don't let anyone control you, don't
worry about little things, don't take drugs, don't
let anger be in charge, don't let failure stop you
from doing anything, because believe me, that's*

239

when you learn the most even though it feels bad at the time. I know that for sure! I have failed in many things, but I try to do better each time. That's all anyone can do. I hope I haven't failed you, sweet Minnie. I hope you know I love you and feel proud.

When she was fourteen:

I know you but I don't know you. All I can say is that I seem to love you more each day, how crazy is that?

When she was sixteen:

I know it's hard when you are a teenager, I remember that time myself, but something you should always try to be, Minnie, is CHEER-FUL. It's underrated, and it's a blessing if you can manage it.

The last letter, when she turned seventeen:

I'm beginning to wonder if I should make a trip to England. As each year goes by, my regret gets bigger. What I did, what I felt I had to do, was the right thing back then, but you will be eighteen soon — time is slipping away so fast. Maybe I will keep my promise to Hope and I won't interfere so that you don't know anything, then your life can just tick on with peace and calm. Maybe I will just watch you from a distance one day? Even if I see you get on a bus or have a

*coffee, I will at least know you are OK, and I'll
see what you've become. I want that very much.*

Minnie put the letters down and allowed the
tears to stream out of her. At last, she had a dad,
and she knew that he'd always thought about
her. She felt buoyed up. Isaac's letters were the
life jacket she needed as she'd started to sink in a
choppy sea of shock and confusion.

She gathered up the precious letters and all
the creased and worn banknotes and started to
put them back in the box to show Lee, when she
noticed that, there, lining the bottom of the box,
was a piece of paper, folded up. She reached in
and pulled it out. As she opened it, she could see
that it was something official, formal. She was
looking at a medical death certificate. It had her
own name on it, 'Minnie Parker', and her own
date of birth, '1– 1– 2000'.

The box where the 'Name of Father' should be
written was scored through with just two lines. No
mention of Isaac. Two lines right through him.

In the box marked 'Cause of Death' were two
words: 'Unknown. Stillborn.'

Minnie was looking at her own death and, for
a brief moment, her own heart did indeed stop.
This is what everything was really about. Little
dead Minnie. The first Minnie.

Minnie felt her heart start again, but now, under
the pressure of truth, it was cracked, in sympathy
with Hope's.

241

Hope and Minnie: Mum and Daughter

Hope wandered around in a daze for a few hours, having coffee in various different nearby cafés as she dodged the autumn rain and cold outside, and agonized over how long to leave it before she ought to return home to the flat and Minnie. It felt so odd to have left her there to read the letters on her own. Hope had been by Minnie's side through all the difficult, frightening moments in her life until now. Hope hated being separated from her at such a key time, but she knew that Minnie would need to process it all.

What was 'it all', actually? Since Hope had resisted all temptation (and it was mighty) to open the letters, she was, in effect, leaving Quiet Isaac and Minnie alone together. She was anxious that the letters might have information that would be difficult for Minnie. What had he told her? What had his life turned out to be?

It didn't help that Hope drank one large double-shot black coffee in each of the five cafés she went to. She was absolutely buzzing. Not the best way to deal with an already stressful situation. Her head was throbbing whilst her worst thoughts clamoured and clattered about inside it. Her biggest fear was that she might have lost Minnie forever. She wondered whether Minnie would ever forgive her? Hope's only chance was to step back and trust that her daughter could work it through in her head.

Hope was forgetting that Minnie was in total shock. She'd only just discovered that everything she thought she knew, she didn't. Her world was topsy-turvy. Hope had had seventeen years of normalizing this utterly strange situation, and it had been Hope's choice. Minnie was only a few hours into her maelstrom and none of it was her choice. Not in the slightest.

Eventually Hope Parker, an ordinarily confident woman who held her head high and her shoulders back defiantly, stood trembling and hunched with worry outside the door of the flat, afraid for the first time ever to enter her own home. Everything that really mattered was inside, and she wasn't sure what she would do if she'd lost it. Either way, there were momentous decisions to be made, which would undoubtedly change all of their lives forever. She needed to summon every last iota of courage, and at this very moment, she found it impossible to remember that she'd ever had ANY. She felt full of fear, as if she had no bones in her whatsoever, as if she was only jelly held together with skin.

Shaking, she slipped the key into the lock and walked in.

Ordinarily, she would call out Minnie's name as she arrived home, but she somehow didn't feel the right to. Only people with bones should be so bold, and Hope was currently skeletonless.

In a meek, small voice, she quietly asked, 'Min?'

'In here,' came the response from Minnie's bedroom.

Hope approached and went in, holding her breath. Minnie was sitting on her bed, next to Lee,

243

in the small colourful room full of strings of pom-poms and Day of the Dead graphics and a messy criss-cross of hundreds of festoons of coloured fairy lights. She'd clearly been showing him the letters, and her face was glistening with tears. Under the beautiful twinkly lights, she appeared so vulnerable and so very young.

'Are you ... OK?' Hope ventured.

Minnie leapt off the bed and straight into Hope's eager arms.

Lee smiled from ear to ear.

'Mum! Thank God you're back. Just for a horrible minute, I thought you might've left ...'

'Min. I will never leave you. Not like that. I just wouldn't. You must know that?'

'Yeah, but I said some stuff ...'

'You're very shocked. I understand, darlin' heart. I really do. It must be awful for you.'

They hugged and hugged, and both of them wept as they didn't let go. Lee looked on, and wondered what on earth was going to happen next.

Hope said, 'What are the letters like? I've nearly opened them a hundred times.'

'Oh Mum, look at them! There's seventeen, one for each year. He's written them on my birthday to let me know he was thinking about me ... Look at this one ... and this ... Isn't it lovely? He says, 'I am your father, and I love you'; he says that a lot. And he explains why he went, so that you and I could be together and so that no one would ever know. I think he wished he could stay.'

'Yes, yes, he did. But he couldn't. He is too honest for that. He chose you over himself really.'

'And he's got a little boy. Elijah. Well, not so

244

little any more — he's twelve now. My brother. God, I've got a brother! Wait a minute, is he my brother?' asked Minnie. 'I dunno! It would be so cool to meet him. Meet all of them. He's married; she sounds nice . . .'

'Right,' said Hope, trying to disguise the antiseptic sting of her hurt.

'God, Mum, sorry. Did you know he was married?'

'No, but listen, I don't have a right to know anything about his life, much less judge it. I'm glad if he . . . found some happiness. He should. He deserves it. Just like you deserved him, but it was my fault you didn't have him, and that bit I'm really sorry about. Are you OK, Min?' Hope clocked Minnie's anguished face.

'Have you . . .' Minnie looked at Hope, then Lee, then Hope again. 'Have you been waiting for him all this time? Did you think he might come back? For you? For us? Is that why you don't try with anyone else?'

Hope had nothing to say. She hadn't really even admitted it to herself — she was an expert self-deluder — but her insightful, clever daughter worked it out in seconds. Hope had indeed denied so much. She'd denied all the hurt she'd caused. She'd denied that she was in limbo, hoping against hope that she might be with Quiet Isaac again some day. Only now, in the cold light of Isaac's news, did she realize how much she'd clung to that hopeless hope. He was married, he had a child, he had moved forward and lived his life. Hope had lived Minnie's life. Only. Minnie was her EVERYTHING, because in Minnie,

245

Hope kept her own dead Minnie AND Florence alive.

In that slicingly clear moment, Hope understood something utterly. She would now have to say goodbye to dead Minnie. She would have to let her lie, because Florence had turned up to claim herself, and Hope could not, should not get in her way. In an instant, Hope grasped the true breadth and width of a mother's love. It was selfless love that meant whatever was right for Minnie would be the right thing. The only thing. Strangely, Hope felt a sense of relief. The future was out of her hands now.

Hope looked at Minnie, and took both her hands in hers. 'I love you so much, Min. You are my reason, and you are my joy. And that's a fact, whatever happens.'

'Thanks, Mum. And soz for the ugly things I said, but . . . y'know . . .'

'I know,' Hope told her.

'Well, this is all a tad wawa, doncha think?' Minnie tried to lighten the moment.

'Yep. Colossal wawa,' Hope agreed. 'What the hell happens now?'

'Tea?' chimed in Lee, knowing what's what — good lad.

'Yeah, tea,' they both agreed.

Hope looked at the envelopes on the bed and one in particular caught her eye: the one with a stamp of Captain Paul Cuffee on it. She knew that face; she knew that image.

'Hey, Min, have you seen this fella before?' she asked her daughter.

Minnie screwed up her eyes and looked closely

246

at it. 'Um, no, don't think so . . . Oh wait, yeah, yeah' — it dawned on her — 'is it that guy in the picture on the wall above your bed? That old picture?'

'Yep. That's right. This is Captain Paul Cuffee. And Isaac really rated this man; that's why he had the picture. It was someone way back in his family or something, I think. You need to check him out. Isaac left that picture. I think you should have it, now everything's . . . y'know.'

'Yeah, I know.' Minnie understood. 'Mum, I know what we have to do. And you know really.'

'Yes.' Hope did indeed know.

Minnie continued, 'We have this cuppa, you get Nanna Doris and Aunty Glory over, you tell them . . . then we have to tell the police. We have to.'

'Hmmmm. Yes.' Hope knew she was right. 'But can we have one last night of normal — get a curry, cuddle on the sofa, have some tunes and a lickle dance — before we do any of that? Maybe tomorrow? One more night with my daughter before it all hits the fan?'

Minnie laughed. 'C'mere, lie down with me, and stroke my arm like I was five.'

Hope moved up the bed, laid her head on the pillow and beckoned her pregnant daughter into the crook of her shoulder. Minnie snuggled in next to her, and said, 'I love you, Mum, you baby-thieving shithead . . .'

Anna: the News

Anna whizzed up some healthy green goo in her Nutri-Bullet. It was broccoli and kale and spinach and a dollop of honey to make it palatable. It wasn't palatable. She couldn't understand how some vegetables, which she ordinarily loved individually, could taste so vile when blended together. Nor did she really understand why she was putting herself through a food trial akin to jungle celebrity awfulness when she could instead have a plate of steamed loveliness for surely the same amount of calories and nutritional value?

It didn't escape Anna that this was a good dilemma to have. She was aware that a great many of the things she did in her life were simply to occupy time and distract her from falling into the well of sadness which sat inside her, but her therapist Maddy helped when she explained, 'There's a simple reason you won't fall in, Anna. Because you acknowledge, fully, that it's there.'

'Yes, I know it's there. I so know.' Anna had been sitting on the wall of the well with both feet dangling dangerously in, way back when she had been married to Julius, but now that she wasn't, and hadn't been for years (although, God knows, she sometimes felt that she was sleepwalking through her life), both feet were planted firmly on the ground beside the vast drop. She could see in, but she wasn't on the precipice any longer, and she had a strong will telling her it would be

248

horrific to fall in. Telling her not to. So, she had coping mechanisms. One misguided method was alcohol, for a while, but she had since decided that her future would be alcohol-free. For now, anyway. She wanted to see ahead through clear eyes, and she wanted to be healthy.

As she tried to gulp down the repulsive smoothie, she sauntered over to the window of her first-floor flat and looked down at the street. A police car was parked up directly outside. Her eye was drawn to it immediately, like a moth to a flame. She shuddered. She hated seeing police cars; they brought back too many difficult memories. She was about to turn away when the door opened and, to her astonishment, out stepped the newly appointed, and hardly changed at all, Inspector Debbie Cheese, who started to make her way up the path towards the front door of Anna's building. Anna froze. Oh God. Seventeen years went by while Anna waited for Debbie to come up one set of stairs. Or so it seemed. It was in fact only a minute before the thunderous knock came on her door.

Anna had to persuade her legs to work, which took a few seconds. As she opened the door, she scanned the policewoman's face so hard she thought it might hurt her.

'Breathe, Anna,' said Debbie. 'Can I come in? It's just me.'

'Yes, yes, of course. God, yes, yes, yes,' said Anna, burbling nervously as she led Debbie Cheese into her front room.

'Sit down, Anna.'

'Is she dead? Just tell me. Is Florence dead?'

'Please sit down.'

She did.

Debbie continued, 'I hoped so much this day would come, Anna, but if I'm honest, I wasn't convinced it ever would. We've found Florence.'

Anna was breathing fast and she was grasping the edge of the sofa very tight.

In. Out.

In. Out.

In. Out.

Had Debbie really said what she just said?

Anna considered that she might be hallucinating, or dreaming. She felt slightly dizzy.

'OK, now you're breathing too much,' said Debbie, reaching out to touch her. 'It's true, Anna. At last. Florence has been found.'

Anna had imagined this moment over and over again, and this was nothing like she thought and hoped it would be. She thought she would feel an overwhelming gush of relief, and joy. That wasn't it at all. What she truly felt was an inner collapse, as if the ceiling had come down on her in an inner room. The effort to keep the ceiling up was over, so it fell in. Surprisingly, there wasn't an opening above it to a sunny blue sky. There was another ceiling there. A new, different, higher one to keep up.

Anna was so grateful to have Debbie's hand to hold on to, and she remembered that it was indeed she who had put a comforting hand on her shoulder in that stuffy little maternity suite all those years ago. She allowed her tears to come, and when they did fall down her cheek in huge plopping drops, quietly and constantly, Anna couldn't stop them.

Debbie fished some tissues out of her bag, and said, as she handed them to Anna: 'I asked if I could be the one to tell you, Anna. I wanted to share the good news with you, yes, but I also felt that you ought to know that I blame myself for what happened . . . '

'What? Don't be silly, it wasn't your fault.'

'No, it wasn't my fault she was taken, but I think it was my fault she wasn't found.'

'What?' said Anna. 'Don't blame yourself, Debbie, you all did your best . . . ' She was flummoxed.

'No, Anna. I did not do my best. In fact, I can honestly say I think this might well have been the worst policing in my entire career.'

'What are you talking about?'

'First off, we were all too quick to blame an entirely innocent group of people. We were narrow-minded. And prejudiced. Beyond belief.'

Anna tried to make sense of it all. 'Hang on, are you saying she wasn't with the Romanians?'

Debbie Cheese hesitated. 'No, she wasn't. We spent a great deal of time and resources trying to find, infiltrate and investigate that group, but they are itinerant, and extremely wary of us, so we never entirely got to the heart of it. We assumed she'd been handed on. Trafficked. Out of the country.'

'You assumed?'

'Yes. To our shame.'

'Where was she? Where is she?' Anna's volume was rising.

'She was taken by a woman called Hope Parker who was on the same ward as you. She had a stillborn child the same time as Florence was born. She took Florence on her way out of the hospital.

It's unbelievable that no one saw her.'

'Oh my God. Has Florence been in London?'

'That's the thing. As part of the due process, and because she left the hospital around the right time, I . . . I went to visit Hope.' Debbie hung her head and continued, 'This is where I failed you, failed her, and I'm so sorry, Anna. So sorry. I went with a colleague and we searched the flat. There was no sign whatsoever. There was no . . . baby.'

'Where was she?'

'Apparently, the father took her out.'

'He's not the father!' Anna snapped.

'No. Sorry. Hope's partner. He took the baby out.'

'And you didn't think to check him out?'

'There was no reason — '

'THERE WAS EVERY REASON!'

'Yes, I know,' Debbie agreed, 'but really we were eliminating suspects, and there was absolutely no evidence of Florence there. And Hope was . . . '

'WHAT?' blurted Anna.

'She was devastated from her own loss that very morning. It seemed unfair to be loading more misery on to her with accusations. She was . . . so sad, Anna.'

'She had MY baby!'

'Yes. She did.'

Anna's mind was racing. 'Has Florence lived here? All this time? Nearby?'

'No, Florence's home is in Bristol.'

'Florence's home is not in Bristol, Debbie, Florence's home is here, with me!' Anna cried.

'Yes, Anna. I'm so sorry. I don't really know the right words. She has been raised in Bristol.'

252

'Is she all right?' Anna muttered as she tried to stay calm. 'Is she healthy? Has she been happy?'

'Yes, I think so. Hope is a kind person, it seems, and they both came together to their local cop shop. Florence has only just found out, apparently, and she's the one who encouraged Hope to hand herself in.'

'Right,' said Anna, wiping away tears and beginning to take it all in. 'Does Julius know?'

'Detective Inspector Thripshaw is with him right now,' Debbie replied.

'Have you seen her?' Anna was desperate to know.

'Yes. I have.' Debbie saw that Anna was hungry for any information about her lost daughter, so she tried her hardest to furnish her with a description. 'She's extremely beautiful, very unusual and exotic; she was wearing bright-coloured things and had her hair up in a sort of big bow thing with a huge mass of curls coming out. Orange curls. And she has freckles, and a lovely happy face. She seems to be very bright. She was a bit nervous, understandably, and she is pretty protective about Hope. She doesn't let go of her much. She's worried about what's going to happen. They both are. Oh, and you ought to know that she's pregnant.'

Anna was shocked. 'She is pregnant? She's only seventeen! Oh my God.'

'She seems fine with it. The dad-to-be was there. He seems fully on board.'

'Is she called Florence still?'

'No. Her name is Minnie.'

'Minnie? Who is that? Minnie . . . ?' Anna rolled

253

the name around in her mouth, trying to wrap some understanding around it. 'OK, Minnie. She is Minnie.'

Julius: the News

Julius was holding forth at a small press dinner, in a private room at the Dorchester. He was in his element; he'd made a short speech about the success of 'Clarke's Law', which was old news now, but that didn't stop him gloating about his success with it. The one aspect he liked about his current job as a consultant to the Brexit Select Committee was that he appeared to be interested, compassionate, heroic even, and that had become his brand. He saw someone senatorial when he looked in the mirror, he impressed himself, he could almost be jealous of himself, so slick was he.

Julius sat down at the table of twelve, satis-fied his comments would be well reported and well received. Job done. He could now relax and schmooze with these journalists, networking with them for his own gain, and enjoy the free three-course meal. It didn't escape his notice that sitting at the centre of the large but intimate table, he was the tiniest bit Christ-like, wasn't he, with his Brexit disciples surrounding him, attending to him? Yes, he liked how important he felt; he liked the attention. He wouldn't be deigning to notice how swiftly they all wanted to leave. He was skilled at editing uncomfortable stuff out of his life. He'd edited Anna out almost immediately after the split was announced, and he was quick to manage the PR around it, manipulating the press release to make it seem as if he were blameless, as if they had simply drifted apart. He knew Anna wouldn't object. What would it benefit her to scatter the bleached bones of their failure so publicly?

As the gathered few mercifully took their leave, Julius noticed a figure in a dark coat, hanging back near the door. He presumed the man was a driver come to collect one of the reporters, who'd boldly wandered into the room.

Julius was annoyed at the breach of protocol, never mind the security risk. 'Excuse me, matey, if you're here to pick someone up, you should wait outside. Surely you know that?'

'Good afternoon, Mr Lindon-Clarke, perhaps you don't recall me?' The man stepped forward. 'I'm DI Mike Thripshaw.'

Julius furrowed his brow. This name meant nothing. DI Thripshaw helped him out. 'It's been seventeen years. I was the head poncho on the investigation into the abduction of your daughter, Florence.'

'Oh God, yes, sorry.' Julius's heart (or place where his heart should be) sank. This idiot. Again.

'Don't worry, I'm not a pigment of your imagination, so it would be grand if you could sit down, please, sir.' DI Thripshaw was firm. Julius didn't argue. 'And if we could have the room to ourselves?'

Julius ushered the remaining couple of journos, who were dawdling and gulping down the last of their crèmes brûlées, out.

'Well?' said Julius impatiently. 'Is there some news on the gypsies?'

'Ah well, that's one of the things I've come to tell you. There's been a big seed change in the investigation and we had to change tact entirely.'

'What do you mean, man?'

'Well' — Thripshaw coughed — 'these past years have been a steep learning kerb for us at the Met and we have to acknowledge that in our determination to dissolve this mystery, we resumed that we had our suspects, the Romanian group, but they alluded us and there was flatly no further intel coming from there. The tail went cold. Nothing. Nada . . .'

'Yes. Yes . . . so?' Julius remembered just how much he had wanted to punch this irritating bozo back then, but just what the hell was he doing here, now?

'Listen, I'm not looking for an escape goat, but it was our superiors who told us to lay off it. But to be honest, this particular case has stayed with me. I've never once taken for granite the misery that's been caused to you —'

'For God's sake, man! Is there some news, or have you come here to torture me?'

'No, no, my apologies, Mr Lindon-Clarke, I'm not a stranger to going off on a tandem, I'm aware of that. No. The fact of the matter is, Florence has turned up.'

'What! Turned up? What do you mean?' Julius exploded.

'She and her mother walked into a police station in Bristol this morning.'

'She was with Anna?'

'No, no, the woman who took her and raised her, a Ms Parker.'

Julius paused and thought hard. He was in a curious liminal space, acutely aware that this was giant news. His daughter had returned. He knew instantly what he wanted to do.

'Kirsty!' he shouted for his PA, who came rushing in. 'Grab any of those journos who are leaving. There's something they'll want to know and we need to do it now to catch the evening papers. Go! Now! Quick!'

No fool, she headed straight for the bar.

Julius turned to Thripshaw. 'I want that Parker woman arrested immediately!'

Back Home:
Hope and Minnie

It had been a long day at the police station. Once the officers believed Hope, and cross-checked her story with the Met police in London, they interviewed her in great depth.

She was provided with a legal-aid lawyer and she was interviewed on camera, under caution, and then released on bail to go home with Minnie, who had sat patiently waiting by the front desk for her mother. Hope was warned that some officers from London might wish to talk to her, and that she should not leave Bristol for any reason.

Hope had no intention of fleeing although Minnie had suggested it when they cuddled up on the sofa the night before.

'What about if us three got on a plane tomorrow, instead of going to the police station? What about if we went and lived somewhere on the other side of the world?'

'Like where . . . ?' said Lee.

'Like, I dunno, like Spain or something. That's where criminals go, isn't it?'

'Hardly on the other side of the world, hon,' Hope reminded her, 'and besides, you don't have a passport. I couldn't get you one. Always been sad about that.'

'Oh yeah. I've never really travelled anywhere. I'd like to some day,' Minnie said dreamily.

'Maybe now you can,' Hope the optimist told

her.

They held hands. They held on.

★　★　★

So now they were back home, in a house-arrest limbo, waiting to hear how Minnie's biological parents would take the news.

Hope was well aware that the future didn't look too bright for her. She toyed with the idea of contacting Isaac, to let him know what she'd done, but then it occurred to her that it might be best to leave him in blissful ignorance. While she honestly didn't know his whereabouts, she could truthfully tell that to the police. They didn't need to know about the letters, they didn't need to know that Minnie COULD find him. Just as he had stepped away in order to preserve the secret and allow Minnie and Hope to be together all those years ago, Hope would now do anything she could to protect him. Minnie also agreed to defend Isaac by staying quiet about him. She was facing the very real possibility of being separated from her mother; she wanted to at least leave the chance of a relationship with her father open, especially now that she knew he had been with her all along.

Lee was at home, checking on his sister, so Hope and Minnie cooked pasta and chicken and shared a relatively peaceful contemplative evening together. The calm between two storms.

As they sat down, Minnie put her bowl of food aside.

'You OK, Min?' enquired her mum.

'Yeah, think so. Feel a bit weird.'

'That'll be the baby. They tip everything up. Nothing feels the same any more. I was quite sick with you. Well. Not you. Y'know what I mean. With the baby.'

'Yeah. With Minnie. I don't feel sick actually. I feel ate up. Not right. Crunchy. Don't want this food suddenly, and it's my favourite pasta. Not fair,' Minnie said grumpily as she returned her dish to the worktop in the kitchen, and clattered it down. 'I legit feel weird. Sort of here.' She pointed at her general chest area.

'Come and sit down. It's probably all the stress; it's been crazy these last couple of days. I'm sorry, Min. It's all my fault. You'll be fine.'

Minnie plonked down next to Hope. 'Thanks, Mum.'

Hope took her in her arms, and could feel her breathing fast and shallow. 'Calm down, Min, seriously.'

'I don't know what's wrong,' said Minnie breathlessly.

'I think it might be a panic attack, so just breathe nice and easy, darlin' girl. Big deep breaths. That's it. Steady.' Hope was starting to feel concerned. 'This will pass.'

'Will it?' Minnie needed reassurance.

'Yes. It will. No doubt. Listen, because of me and the bad-but-I-don't-regret-it-for-one-second thing I did, your entire body is probably in trauma. No wonder you feel strange. Don't worry, Minnie Moo, I'm here.' Hope clasped Minnie's head close to her and stroked it comfortingly, as she'd always done since she was a baby.

'I don't think you will always be here, Mum,'

Minnie whispered.

The awful truth of that landed squarely on Hope. There was going to be a huge price to pay for what she'd done; she knew that.

'Hush now, come on. Whatever happens, Min, we will somehow get through it together. We're joined. Heart to heart. You know that.'

'Yes. I know. I do know.'

'Is it getting easier . . . ?' Hope noticed her breathing was gentler.

'Yeah. Think so. God, that was so random.'

'You'll be fine, but just to be sure, we'll check in with the doc tomorrow. Could be something or nothing. Blood pressure maybe? Or a little anxious thing? Or something? Let's just look after you and Bean and be sure. I'll call for an appointment.'

'I'll get Lee to take me.'

'Oh, right, yes, of course. I have to get used to the daddy being involved!' Hope chuckled.

'And you, Mum. Course you should come with us. You're my mum. This is your grandchild.'

'That's right, Min. And I can't wait!'

They sat in silence.

'Fuck, Mum. What's going to happen?'

'More interviews, more police. I just have to tell the truth.'

There was a soft knock on the door, and Hope went to answer it. She knew who it was; she'd invited them over.

'Hey,' said Hope as she answered the door to Doris and Glory. They greeted Minnie and bustled about making coffee in the kitchen.

Doris said, 'So what's the big deal? What do you need to tell us?'

262

Glory said, 'Yeah, sounded so mysterious on the phone — wh'appen?'

'I think you'd better forget the coffee, and come and sit down.'

The Morning After

Nobody slept much that night. Nanna Doris and Glory found the shocking news difficult to process and they'd had a million questions for Hope, all of which she'd tried to answer as openly and honestly as she could, however difficult or intrusive.

The whole night was a roller coaster of bewilderment, anger, blame and resistance. There were raised voices and stomping off and tutting and crying and hugging.

Lee arrived back at the flat around ten o'clock, and became the waiter, providing cups of tea and slices of pizza as the night wore on. He spectated the roasting of Hope. It wasn't his place to join in. This was serious family territory.

There was a barrage of questions:
'How did you get her out of the hospital?'
'How did no one see?'
'How did you hide her from the police?'

Those practical enquiries were simpler to answer. When Nanna Doris asked, 'What happened to your Minnie?' and Glory asked, 'So who is Minnie to me now? Is she still my niece?' it was devastating. Glory saw the look of anguish on Minnie's face and adjusted her words, 'I mean, of course she's still my niece! We all love you, Min, exactly the way we always have. It just feels like there's something different.'

'Are you saying'—Minnie needed to know—

'that I'm not part of the family now? That I don't belong any more? Oh my actual God . . .'

'Of course you're part of our family, that doesn't change,' Hope tried to reassure her.

Minnie thought for a moment, and said, 'Well, I'm not part of anyone else's family, that's for sure.'

Nanna Doris weighed in, 'Everyone can just shut the fuck up. Minnie isn't PART of this family, she IS this family. She's in it, right at the heart, and that's the end of it. My bloody fear is that she could be removed from us, she's still a minor.'

'God, Mum, could that happen? I don't want to go anywhere . . .' Minnie panicked, and grabbed Lee's hand.

'No one has suggested anything like that. Min, the police told me to wait at home with you. We have to see what'll happen.' Hope was keeping it all very cool, although the thought of Minnie being ripped away was her worst nightmare.

Nanna Doris gave everyone a reality check. 'Let's not forget, in the craziness of all this, we've lost a child. My granddaughter. Your daughter. One of us is gone. We must remember her.'

The three generations gathered each other up in a family hug and spent the night talking and sleeping and talking and eating and talking, and Hope made sure they finally understood who Quiet Isaac really was and why he did what he did. At last.

★ ★ ★

265

The next morning, Lee left to go to work as usual, but returned twenty minutes later with an armful of different newspapers.

'Sorry to ruin your morning, girls, but thought you ought to see these . . . ' and he flumped the pile down on the counter. 'Seems like your dad, your birth dad rather, is some famous dude,' he said to a very sleepy Minnie.

The front pages of pretty much all the newspapers were splattered with huge photos of Julius. It was the same image in each one: he was looking directly at the camera, with his hands clasped together, as if in prayer, in front of his chest, and there was a hint of brimming tears in his eyes. It was mawkish to say the least, but it was pure Julius. The head-lines varied from ''The heartbreak is over,' says ex-MP Julius Lindon-Clarke' in *The Times*, to 'My baby girl is back' in the *Mail* to 'Put the monster who stole my daughter behind bars!' in the *Sun*.

Doris, Glory, Hope and Minnie were speechless with horror. They were all drowsy from the lack of sleep until they saw these. They woke up fast.

'God, Mum, is this him?' ventured Minnie.

'I suppose so, yes,' replied Hope as she hurriedly flicked quickly to the pages inside where Julius had clearly written his statement. Luckily, he hadn't named her, but he told the story of what happened seventeen years ago, and didn't hold back on the emotion and drama. Glory read part of it aloud, over Hope's shoulder.

'My life has never been the same since,' said the grieving ex-MP, desperately fighting back

266

tears. 'The huge stress of it all has weighed heavily on me especially. My ex, Anna, has thankfully moved on with her life, but I simply couldn't. I have been stuck in the sadness of that awful day and, truthfully, I think my heartbreak was the reason our marriage failed in the end. So very sad . . . '

There was no sign of anything directly from Anna. She hadn't spoken to the press at all.

Just Julius. All about Julius.

Minnie was fixated on the photo. 'Look, he's sort of crying. God, I think I've got his nose, and deffo those eyebrows! It's so random . . . ' She was eating the image with her eyes, scanning every inch of it for any clue to the person in it, and thus to herself, vicariously.

'Look at this,' said Glory, as her finger followed the piece in the *Daily Mail*. 'It says here, ' 'I've lived my life ever since that day in the pursuit of safety in hospitals, so that no one else should have to suffer what I did,' said the Great Man himself.' That's weird because it says it was written by him, so has he called himself 'the Great Man'? Do you know his face, Mum? Is he like really important or something?'

Doris replied, 'Never heard of him. But tell you what, he'll hear of me if he continues to call my daughter 'a monster'.'

Minnie chimed in, 'YES, that's terrible. How is he allowed to do that? You're not a monster, Mum,' and she put her hand on Hope's.

Perhaps, Hope thought, she WAS a monster.

A monster.

Hope and Minnie to the Hospital

Three days later, Hope and Minnie sat in the waiting room outside Dr Chandra's office. Hope was convinced people who looked at them knew their whole story, but Minnie reminded her that there had been no pictures of them or any names used as yet in the news. Hope was naturally uncomfortable in hospitals. In fact, she hadn't been back to one for seventeen years. She didn't like anything about them. She still found herself scrutinizing the cleanliness; it was an old habit. Southmead Hospital in Bristol was passing the test — she was impressed. All of those thoughts were distractions, she knew that, as she found herself counting the amount of people who used the hand-sanitizer when they entered the waiting room.

Hope smiled at Minnie, remembering with a jolt why they were here. At the local surgery, the GP had examined Minnie when she went in for her appointment, and was concerned to hear a 'murmur' she didn't like. That, coupled with Minnie's chronic tiredness, had put Minnie on to the fast track for an appointment with Dr Chandra, the most senior cardiologist in the department.

They'd been at the hospital all morning while Minnie had an echocardiogram and an ultrasound scan, and now they were waiting anxiously for the doctor to tell them the results. Hope felt for Minnie. All this on top of the startling news she'd had to deal with in such a short space of time: no wonder her heart was under pressure. Hope considered whether she'd been an utter idiot to reveal all as she did. She could've kept the secret for longer and spared Minnie the hell, but sooner or later, and likely sooner, Minnie would need documents Hope couldn't give her; and she was entitled to know her medical background now that she was pregnant, Hope knew that. Perhaps, though, she'd underestimated the seismic quake of shock that would course through Minnie, culminating in the two of them sitting here, waiting, like this.

Hope squeezed Minnie's hand. ''S OK, li'l Min. 'S gonna be OK. You are mighty, don't forget that.'

'I bloody hope so, and I hope Bean is.'

'Nothing's going to worry her. Little warrior,' Hope said, more as a wish than a certainty.

They were called into the doctor's office, and they sat in two uncomfortable chairs opposite the very tall, smiley man.

'Now then,' he started. Already Minnie liked his kindliness, but she instinctively knew it was the introduction to something tricky. 'As you can probably tell from the speed with which we've reacted, there is a little bit of worry around you, Ms Parker.'

'Minnie, please.'

'Minnie, OK,' he continued. 'Tell me, have you had this shortness of breath and fatigue for a long time, or just recently?'

'Umm, well, I think it's been forever really, but sort of worse recently. I mean, I didn't do sports 'n' stuff at school, I always had tired legs, didn't I,

Mum?' She turned to Hope.

'Yes, yes, you did.'

The doctor continued, 'And did you see anyone about this at the time?'

Minnie looked at Hope, who appeared speechless. Eventually, Hope said, 'No, doctor, and that's my fault. I thought she was just not very sporty, she's more of an arts kind of girl. Happier writing and drawing? So, no, she didn't see any doctor. I'm sorry. I tended to her at home. I had my reasons ...'

'I'm not here to judge you, Mrs Parker,' he said, 'but we need to concentrate hard on your health now, Minnie, because I'm pretty sure you have something called coarctation of the aorta. It means that an important flow of the blood from your heart down to the rest of your body has become very tight, sort of pinched, restricting the blood flow.'

'Right,' said Minnie, in a very small voice indeed.

He continued, although both women were deep in their own respective brain fugs, trying to process all this.

'Your heart has been working very hard,' he said.

It was certainly working very hard right now, Minnie knew that, because it was pounding away like a jackhammer; it felt as though it was trying to exit her chest right then.

'Poor old heart' — he tried levity — 'or rather poor young heart. And THAT is the reason it's going to be all right, Minnie. You are young and strong and your heart is trying to do the best for you and now for your baby as well, so we need to give you all the support we can.'

'OK, yes, please,' Minnie replied in an even smaller, hardly-there voice.

'Yes, please,' echoed Hope, in a definitely-there big voice. A voice that she hoped would underpin all the confidence of this wonderful man who was going to save two lives if he could . . .

Hope didn't want to reveal her anxiety, so while the doctor was explaining, she kept focusing on things, real things in the room, to keep her anchored.

His tatty briefcase on the floor by his desk

The pile of grey cardboard bowls on the shelf

The small yellow bin with 'SHARPS' emblazoned on it

His wide gold wedding ring

Minnie's red trainers

The sun hitting the pillow of the examination bed in the corner

The pleats in the plastic curtain that goes around it

The doctor was still talking. 'We will monitor you very closely, so that your blood pressure is managed, and so that if there WERE to be any heart failure, we could get amongst it immediately. What we want, ideally, is the least invasive process for your baby, and of course for you. You may need serial echocardios like you've had today, but the team will inform you of that, OK?'

FAILURE. Heart failure. The word clung to both Hope and Minnie like a burr to a cardigan.

'Can I . . . go home?' asked Minnie.

'Certainly. We'd want you to rest as much as

possible, and you'll have direct access to me and all the guys here. We will get you through this, Minnie. Now we know what we're dealing with.'

'Is it going to get better, my heart?'

It didn't escape Hope that the question was huge, on every level. Hope stopped breathing . . .

'Well,' said Dr Chandra, 'you see this eye?' He pointed at his right eye. 'It's very beady and it's watching you very closely, and I think we will get this lovely healthy baby born and then we will think about our options when we know how your heart is then.'

He was being careful. Minnie sniffed it, and needed to know more. Now.

'Sorry, doctor, but what do you mean, 'options'?'

'I mean that if your heart feels like it's done its job, we can get you a new one.'

Now Hope's heart also stopped. She was floating in limbo. What had he just said . . . ?

Minnie managed to stutter, 'A *new* one?'

'Yes, a transplant. We can absolutely do that, but, Minnie, listen, that's way down the track. For now, it's working, it doesn't know it should be easier, so it's working hard, like it always has. No need to panic. I'm watching, OK?'

'OK. Yeah, OK,' Minnie replied.

Hope's heart started again.

And breath came out of her.

The doctor continued, 'I'll send all this info in a letter. It's hard to take it all in. Out of interest, has anyone else in the family ever had any heart disease, because this condition can often be inherited, genetic?'

Hope and Minnie looked at each other.

272

Hope jumped in: 'Ah. You see, that's not something we can easily answer, doctor, but I want to tell you why. Do you have five more minutes . . . ?'

Nesting: Hope's Flat

The next months were treading water for Hope and Minnie and Lee. The flat was their haven and their sanctuary to be together, to keep Minnie and Bean safe. A new term was starting and Minnie wasn't at school to begin her final A-level year. Other than her belly growing and some slightly increasing tiredness, she actually felt quite well physically, and had asked her mum if she could at least pop in there to see her mates, but Hope put her foot down. The doc said she should rest, so she would rest. When Hope decided, frankly you didn't argue.

In truth, Hope was feeling increasingly afraid of the consequences of what she'd done. She was angry also. Angry that she was going to miss out on Bean.

She wanted to be the best grammy, to know Bean better than anyone other than her parents. She wanted to have special secret codes with her that were known to just the two of them. She wanted to introduce her to *Toy Story* and *Up* and be there to comfort her when she first saw the Child Catcher in *Chitty Chitty Bang Bang*, and the Other Mother in *Coraline*.

She wanted to make Saturday soup for her with alphabet pasta in it.

She wanted to teach her alternative swear words.

She wanted to braid her hair.

She wanted to read her to sleep.

She wanted to google Captain Paul Cuffee with her.

She wanted to put a plaster on her hurty toe.

She wanted to take her to Center Parcs.

She wanted to apologize to other shoppers in Tesco when Bean ran around; she wanted to say, 'Oops, sorry, she's a wild one, my granddaughter!'

She wanted to count her fingers and toes.

She wanted to dance the reflection of light from the biscuit-tin lid on the walls and make it their own personal fairy.

She wanted to teach her about 'wawa'.

She wanted to shout out 'BUMS!' extra loud any time they were in a quiet place, to make her laugh.

Yes, Hope wanted all that and plenty more, but she wasn't going to get it, not for a long time, it seemed.

Hope had meetings with her officious legal-aid defence lawyer each week to clarify exactly what her defence was going to be when they eventually got into court. There were pre-trial meetings and planning meetings, and further interviews and lots of waiting for Julius's lawyer and the Crown Prosecution Service to decide what the charge was going to be.

Hope had given up her jobs. She wanted to watch Minnie as closely as possible while she could. This pregnancy had to go well. Lee offered to give up his job too, but the Parker family persuaded him not to, and they reassured him that they were all there for support, which they certainly were.

Glory and Ky and Princess came round to cook

275

and play on the PlayStation and help Minnie continue to do all her appliqué and clothes customizing. Nanna Doris brought DVDs (mainly of films she wanted to watch) and old photo albums to browse through with Minnie, to distract her. Her uncles came over and hosted card games with betting for pennies.

It felt strange and normal at the same time. Everyday stuff happening on the surface, whilst life-threatening ill health and life-changing court procedure were chugging on below. Occasionally, Hope would stop to consider it all, lock herself in the bathroom, breathe deep and sob at the enormity of it all, wishing she had someone to share it with, but mostly she just got on with it, moving from one cup of tea to the next, doing her best to keep it normal.

In between those cups of tea, ordinary extraordinary family life was taking place, where Minnie could feel comforted and as safe as she could be in light of the craziness. She had regular hospital appointments, which Hope went to with her. Hope wrote every word down in a notebook so she might better understand the confusing world of medicine.

Hope learnt a lot. The difference between doctors and consultants and surgeons. The difference between the various scans. How the blood pressure and heartbeat are monitored. Hope took every transplant leaflet home and spent hours online, researching the whole organ-donation world, and educating herself about the intricacies of blood groups and tissue-type compatibility and all the sundry complications. She urged everyone in the family to sign up for organ donation, once she realized how understocked the system was. She became a transplant bore. She wanted Minnie to be well informed and positive, but she also knew that time was limited, and she wanted Minnie to have plenty of slobby seventeen-year-old time, whenever she could.

Social services had allocated a support team to Minnie since the news of her discovery was now becoming daily tabloid fodder. No one had yet identified her or Hope, but it wasn't going to be long. Minnie was the top of the pyramid when it came to priorities. She was labelled the 'victim'.

Then came Julius and Anna, her parents, also referred to as 'victims'. Hope wasn't anywhere on the pyramid. She was buried underneath, the lousy 'criminal'.

They knew much more about Minnie's biological parents now. They knew the couple had since divorced. Hope could put names to the sleeping woman on the bed and the snoring man in the chair in that fuggy hot room all those years ago. Minnie rolled these names around in her head. Julius. Anna. They were strangers to her.

★ ★ ★

Minnie was in her PJs one day with Cat curled up on her bed near her. Cat had been off her food recently. When Hope and Minnie returned from a hospital appointment, she was standing in the hallway with another dead Mouse in her jaw. If this was any other cat, it would be a normal sight. Cat catches mouse in garden, kills it and brings the trophy home to show human mother. A conquest. Not this Cat. This Cat was holding the corpse of her companion Mouse, who had simply conked out from old age and natural causes, as had all the descendants of Mouse every eighteen months or so, since the very first one. Cat had not been without a Mouse for five years now, and it looked like this was going to be the last since there were no more babies to raise. Cat had taken to shadowing Minnie everywhere she went. Their bond was stronger than ever; just when Minnie needed it most, she had a purring chum. Hope came in and sat on Minnie's bed, gently shoving Cat over.

'I need to talk to you, Min,' she said.

'OK. But, like, no more huge revelations, OK? I can't deal with it. Like, are you going to tell me you're a man or something? If you are, can you delay it 'til Bean's born? Keep a lid on the stress? I'm really trying to convince Bean she's going to come into a boring, regular family who are just, y'know, a family without dramas, nothing extra. I talk to her all the time.'

'You are going to be such a beautiful mum, Min. Look at you doing it already, looking out for her,' Hope said.

'Yeah, well. You do, don't you, if you love your kid, you know that.' Minnie touched her mum's hand.

'I just want to say a couple of things, Min, that's all. There's going to be a trial, pretty sure of that, so before it all gets out of our control, I want to be sure you know some stuff. First, the request is here for you to meet Anna and Julius. Feels weird even saying their names . . .'

278

'I know.'

'And listen, Min, I've been thinking that you might be avoiding meeting them to sort of spare my feelings . . . and you really don't have to do that. I'm the one who made all the decisions about this. Not you. Not them. So, I am the one who should sit with all the wrongness of it, not you. You are fully entitled — hear me now, FULLY ENTI-TLED — to meet your biological parents. Truly. It's natural curiosity. I am the one who has to deal with who I was, what I did, and what I've become. We are all the result of every choice we make, and I've had years to make friends with what I did. I'm OK with it. I'd even go so far as to say I don't regret it. I really don't. The only remorse I have is for their pain. They lost out on you, and I did that. For that alone, I will hold my hand up, hold my head up, and take whatever's coming my way. But for having you in my life? No regrets. Not one.'

'Oh Mum.' Minnie started to weep.

'I'll cope, Minnie Moo, I will, because look at us: I know what it is to have love, and to give it. I know the sweetness of it. I know now, more than ever, what it's like when love lives in you, and you are the one who's taught me all of it. Little mighty Minnie, full of light and love. You are the best blessing, such a gift, and I'm never going to be sorry you 'n' me built our home, our life together. This was not your secret, not your lie, but it is your life, and you must grab it, Min. Everything about it. They are part of your story. They deserve to know you too. They do. They should feel the power of all the goodness in you, just like all of us who know you do.

279

'And y'know what? I ain't threatened by them. Know that. I am your mother. I always will be. I'm sure of the love, darlin', and I know you are. That's our foundation, isn't it? It's solid. You can rely on it like the air you breathe and the ground you walk on. It won't change. Not going to be toppled. Reinforced. That's us. Like concrete, my love. Going nowhere. Me 'n' you. Heart to heart. The mother line. Unbreakable. Got it, child?'

Minnie was bursting. She was stuffed with love, fed to her for her whole life from this magnificent woman, who never failed to fill her up with nutritious care, and was now making sure she had a delicious pudding of devotion, to be sure she'd eaten her fill. No hunger whatsoever. No need. No question. No want. All truth.

'I'm scared, Mum.'

'I bet.'

'I won't know how to live without you for comfort. You always make it OK.'

'That's my job, sweet cheeks.'

'I don't know them. I'm not from them. I'm from you.'

'Yes. You are. Which is exactly why you will deal with it. Besides, you know the first rule of Wawa club?'

'What?'

'Never doubt the Wawa.'

And with that, Hope underpinned Minnie with her honest and huge mother-love, forever.

280

1 January 2018

Dear Daughter,
Cushah! So today is your eighteenth birthday.
Little Minnie grows up! How did all these years
flow past without me noticing? I feel cheated
that I haven't been able to see you grow into
your adult skin, but it was my choice to go, so
I have no one to blame but myself, and believe
me, I do that all the time.

Do you drive a car yet? I'd love to know. Your
mother and I had an old Honda Civic years
ago. I can recommend them: they might rust, but
they keep going. We brought you home from the
hospital in it, eighteen years ago. I wish I was
the one to teach you how to drive. I am patient
and prepared to die. That is a joke, which is also
not a joke!

Minnie, I am determined to make a plan
to see you sometime soon, but I don't want to
upset Hope or you or anyone you love, so I will
stay here unless I hear from you. I have no idea
whether you have ever seen any of the letters
I've written over the years. I have left that
decision to Hope. It's the least I could do. On
the back of this letter I have written my details
if you should ever want to contact me. I hope
you do, but I will completely understand if you
don't or can't. I expect nothing, but pray for
everything. God willing, one day, we will meet
again.

Once more, api batde, Little One.

From your loving father,
Isaac xx

The Meeting; the Mirrors

Anna could hear Debbie Cheese calling out to her, 'Ready when you are, Anna!' She'd already encouraged her to come, a few times, but there seemed to be no movement from the bedroom.

Debbie knocked gently on the door. 'We really must make a move, Anna. Can I come in?'

She pushed the door open and saw Anna in her bra and pants, glued to the spot in front of the mirror, with sheer panic in her eyes.

'Umm. Look, I don't think I can go after all.' Anna looked firmly at the floor.

'OooKaay,' replied Debbie, 'but why?'

'Because . . . because I don't know how to be a person. I'm about to have the most important meeting in my life. I'm meeting my daughter for the first time. Who the hell is she going to meet? I have no idea. What is she expecting? Someone mumsy in a floral dress? Or a rock chick in a leather jacket? Who am I anyway?'

'You are Anna.'

'Who the hell is that?' she shouted. 'I knew who Julius's bloody wife was. I knew that costume. Anything bland and expensive that I could disappear into the background in. Anything that would allow him to be the peacock up front! It was my job to disabloodyppear!'

On this day Anna had ripped her way through her wardrobe, discarding all the dull things. And

283

there were many: a mountainous pile of personality-sucking beigy-grey unremarkable clobber was soon going to be gracing the rails of the nearest charity shop. To see the fabric slag heap of her past so starkly in front of her, indicating the alarming extent of desuetude her poor personality had fallen into, owing to lack of respect or attention or love, was sobering.

'That' — Anna pointed at the sad pile — 'is the person I've been for ages, got totally stuck in it, but I don't want Florence to meet . . . THAT.'

The two women stood side by side in silence as they looked at the pile.

'Do you like what I'm wearing?' offered Debbie.

'Umm, yes, s'pose so. Looks . . . normal.' Anna clocked that Debbie was in some plain black trousers and a simple shirt with a jaunty cherry design on. Nothing too challenging. Nothing too boring. She was shocked when all of a sudden Debbie started unbuttoning her shirt and pulling down her trousers.

'Right, put these on. We're close enough in size, come on.'

'What! What are you doing? I can' t — '

'Put them on, Anna. You can work out who you are another time. You're not going to miss out on meeting your daughter after eighteen years because of some trousers. Come on. Please.'

Anna hesitated for a couple of seconds. Debbie was now down to her bra and pants too. It was mighty odd, the two of them standing opposite each other like this. Not so odd that it prevented Anna from noticing that Debbie had a very good pink balcony bra on, encasing lovely small full bosoms. Anna jolted herself out of that surprising observation and took Debbie's offer of clothes from her outstretched hand. She clambered into them immediately, while Debbie rooted around in the old boring Anna pile and found the least awful blouse and trousers, and started to re-dress. Within thirty seconds, both of them were looking in the mirror.

Debbie spoke first, indicating Anna's reflection. 'Ideal. Yeah?'

'Yes. I think so. Yes,' Anna agreed, adding, 'But you look sort of awful.'

'I don't give a toss. Let's go.' And with that, Debbie took Anna's arm firmly and led her out of the door with the kind of assurance only someone in the police force can wield, the kind that lets you know, without doubt, that you will be exiting right now. You will.

★ ★ ★

Meantime, Minnie and Lee were also in front of a full-length mirror in the London hotel room the police had organized for them. The meeting was to be held in this same hotel, in a private room, so Minnie and Lee had travelled to London on the train with strict orders to stay in constant contact with Hope, who'd armed them with a list of hospitals and consultants near their hotel. They were only due to be gone for twenty-four hours, but Hope and Minnie hadn't been parted before, and it was strange and difficult for both of them. Especially in these circumstances.

Hope told her, 'I believe, in every fibre of my

285

body, everything I told you, Min. You and I are mum and daughter forever, come what may. And by the way, look 'pon this face, girl, do I look threatened? Nah! Go on now. Do what you gotta do. I'm right behind you, OK?'

But she knew that this meeting was giant.

For everyone . . .

★ ★ ★

Minnie wore a bright green dress that gathered under the breast and flowed out, allowing for the increasing bump that was Bean. She put on a short denim jacket, which she'd customized herself, and tied her mass of curls up into a bright red bandanna so that they were contained around the sides of her head, but blurted out in a messy explosion on top. This was the authentic Minnie. Bold and colourful.

Minnie knew exactly who she was.

Nevertheless, she was nervous. Would she be the person Anna was hoping for? How could she be the person Anna was hoping for, when she didn't know Anna?

Lee was next to her. In every way.

He reassured her, 'Hey, Curls, you look gorgeous — course you do, you're my bird, incha, and I wouldn't be with any ol' minger.'

'Umm, thanks? I think!' She thumped him.

'You'll do all right today, Min, how could she not love you? Everyone who meets you loves you. And listen, if she turns out to be a twat — '

'Like you.' Minnie giggled.

'Like me, then just tip me the wink, and I'll end

286

her with one swift karate chop. I'll put her closer to her God . . . hoyaa, like that. Two seconds tops. On the floor. Never sees life again. Bye, Anna.'

'Yeah, not sure any of that is relieving my stress, to be honest.' Minnie turned back to the mirror.

He put his arms around her from behind, framing her swelling belly with his big builder's hands, and he kissed her ear. 'All I'm sayin' is — it don't matter what she thinks. If she's nice, it's a bonus: you get an extra mum. If she isn't, it's you, me and Bean, just like it always was going to be. No big deal, OK?' he clarified.

She turned to face him and took his face in her hands. 'Yes. Love you.'

'Love you back,' he said.

'Love you front,' she said.

'Love you sideways.'

'I'm ready. You'll wait here, yeah? See you when it's over.' She kissed him gently and turned towards the door.

* * *

Julius was checking his tie in the mirror. He decided it looked great. Really *great*. He had arrived early at the hotel. He had plenty to organize. This was a huge day. For him.

Thripshaw met him in the designated room. 'Morning, Mr Lindon-Clarke. Well, here we are on this suspicious day. A long time coming, I think.'

'Yes, indeed. Longer than it should've been, thanks to you and your dozy team,' Julius snapped back sarcastically as he took off his coat and handed it carelessly to his secretary Kirsty.

'There's no need for that, sir, my team were, and still are, splendid folk, who've gone above and behind to tie up all the loose holes in this case. Yes, mistakes were made. No one can be the suppository of all wisdom, least of all me . . . '

'Never a truer word,' emphasized Julius.

'But,' continued Thripshaw, 'this matter concludes here today, and is a perfect case and point that, with perseverance and justice, it can always turn out to be rosie dosie in the end. Agreed?'

Julius looked at him, aghast. 'When can I see her?'

'We've asked Mrs Lindon-Clarke, sorry, the ex Mrs Lindon-Clarke to join us in here, and then my colleague Debbie will collect the young lady and bring her down. Then I think it's for the best if we leave you three alone together. We don't want to upset the apple tart.'

'No,' replied Julius, heading back to the mirror to reconfirm how impressed he was with himself.

Anna opened the door mid-preen, followed by a huge dollop of awkward. Julius decided to ride roughshod over all of it by advancing on her with his arms open, exclaiming, 'Darling!'

Anna recognized the familiar sophistry. 'Hello, Julius.' She accepted his hug but returned none of it; she didn't feel obliged to, since it was entirely fake.

'Where shall we sit?' she said.

Debbie arranged the sofas so that they were opposite each other and suggested that they should give Florence her space on one, and that the two of them should sit together on the opposite one.

288

It was good thinking, but Julius was distracted by his phone and he kept nipping out into the hall to answer it. Anna tried not to mind, but she did. She really really did. Eventually, she had to pipe up.

'Julius. Please turn your phone off, and come and sit down. We are about to meet her for the first time in eighteen years. For God's sake!'

Julius was surprised. He was about to initiate the customary ruckus in which his need to be alpha would drive the quarrel, but he suddenly realized that he was no longer married to her, therefore had zero power any more. It wouldn't matter if he won an argument. He compromised and turned his phone to silent.

They sat quietly for a minute or so as Debbie cleared the room out, asking Kirsty and Thrip-shaw to leave.

Debbie turned to them both. 'Are you ready?'

Julius and Anna nodded.

'OK, I'll be back with her in two ticks,' said Debbie as she left the room, sliding a sly wink of support to Anna, unseen by Julius.

The room was still and silent.

Anna didn't want to, but she knew she had to look at Julius. For a fleeting second, they locked eyes and a ghost of a memory passed between them. They had, after all, made this person who was about to come through the door. There had once been . . . something . . . together. Any whisper of rare vulnerability disappeared from his face the moment the door handle turned.

They both looked at the door. Debbie came in first, and in her hand was a hand. Then an arm.

Then she was there.

Anna gasped. The beauty of her. The light.

Here she was. Her daughter.

Minnie froze to the spot just inside the door. She couldn't take her eyes off Anna. Something in her felt profoundly connected instantly.

Julius was the first to clumsily break the magic mother-line moment.

He bellowed, 'Florence! Come and give your dad a big hug!'

Minnie's brain was thrown into complete confusion. Who was 'Florence'? Who was 'dad'?

This felt like an assault. Anna recognized immediately that she was floored, and put her arm out to prevent Julius from lunging forward.

Instead, the ever-sensitive Debbie led Minnie to the sofa and indicated for her to sit down, which she just about managed on her jelly-wobbly legs. Never had she felt so entirely other-worldly. The whole room and everyone in it seemed surreal.

Debbie crept out, closing the door behind her.

The three sat there, looking at each other, drinking it all in. The air was thick with difficult.

Anna spoke, eventually. 'What would you like us to call you?'

'Florence, of course!' blurted Julius. 'That's her name!'

'Shh, Julius,' Anna interrupted, the lioness in her emerging in defence of her cub. She turned back to Minnie. 'Please help us to know what you would like to be called?'

'Well,' replied Minnie, speaking for the first time in this strange room, 'I'd like you to call me by my name. Minnie.'

'What?' he puffed. Anna put her hand up to shush him.

'Of course. Minnie. It's actually a lovely name, it suits you so well,' she said, smiling.

'Um, thanks,' Minnie said, trying to be nice.

Then she didn't know what else to say, so Anna came to the rescue.

'Can I just say, Minnie, I can't begin to know how this must all be for you. It's blummin' weird for me, for us, so it must be a hundred times that for you. None of us know how to do this, so forgive us if we get it a bit wrong, yes?'

Julius looked puzzled. He wasn't going to get it wrong. What did she mean?

Minnie was captivated by Anna's voice. It was softer, posher than she'd imagined. It was different. And lovely. Minnie liked that Anna looked her directly in the eyes, not flinching for a second. Julius, on the other hand, seemed fidgety. He was moving about in his seat, restlessly, illustrating his embarrassment.

Minnie had seen his face already in the newspaper. She had scrutinized it closely. His features were markedly different to the West Indian men she knew in her family. He was darker, and his features were more sharply defined. He was clearly of African descent, more like Captain Paul Cuffee in the beloved picture. This differentiation had always confused Minnie. Her uncles and her grandmother were essentially Jamaican, but they always reminded her that they too were Africans originally, way back when. They were proud of that. Their faces, though, bore the traces of all the different influences that had been evident in

291

Jamaica throughout history, including Indian, Chinese and Taino Arawak people. It was this melting pot of variety that produced the slightly lighter skin and almond eyes of the Jamaicans that Minnie knew.

Now she was looking at an African face that was her direct genetic inheritance, and at Anna's Nordic skin and the whole pearliness of her, a lot about what Minnie saw in the mirror every day started to make sense. Until Hope exploded her world, Minnie had never questioned any part of her identity. The Absent African was the key for her, and she'd never seen Isaac, so she assumed that any unanswered questions about how she looked were to be answered in him.

Yet here they were, her biological parents. The two sets of atoms and genes and flesh and blood and everything that had actually made her. It was overwhelming.

'Of course,' answered Minnie, 'it's all new.'

Anna's heart might have jumped out of the cherry-patterned blouse and straight into Minnie's, she felt such a rush of love for her. Anna had no doubt she would connect with Florence, now Minnie — how could she not? But what she had not predicted was the utter beauty of her, making her completely irresistible. Perhaps, Anna thought, she was seeing herself in Minnie. Was it wishful or vain to consider that? Was it selfish? It was all she could do not to throw herself on to Minnie and gather her up; she so wanted to, but she knew it would be foolish to scare her. She wanted to tread carefully, although she longed for touch.

Anna said, 'With time, Minnie, I hope you'll

292

come to know us, and we'll know you, but only in your own time, OK? We're not going to hurry anything. It will all be at your pace. You are in charge.'

'Thank you. Yes,' Minnie replied gratefully.

'I can't wait to show you the couple of pictures we have of you when you were only a few minutes old. You were so beautiful, so perfect. You ARE still . . .'

'Oh my God. I didn't think about that . . . WOW,' Minnie answered, her smile a reflection of Anna's.

'We've only got two,' Julius interjected, 'because, of course, we didn't have you long before —'

'Julius!' Anna gave him a shot across the bows, but he ploughed on like the bull he was.

' — before you were stolen,' he said, emphasizing the last word, throwing it at Minnie like a dart. Julius had the moral bit between his teeth now. 'I'm so happy to see you again, Florence — '

'Minnie,' Minnie corrected him.

'Well, you're Florence to me. That's what we named you, and you ARE our daughter, after all, but excuse me, I will take time to get used to that name. But the most important thing to take away from this meeting today . . .'

MEETING? Anna was starting to boil. He needed to shut up. He was in danger of tipping the whole thing up, the fool.

'. . . the most important thing,' he continued, taking the floor, 'is that you are back now, in your rightful place, with us. Obviously, there's a lot to sort out, not least what the consequences are for Ms Parker — '

'My mum,' Minnie corrected him.

'For Ms Parker, who, I'm afraid, committed a

293

very serious crime indeed. I mean, in truth, for all these eighteen long years, Anna here has been wilfully DENIED that chance to be your mother, which she was so longing for. As was I wanting to be your father . . .'

Shut up, Julius, you fake. Anna was seething. She could see Minnie starting to recoil, she had to interject, 'Julius, now is not the time.'

'Well, when, Anna?' he blustered on. 'It's only fair on Florence that she gets the truth . . .'

'Listen, Julius, please,' Anna pleaded with him in desperation as she felt the moment collapsing under the weight of his clomping boorishness, 'the fact is that ALL of us stand in need of kindness and forgiveness here, except Minnie. She is the one shining truth. She is innocent of anything. Please tread carefully . . .'

'I am guilty of nothing, Anna,' he snapped. 'How dare you?'

Minnie saw the giant fissure between them start to physically crack open in front of her. She was unfamiliar with this jarring type of squabble. She only had one parent. Hope didn't argue with anyone except her, and even that was forgivable, always. This was different. It was spiteful.

'Look,' said Julius, standing up. Minnie thought for a moment that he was going to calm the situation and maybe say something clever and kind to make it all right. That's what fathers did, after all. Maybe he was going to come through heroically?

He continued, 'I think we need to just calm down. I'd like to suggest that we get the interview and the pictures out of the way, and perhaps then

294

we can get a nice afternoon tea or ice cream?'

'Sorry, Julius.' Anna jumped on this immediately. 'What pictures? What interview? What the actual fuck are you talking about, you git?'

Minnie was shocked. Perhaps Anna wasn't so soft or so posh after all? But she was glad Anna seemed to be sorting it.

Julius replied, 'I just thought it would be a lovely story — to tell everyone, after all these years of asking for their help to find her, to show that Florence is back where she belongs. The guys are all set up in another room up the hall.'

'I can't believe you'd do this; you are beyond belief. You're a venal cur. That's what my father called you when we split up and he's right. You are toxic, Julius!' Anna shouted at him.

Minnie stood up. Anna and Julius stopped squabbling for a moment.

She opened her mouth to speak to both of them. 'I am Minnie. I'm not a story. I'm a person. Who is leaving now, to go back to my mum, who knows how to love me.'

And with that, she left.

Anna cried after her, 'Minnie! Please!' Then she turned on Julius, all guns blazing. 'Why, and may I emphasize the FUCK, would you do that? You've ruined it, just like you ruin everything. Oh God, I've lost her again, and I didn't even get to touch her!' And with that, Anna started to weep.

By now, Thripshaw had entered the room, having heard the furore. He spoke directly to Julius, who was pacing up and down in exasperation.

Thripshaw didn't hold back. 'Well, Mr Lindon-Clarke, that went well, didn't it? Truly, I've met some pricks in my time, but you, sir, are the full cactus.'

The Trial, London

Hope was on the phone to Minnie, in the fuggy anteroom where she was waiting with her lawyer for the trial to start. The couple of weeks since Minnie had met her birth parents hadn't been easy, and now this.

'Hi, Min. How you doing this morning?'

Minnie's voice was wobbly on the phone. 'Hey, Mum. Oh God, I wish I was there with you. This is so wrong.'

'I know, but look, I can handle this; you need to look after you and Bean right now. What did Dr Chandra say?'

'He wants me to stay put here in the hospital for another couple of nights, just to get my breathing sorted. They're doing regular blood-pressure checks and I've got another echo this afternoon, but I'm OK and Bean's doing OK, and Lee's here. He brought me a Happy Meal in from Maccy D's. I've got a free toy. Couldn't be happier,' she lied, then faltered, 'Oh Mum, I can't believe it . . .'

'I know, Min, I know. But honestly, it's best you're not here anyway. There are tons of press outside. Cameras flashing everywhere. That's me in the papers now, I reckon. They've got pics of the Monster at last.'

'Yeah, the Monster. That's you all right.'

'I have to go now, Min. Remember everything I've told you. Stay gentle and keep in touch with me, OK?'

'OK.'

'And Min . . . '

'Yeah?'

'I'm sorry.'

'I know, Mum.'

'Love you.'

'Love you too.'

'Wawa forever.'

'Wawa for always.'

'Bye.'

'Bye.' And she was gone.

Hope took a very deep breath. She didn't want to be in court in London. She wanted to be at the hospital in Bristol with her daughter.

Hope had instructed her lawyer that she wanted to enter a guilty plea. They'd been discussing it all for weeks, and her counsel were advising caution and patience in the hope that they might be able to mitigate in her defence in two ways.

Firstly, that allowance should be made for her state of mind when she took the baby, but considering that she had kept 'the baby' for eighteen years afterwards, they felt she would be on shaky ground with that.

Secondly, they believed that they could argue that Minnie/Florence (Julius had insisted she be referred to as the latter throughout the trial) had never experienced violence or cruelty or sexual assault, so that, in effect, her upbringing had been relatively normal, and that, in fact, there was a case to be made that she might well even have had a WORSE childhood had she remained with her original parents. Who had since divorced.

Hope had considered this very seriously as it

could possibly help to reduce her sentence considerably; also, Minnie's account of how broken the relationship was between Anna and Julius, as evidenced in their meeting with her, was sadden-ing. Julius didn't sound like a kind or good man. Hope believed it was absolutely true that Minnie had been better off with her.

BUT.

Minnie's description of Anna prevented Hope from using this argument. Anna sounded like a decent person. Minnie liked her. Hope did steal her baby. She couldn't add this dire insult to the already deleterious injury. Woman to woman, despite the evident benefit to herself, Hope couldn't allow her team to use this argument in her defence.

She said a resolute no.

So, because she'd not pleaded guilty at the earliest opportunity, Hope missed out on the larger reduction on her sentence.

But Hope was fully ready to pay for what she'd done. And pay she would, if Julius had any say in the matter. He was ravenous for revenge.

Julius had wanted to arrive at court with Anna, hand in hand, but Anna refused to continue the façade, so she arrived very early and sat drinking endless awful coffees until it was time to go in. Everyone had agreed that neither Anna nor Julius would be called to testify, but that their victim statements could be used by the prosecution.

Julius wasn't happy that he was going to miss out on his chance to rail and shine, so he decided to make the most out of his arrival. When his car first pulled up outside the court, he was a bit early, so there was only a smattering of press present. He instructed the driver to go once more around the block, so that his entrance might be more impactful, and when he eventually climbed out of the car, he had his best pained face on, and kept claiming, 'Guys, seriously, this is a difficult day, both Anna and I would appreciate it if you respected our privacy . . . ?' He was more than a bit miffed when they did just that, and backed off, trickling away one by one.

* * *

Inside the sombre building, Julius hunted for Anna, and found her drinking thin coffee and trying to hide in a corner. He saw her across the large main hallway, and he started to approach her. Just as he came close, help loomed into view, in the shape of Inspector Debbie Cheese, who'd agreed to stick by Anna all day.

'Morning, Julius,' Debbie said, too loudly, too cheerfully, heading him off at the pass. Julius tried to ignore her.

'Anna, may I speak with you?'

Ignoring Debbie was akin to ignoring a tsunami. Impossible.

'I'm afraid Anna is currently out of the office, can I help at all?' she replied as she stood directly between them.

'Don't be ridiculous, let me talk to her . . . '

'Perhaps you didn't quite hear me? Anna is out, unavailable, engaged, occupied or dead to you. Choose any or all from the above. Either way, you can't speak to her right now, capiche?'

Anna felt a mammoth wave of gratefulness

300

wash over her.

This woman was stupendous. She leant out from behind Debbie to see what Julius's face was doing. It was puffing and dark red. His eyes were wide with outrage, but he was clearly too gobsmacked to speak.

Debbie turned back to Anna. 'Come on, it's time to go in.' And with that she nodded to indicate that they should move away.

Anna stood and, contrary to everything her manners dictated, she walked away from Julius without a backward glance. She took Debbie's arm for courage, and they went into Courtroom No. 1, and sat down on a green leather bench side by side.

Hope, since she was firmly pleading guilty today, was anticipating some degree of leniency. The trial would not be as huge and awful as it could have been, though she was nonetheless shaking when she was led in.

As Hope entered the courtroom, her life, which ordinarily travelled at normal living speed, suddenly switched to the kind of pace at which treacle travels. Even her blinking was slow. She felt as if she'd been drugged with Rohypnol. She could hear her own sluggish breathing, and her head was so heavy, swivelling in slow motion on her neck, as she took in everything to her left and right. She was acutely aware of the smell of musty suits and recently applied perfume and wood. She had chosen to wear a smart navy-blue trouser suit with a soft yellow blouse beneath which fastened at the side of the neck with a large bow. She wanted to be smart, look businesslike, so that no one could accuse her of being sloppy or crazy. She wore heels and this was the main sound she could hear as she entered, her heels clomping on the old parquet wood of the courtroom floor.

Clomp. Clomp.

All heads turned to see the Monster. She wondered if she might have sprouted horns maybe? She felt as though she was looking out of a mask called her face, so she couldn't be sure how it appeared. She knew her breathing was heavy. Maybe she was actually breathing fire from grotesque flared nostrils after all?

She sat in the dock with a police officer beside her, and her legal team in front. She scoured the surroundings. Hope gasped when she immediately saw that Doris and Glory were there. She'd instructed them to stay away, but of course they'd ignored her. They were clinging to each other, and trying desperately to beam some encouragement at her. Hope hated witnessing their fear.

She mouthed, ''S OK. Love you.'

Her mother and sister smiled back, feebly.

There were plenty of strangers there. Press, and nosey parkers. Higher up, there was a row of seats in front of a huge window, so the outlines of the bodies in those seats were in silhouette, but she could tell the row was full. This case had caused a stir, no doubt about that.

Hope's nervous reconnaissance around the courtroom ended when, after scouring the benches eagle-like for that one person, she saw her.

She saw Anna for the first time.

Sitting one seat away from Julius, with the policewoman in between. Hope couldn't stop looking at Anna, and Anna was returning the laser gaze. Hope expected to see hatred there, but Anna's face was full of worry; she even attempted the tiniest smile. Hope felt overcome with gratitude that there was clearly mercy in this woman. That was going to make whatever came next a bit more bearable.

Julius, however, was glowering at her. He looked as though he was bursting to have his say. He looked like an over-filled balloon, shiny, tight and fit to explode.

Hope had never been in a room such as this. She'd never before been the object of so much unwelcome attention, and although she felt humiliated and uncomfortable, she remained calm.

The strange slow motion she experienced jolted into real time the second they all stood up as the judge arrived.

The guilty plea was entered and Hope had to confirm that was what she wanted to do.

The judge then explained that she'd read all of the relevant documents, and that she had to decide if this case was one of child abduction, or the more serious one of kidnapping and false imprisonment.

When the bun fight of defence and prosecution statements was finally over, Hope's defence pointed out:

- She was very young and in a terrible heightened state of shock when it happened
- She had no previous convictions
- She had fully admitted her crime to 'Florence'

- She had volunteered the truth to the police (albeit eighteen years later)

The prosecution countered with:

- 'Florence' had never consented to being taken
- She'd been kept in ignorance all these years
- She'd been taken by fraud
- The impact on her original parents was considerable

Hope listened in a daze. She sat up sharply when the three 'Victims' Personal Statements' were read out.

Julius's was full of vitriol and drama. In it, he claimed:

That baby thief not only stole our darling little newborn daughter, she stole our happiness and any chance we had of a contented and robust marriage. She ruined us.

Anna's contained:

Although I have spent the last eighteen years looking for my daughter and it has been very difficult to live through this, I find comfort in the fact that I now know she has always been lovingly cared for. 'Florence's' was full of:

I need to state that my mother, Hope, is the kindest, most nurturing person I know. There isn't a better human in the world. I was shocked when I first found out about Anna and Julius, of course, and I didn't want to believe it of her, but there is no doubt whatsoever that my heart is my mother's. I have no intention of being Florence. I am now, and always will be, Minnie.

Anna was weeping and Julius was apoplectic with rage. He hated that he had to remain silent. And listen to all this inconvenient truth. She'd stolen their baby, for God's sake!

Eventually the judge turned to address Hope.

'Ms Parker,' she started, 'in the absence of any real mitigation for the terrible thing you did all those years ago, a young woman's lifetime ago, and in light of the fact that no trace can be found of your partner in this crime — who I am led to believe disappeared back home to Africa and hasn't been heard of since — I am compelled to classify yours as a 'grave crime', that of kidnapping and false imprisonment.

The maximum sentence for this is life . . . '

The courtroom gasped. Doris let out a woeful moan. Julius clenched his fists.

'However, having considered your defence and heard the statements, and with a partial credit for your guilty plea, I am reducing that to eighteen years. One for each of the child's life. This very sorry case is dismissed.'

BOOM.

Hope always knew she would do time in prison. She hadn't thought that it would be that much.

The whole courtroom stood up as the judge and other officials filed out. Hope looked up at the very ornate ceiling as if she might find some support there for her breaking heart. The police officer tapped her on the shoulder to lead her away, and as she turned her head, her eye caught sight of a figure silhouetted against the big window. He was standing still whilst all around were moving past him to leave. She blinked against the light.

Who was that familiar man?

Then she knew.

Older. Wider.

It was Isaac.

Anna and Hope: April

Anna sat at the table, waiting. She was extremely shaken. She'd never been in a place like this before, and she'd not ever imagined she would experience the strangeness of the last thirty minutes, where she'd been detained in the prison's visitor centre while they double-checked the validity of her Visiting Order, requested that she put all personal belongings in a locker, checked her passport for ID and took her photo and fingerprints. She was then patted down back and front and left feeling as if she were herself a convict, and somehow humiliated.

The visitors' room was large and grim with neon lights, plastic tables and chairs, and a joyless tea bar at one end.

Anna had been warned to use the toilet in the visitors' centre, which she had, but she was now acutely aware of needing it again. It was only nerves. She could cope.

She looked around. There were visitors waiting at only three other tables. That struck Anna as possibly the saddest sight she'd seen for years. This prison held over a thousand female inmates. Only four of them would have a visit today.

At least she knew Hope was willing to see her, because it was Hope who initially had to fill in the Visiting Order. She could've blankly refused, but she didn't. So, here Anna was, waiting for her to come through the door.

307

Eventually, when she did, it wasn't the momentous occasion Anna anticipated. Something about the surroundings dulled everything.

A woman came through the door.

The woman was Hope. That's all.

She came over to Anna's table. Anna stood up.

'Hello,' said Hope, nervously.

'Hello,' said Anna, nervously.

They sat down on opposite sides of the table. Two prison officers watched them and everyone else, from a distance.

'Thank you for letting me come,' Anna said quickly. 'I wasn't certain you would.'

'Oh. YES. I definitely wanted this . . . moment,' Hope replied, rather surprised. She felt she ought to be the one thanking Anna.

'I suddenly don't know what to say. I had a million questions. I don't know what any of them are now. It sort of . . . doesn't matter.'

'It does matter, Anna. I took your baby. I should answer anything you want to know.'

'I want to know . . . not why . . . I think I know that . . . but why you didn't give her back?'

'I couldn't give her back. She was entirely mine in minutes. I loved her. I love her so completely, it would've been as unthinkable as stealing a baby. So I didn't think about it. I let it all be normal. It was normal. She grew up in my family, they are her family, they love her and she loves them.'

'But I loved her, Hope.'

'Yes. I know. I had to forget that. I had to decide that my love was better than yours. That my home was better than yours. Trumped it.'

Anna was dumbfounded; all she could do was

308

stare at Hope. Looking right into her.

Hope's eyes brimmed with tears. 'I'm sorry.'

Anna knew that Hope meant it, that this was the most real apology Hope would ever make and that, should she accept it, it would be the most important allowance both she and Hope would ever know in their respective lifetimes.

The two women were utterly conjoined in this key decision. It was a testing moment of supreme forgiveness that could open a future up for both of them.

Anna's hurt was ancient, familiar, righteous and hard to let go of. How ironic that her emotional skeleton was made of pain, the very stuff that would not support her — it couldn't. Pain is not galvanizing, it's corrosive, so she would eventually rust. It was already happening and she knew it. All the parts of her held together by pain were deteriorating. She needed new reinforcement if she was going to claim her future without alcohol or sleeping pills or fear or endless crying.

Anna needed to bestow this forgiveness.

And mean it.

'The sad truth is that it's probably true. Your home may well have been better than mine,' she said, 'but that didn't give you the right to steal my happiness. She was my way out. Without her I was lost again. Just like before her. I got stuck eighteen years ago when you took her . . . but I'm not stuck any more, Hope. I'm here, in front of you. And, thank you, God or whoever makes love happen, I don't hate you. Not at all. I'm grateful to you. Not for taking her. Not that. But for raising her in love. So, here's the thing, I can forgive you,

Hope, but you have to help me.'

'Help you?' Hope was confused.

'Help me to know her. She's related to me, but she has a relationship with you. Of course. May I have your permission to build a relationship with her, if she wants it?'

Hope knew, in that moment, that Anna was remarkable. A rightful mother. She reached out over the table and touched Anna's hand. The guard shook her finger. Hope retracted her hand.

She said, 'She definitely wants it, Anna. She really liked you when you met. Julius worried her — I'm not going to lie . . .'

'I know, but she can take or leave as much of him as she likes. He's not a bad man, he's just fantastically self-centred. Harmless really, so long as you keep a distance . . . He's like a budgie: loads of talk, until it sees a mirror.'

Hope burst out laughing at that. So did Anna, who said, 'Can I buy you a coffee?'

'Yes, please,' said Hope, 'and a biscuit, please.'

'Just one?'

'Yep. I had an snackident this morning.'

'What?'

'Y'know, when you inadvertently scoff a whole packet of custard creams when you only intended to have the one? That was my week's allowance . . .'

Anna smiled broadly. She liked Hope. How did this happen? She actually LIKED her.

When Anna returned to the table with the coffees and many biscuits, Hope had some things to say.

'Look, Anna, you say you need my help. Well, I

will do everything I can for you, truly, but I need your help too.'

'Anything,' Anna offered. And meant it.

'I don't want Min to visit me. She's not so well at the moment. She's got this weird thing called coarctation of the aorta. It means — '

'I know what it means. Julius had it as a kid. It was corrected. Shit, poor Minnie.'

'Right, yes, that explains a lot. You know she's having a baby?'

'Yes.'

'So she needs to stop stressing herself out thinking about coming here; she needs to stay at home with Lee and rest. She could get into serious trouble with it as the pregnancy goes on. My mum's there, and her auntie, but . . . she could do with a mum? Can you keep an eye out? And maybe be there when Bean is born?'

'Bean?'

'Yeah, I know.' Hope chuckled.

''S cute.'

'Yeah. I'm thinking that I never want Bean to come here. See me like this. But anyway, listen, can you? Be there? And let me know how she really is? Everyone's fudging it at the moment, protecting me. I don't need that.'

'You want me to be her mum for you?'

'Yes.'

'There is literally nothing I want more,' Anna replied quietly. 'You can rely on me, Hope. I will take the best care of her I can. I'm not experienced like you, but I will do my very best — know that.'

'I know already. Thank you. I can do this

311

because of you.'

It was a truth, an endless sureness.

A perfect forgiveness.

Mother to mother.

'You will never regret it,' said Hope. 'You made an extraordinary ray. There's no one like her.'

★ ★ ★

To leave Hope there was a dreadful wrench.

Hope was strong. Hope was courageous.

But how does anyone deal with what she was going to face now for so long? It wasn't so much the incarceration, it was the primal tear away from Minnie that would be so crushing.

Her words rang in Anna's ears as she left: 'I can do this because of you . . . '

As Anna left the prison, she felt elated and perturbed. For the first time in eighteen years, she knew her purpose and was determined to fulfil it. For Minnie, for Hope, for Bean and for herself.

Minnie in Hospital

As per Hope's request, Anna immediately contacted Minnie after her visit to the prison, and she was so glad she did, because Minnie was in trouble. Minnie had been admitted to hospital at twenty-eight weeks pregnant. She'd collapsed at home the night before Hope's trial, but hadn't wanted to tell her. She'd given Hope a version of the truth on the phone, but omitted to tell her the whole truth. Not the truth, the whole truth and nothing but the truth, as Hope would've sworn in court. Instead, a bit of the truth. Enough for Hope to be informed but not to further burden her, because, after all, what could she do?

Anna went to see Minnie in the hospital. After fairly awkward, tearful hugs with Doris and Glory and Lee, they were left alone together in the small room where Minnie was being closely monitored by Dr Chandra and his team.

Anna said, 'I'm sorry it was so awful when we last met, so sorry; we could have handled it all so much better.'

'It's OK,' Minnie replied, 'it wasn't you, it was . . .'

'Dickhead Dad,' Anna finished her sentence, and Minnie laughed, although it sort of hurt to do so. Minnie was hooked up to various machines monitoring her heart and checking every aspect of her health.

'How are you, Minnie?'

'Yeah, OK, bit scared. Wish it wasn't like this, not really sure how it's going to go. My heart is only just coping. I don't want Bean to have any distress. I don't want Mum to have any more distress . . . Oh, sorry . . . I mean . . .'

'No, that's right, Minnie. She is your mum. I know that. Call me Anna, that's just fine.'

'Oh, OK, thanks. Easier. Yeah.'

'Of course. Look at you trying to look after everyone, Minnie. Well, I'm here to tell you, direct from your mum's mouth and your mum's heart, that you have to stop that, and ONLY think about you and that little Bean. The rest of us will cope. Your mum has asked me to be here for you, if you want me to?'

'Yes, yes, I want you to. I really do, please.'

'I don't want to be anywhere else, Minnie. I've got your mum in my pocket; we're both here for you. But there is a condition . . .'

'What? What d'you mean?'

'She wants to know everything, Minnie. Being kept from the truth, the reality of it all, is what's wrecking her. She's a big girl, seriously, she can cope with anything true; she can't manage lies any more. She's had a lifetime, your lifetime, of that. She's exhausted from it. Do her a favour and let me include her on EVERYTHING, yes? Not filtered, not edited. She needs to be part of it for real.'

Minnie's beautiful face started to crumple. Lee, who had been standing sentry outside, saw Minnie's concern, and rushed in, demanding, 'Hey, hey, what's going on? You can't come in here,' he said pointedly to Anna, 'and be upsetting her, for

314

God's sake!'

'No, hon' — Minnie took his hand — 'no, you've got it wrong. Mum's asked her. It's OK. It's OK.'

Lee looked between the two of them and trusted that all was in fact well.

'Yep, you really are the marvellous chap Hope told me you were, Lee. She's pretty much right about everything, isn't she?'

'Umm . . . yeah!' Minnie chimed in. 'Except she did steal a baby. She ain't no angel. None of us are.'

'None of us. True,' Anna easily agreed, 'but I'm going to be the human bridge between you and her, so that you can get on with bringing this baby here safely, and not worrying about anybody or anything else. Want that, Minnie?'

'Yep. I want that, Anna. Yes. Thanks.'

'I'm here now. For anything you want. It's my privilege. Now, what's first up? What d'you need?'

'Umm . . .' Minnie thought a moment. 'Oreo cookies?'

'You are your mother's daughter, darling, you really are.'

★ ★ ★

Anna stayed at a little boutique hotel in Bristol and was with Minnie whenever she wanted over the next week, filling in the gaps where Doris and Glory couldn't be there, or when Lee had to be at work. She watched everything very closely, and noted down all the medical details of every step the team took, every decision, every bit of advice,

315

and she relayed it all to Hope in phone calls whenever she could. Hope didn't miss out on a single detail, and she sent messages to be relayed back to Minnie. Sometimes, they were wawa messages. Anna retold them exactly as directed and never once questioned it. She knew it was their exclusive club, their secret code, and she didn't presume to interfere.

Anna's most prized moments in amongst the chaos and tension of the hospital procedure carrying on all around were when Minnie would nod off, which she often did. Hosting her racing heart was exhausting. It was in these sleepy moments that Anna nabbed her moments of joy. Watching her sleep, stroking her hair, holding her hand. All the little things she'd ached for with her stolen daughter, over the long and painful years. Little things that meant everything.

One time, Anna herself fell asleep holding Minnie's hand. She only woke when she felt Minnie move. Minnie was awake seconds before Anna and saw what was happening. She smiled at Anna. It was OK. It was comforting. Baby steps.

Anna was about to leave the hospital late one night when, as she passed the nurses' station, she heard a man asking for directions to Minnie's room.

'I'm here to see Minnie Parker, please,' the man said, very formally.

He had an accent which caught Anna's ear.

African, undoubtedly.

Anna hung back.

The nurse pointed towards Minnie's room. As he passed Anna, the tall handsome man with the high forehead and polished ebony skin exchanged a cursory glance with her. Anna saw the flash of green lightning in his right eye. Sudden green in the dark dark brown. He walked past her, towards Minnie's room.

Anna decided to double back. She needed to know if this stranger was friend or foe.

He approached the door to Minnie's room, and hesitated.

He was looking through the glass at her. Then he knocked lightly and went in.

Anna approached the door and saw Minnie look up at him.

'Dad,' she said, 'you've come!'

'I'm here,' said Quiet Isaac, 'I'm here.'

Anna backed away slowly to let them be together.

So, this was the Absent African.

Returned.

Anna's heart plummeted. Was she about to lose her daughter again?

The Birth

As Minnie drifted in and out of sleep and worry, she wondered if she would always remember the safety she felt when she saw Lee's lovely face as she woke up.

'Hello, Curls? Still in bed bein' a lazy mare?'

A few days later, everything changed for Minnie. As Bean grew inside her, even though Minnie was resting, the strain on her heart became impossible for her to withstand.

Minnie was desperate to walk around, but she became frighteningly breathless and it was obvious some action had to be taken. It was suddenly urgent.

Dr Chandra asked for the whole family to gather in Minnie's room, with the machines beeping around them. Glory, Doris, Lee and Anna were there, and just as the doctor was about to speak, the door opened and Quiet Isaac stepped in. Minnie smiled and said, 'This is my dad, everyone.'

'Ah,' said Dr Chandra, 'so you are the chap who had the coarctation corrected as a kid?'

'Umm. No,' replied Isaac calmly.

'No,' Minnie butted in, 'that's the other one, the biological, what'you call it, genetic one. This is my real dad.'

Isaac beamed.

'OK, got it,' said Dr Chandra, and he went on to explain that this situation with Minnie's heart could not continue, for her sake or for Bean's

318

safety, so they wanted to take her down to theatre for a caesarean section right now. He would be there, watching how Minnie's heart responded. Lee would be allowed in, and obviously the obstetric team would be there to deliver the baby. All others would have to wait up here on the ward, and would be informed of everything.

Dr Chandra looked Minnie directly in the eye and said, 'We're going to get this baby born, Minnie. You need to trust us: it might be a bumpy ride, your poor tired heart is working too hard for both of you, and we have to help it now.'

'I know. And I trust you. Thank you,' Minnie replied, obviously terrified.

'Right, let's get going,' Dr Chandra said purposefully as he left the room.

'Oh shit,' said Minnie, the second he was out of the door, 'this is it, this is full-on wawa.'

There was a clucking flurry of 'You'll be fine' and 'See you when Bean's here' and eventually Anna and Isaac were the last two to leave; they both hovered near her, reluctant to go.

'Thanks, Dad. Thanks . . . Anna,' said Minnie.

'I love you,' said Anna.

'And I love you,' said Isaac.

'Me too. Tell Mum what's happening, yeah?' Minnie said breathily. It was getting more difficult for her to breathe by the minute.

'Absolutely,' confirmed Anna as she and Isaac left the room whilst the team buzzed around Minnie, getting her ready for surgery.

Lee's mouth was dry with fear as the nurses gowned him up for the most astonishing moment of his young life. He had no jokes in his stockpile to suit this serious situation. 'Um, yeah. Put this on. Yeah. It's time. Yeah. Put arms in. Tie it up. Yeah,' was all he could manage in his terror.

The next couple of hours were extremely tense. Upstairs on the ward in the dayroom, the family sat in huddles trying to comfort each other and stay calm. It was an unfortunate but welcome opportunity for Doris and Glory to talk to Isaac and know him. Anna did all the coffee runs and fussed around them all, until eventually she had the chance to sit quietly with Isaac.

'I owe you an apology so big it's impossible to make,' Isaac said.

'Hope has told me all about you and what you did, Isaac. I understand it. I can't say I approve, but I do understand . . . and . . . Look, we're here now. It doesn't matter any more. This does.'

'I have struggled to make it right with myself and my God for many long years, Anna. It means everything for you to say that. Everything.'

'We need to just be the best parents we can be for now,' said Anna.

Isaac nodded, and whispered, 'Being here, waiting for a baby. It feels familiar. I can't say I'm not unafraid. It didn't go so well once upon a time . . . ' Isaac was wringing his hands.

'Oh Isaac. Of course, yes, Minnie. The first Minnie.'

'Yes. I will never forget how . . . small . . . and . . . still she was. Our little daughter. Sleeping. She didn't ever know us, know how much we loved her, not like this Minnie. She knew. She knows.'

'Yes, she surely does,' Anna said. 'Maybe you can think of that time back then as a sort of scar.

It's still there, evidence of something tragic that happened, so that you won't forget it, or forget her. But you are allowed to heal, Isaac.'

'Yes. Yes,' he said, fighting back tears.

'And you are here for this Minnie. Your . . . daughter. I saw her face when she saw you: she lit up. You've shown her devotion and courage in coming. And listen, she will be OK . . . and so will Bean. I'm her mother too, and I say so, so IT WILL BE SO. Get it?' Anna said in her bossiest voice, so wanting to believe it.

Isaac chuckled.

Anna's optimism was infectious.

All of them spent every minute looking up at each doctor that walked by, just in case there was any news.

Sixteen repulsive hospital coffees later, Dr Chandra finally came in and shut the door.

Ominously.

'OK, folks. It was tough. The baby is here. It's a girl, she's just under five pounds, but she's fine. Lee is with her. Minnie's heart is trashed, but it's limping along, with help from what we call a mechanical heart, a kind of pump. She's OK, but this is a critical time now, and I've bumped her up to the top of the waiting list for a donor heart, so she's now officially what we call 'bridge to transplant'. The next forty-eight hours are crucial. She's in the ITU and is not conscious, so to be honest it's best if you guys leave the team to get on with looking after her. Someone will come and fetch you to see the baby . . . '

'Bean,' said Glory.

'Bean. Yes, someone will bring you down to Lee

shortly. I must go. Hopes and prayers, guys, she's a strong one. I have faith. So must you . . . ' With that, he left.

'Lawd a mercy,' said Doris quietly, and she sat with her head in her hands.

Anna slipped away; she knew she had to put in the call to Hope, but she really didn't want to.

Meanwhile, in a small hot room next to the ITU, Lee held his new daughter in his arms and his soft tears dripped on to Bean's little brown fingers. He'd never been so grateful or so scared. 'Don't die, Min. Please. You mustn't die.'

Hope

Aunty Betty heard Hope's profuse gratitude as she stood next to her by the phones in C Block. Aunty Betty was leaning her considerable frame against the cold wall to relieve the arthritis in her knees.

'Thank you. Thank you. Thank you, Anna. I hope you know how much I appreciate . . . yes . . . thank you.'

Hope replaced the phone. Her allotted time was up.

'C'mere. It's not easy,' Aunty Betty said as she gathered Hope into a hug, during which she furtively smuggled the contraband Hope had bought from her with her commissary money across from under her prison-issue blue tracksuit top to under Hope's. All the while, Aunty Betty kept her eye on the CCTV camera at the end of the corridor.

Aunty Betty was the biggest-hearted 'bossiest bitch' on her wing. She and Hope had become firm chums in the time Hope had been inside. She was the only woman Hope confided in.

To all others, Hope was a mother figure.

To Aunty Betty, she was a sister.

It was only Aunty Betty who knew Hope's deep deep fear of not coping for so long a stretch. Hope told her that she couldn't imagine making it to the end, couldn't picture ever walking out, couldn't see it.

'Thanks, Aunty. So. Ten past eight. On the dot.

323

OK?'

'All right, m'duck, will do,' Aunty Betty replied. 'Love you.'

Hope squeezed Betty's hand and, keeping her secret purchase carefully hidden, made her way back to her cell. Once in, she sat down with her notepad and pen quietly, to write to Minnie. This letter would be very important. It was going to be mother to daughter to daughter.

Heart to heart to heart.

When she finished it, she put it in the envelope. She kissed it and licked it closed . . . She wrote another note and left it open. She watched her small clock. At 8 p.m., she retrieved the smuggled lighting flex from under her mattress. She climbed up on the stool and attached it to the window fastener. She prayed it was sturdy. She tied the flex around it, and around her neck. She thanked the air for all the good things in her life, and she kicked away the stool.

In her cell, Aunty Betty was watching her own clock through a mist of tears.

At ten past eight, she shouted out to alert the guards to an emergency.

All hell broke loose as they rushed to Hope's cell, where they found Hope, only just dead, with a sealed letter and an open note on her bed.

The note read:

I am Hope Parker. My daughter is Minnie Parker. She is in hospital in Bristol. She needs a new heart. I want her to have mine. Please, please do this AS SOON AS YOU FIND ME.

Beneath this, Hope wrote the details of:

The hospital where Minnie was

The address of the clinic where she'd had all her tests: blood group, tissue-type, etc., to be sure she could be a suitable match

The details of all that testing

The sealed letter had 'For our daughter Minnie' written on the envelope.

Minnie's Heart:
A Week Later

Lee was doing all he could to physically hold on to Minnie while she shrieked, and beat the ITU bed with her clenched fists. It had only been a week since her operation, and she was still so fragile.

'You selfish bitch! How could you?

'I hate you! You left me — you promised you never would! I need you!

'I. Hate. You!'

It hurt so much when she cried, but she had to, she had to. She couldn't believe the awful news Nanna Doris had told her. Lee placed Bean on her, and, because she didn't want to upset her daughter, Minnie gradually calmed down.

Anna, Isaac, Doris and Glory were all there when Anna handed her the letter.

'Do you want us to leave you alone?' Anna was trying to be sensitive.

'No. Never.' Minnie was still whimpering; she hurt so much, so much. 'Please, Anna, can you read it out?'

'Oh God, Minnie, are you sure?'

'Yes. Please.'

So she did:

'My darlin' daughter, Minnie, the extraordinary ray, the everything that mattered in my blessed life, when you read this, I will be gone, and if they all do what I ask, my heart will be

ticking away inside you. I so hope this is what has happened, and that your body has accepted part of mine.

I know things will seem very dark right now, but believe me, the sun will come out soon and it will all change and brighten up, and little Bean will be a huge spark in the darkness to light your way.'

Minnie held Bean tight and looked up at Lee for reassurance.

'My biggest regret, my only regret, is that I won't know her, but I've accepted that. I didn't want her to visit me here so . . . it's OK.

Here's the thing, Min. I took you. I shouldn't have, I know, but you brought a love into my life like I've never known. You are made of goodness and beauty, and the world is lucky to have you, and I have been the luckiest mum of all. Anyone who meets you automatically becomes a better person. I did. Thank you for that.

So, my lovely daughter, as you enter your next chapter, there are some things to say:

1. *Know that your father Isaac is the very best of men. Go to Africa to visit him and know his family, and his ancestry, your ancestry*
2. *Keep a watchful eye on Nanna Doris and Glory. They are your family, your tribe and they love you*
3. *Be curious and live adventurously, never hide your beautiful unique light, show up*

in the world in your own Minnie-ish way, unapologetic

4. *Love Lee and love Bean. Make more babies from your love and all be kind to each other*
5. *Go back to school and go on to uni if you want to. Anna and Nanna Doris will help with Bean. Promise me this*
6. *Don't fight all your difficult emotions, including those you're having right now; all your feelings are valid. Feelings are how we know we're alive*
7. *NEVER EVER forget the WAWA!*

So, please carry my words and know that I will always be with you. I will be a gentle movement within you, every other heartbeat, every other breath.

Everything that's happened has proven that it doesn't matter WHO you are from, Minnie, but WHAT . . . and you are from love, my sweet child.

There was another Minnie before you. For her, for me and, most of all, for you, please have a good, honest, optimistic life, and laugh a lot.

Remember this also, Min: I can go because you have Anna. She is your home whenever you need her.
She is a fantastic person. She is your mother too. Please call her mum if you want to, pronounce her name loud and strong, 'Mum', and I'll be there too, when you do.

Believe me when I tell you that I rest in soft peace. I've done my job the best I can. I live on in you. So, I can go home now.

I love you so very much,
Your mum
Hope (Chairperson of the Wawa Club)
XX'

Anna looked up.

The room was silent.

Hope's words to her were ringing in Anna's head: 'I can do this because of you . . .'

Minnie rang the buzzer on the side of her bed, and it was Dr Chandra himself who rushed in. Minnie asked him to come close. He leant in; she kissed his cheek and whispered, 'That's from my mum,' and she took the stethoscope from around his neck. She put the ear tips in her ears, she gave Bean to Lee, and she placed the flat diaphragm on her chest. She listened. There, loud and clear, was

Hope.

Acknowledgements

THANK YOU SO MUCH

Malcolm Dalrymple-Hay — heart stuff
Veronica Eagles — registrar stuff
Judge Angela Du Sautoy — legal stuff
Claire Hamilton-Russell — divorce stuff
Amy Dunstan — midwife stuff

Emma Kilcoyne, Carol Noble, Jon Fink — friend/
   writer encouragement stuff

Louise Moore — editor stuff
Jill Taylor — more editor stuff
Liz Smith & all who look out for me at Penguin
   stuff
Maureen Vincent — agent stuff (& so much more)
Robert Kirby — literary agent stuff
Neil Reading — PR stuff
Sammy, Dave, Mike & Karen — home-front stuff
Biggs — for claiming it's his book stuff
The Mighty B.F. — sanity stuff
LAST & BEST: Sue — for other-half-of-me stuff
   and all the bleddy endless typing!